Secrets & Lies

ANNIE JOCOBY

VINCI
BOOKS

By Annie Jocoby

Fearless

Fearless

Secrets & Lies

Trapped

Vinci Books

vinci-books.com

Published by Vinci Books Ltd in 2026

1

The publisher and the author have made every effort to obtain permissions
for any third party material used in this book and to comply with copyright
law. Any queries in this respect should be brought to the attention of the
publisher and any omissions will be corrected in future editions.
A CIP catalogue record for this book is available from the British Library.
Paperback ISBN: 9781036703066

The EU GPSR authorised representative is Logos Europe, 9 rue Nicolas
Poussion, 17000 La Rochelle, France
contact@logoseurope.eu

Chapter One

Dalilah

Today would be the worst day of my life. Bar fucking none. I would have to break the heart of the kindest boy that I have ever known, and the one person in this world who has been able to bring out my absolute best. All because of my fucking stupidity. I had the best of intentions, of course. I mean, I would like to think that I wouldn't have done what I did without having a good cause behind it. But no matter. The outcome was more tragic than I ever could have imagined. And the outcome was really all that mattered.

Already, Luke had called me and texted me excitedly about my coming over. I had begged off posing for him in the morning, texting him that I had a migraine headache and didn't want to be disturbed.

He texted me back: "Let me bring over a cold compress for your head. My mom used to get them, I know just what to do."

My heart was in my throat, and tears were streaming

down my face as I texted: "Thanks, but I need to be alone right now. In a dark room." And that was all. I didn't want to lead him on, so I didn't put my usual "xoxoxoxo" at the end of my text.

He texted back a frowny face and "45683968," which was our secret code for "I love you." The numbers corresponded with the letters I-L-O-V-E-Y-O-U on our phone pads.

I shook my head, willing myself not to text him "45683968" right back. Willing myself not to tell Nottingham to go to hell, and not to go over to Luke and just let him hold me in his arms. That was what I was absolutely craving at this time.

No, Dalilah, you can't do that. You can't ruin him like that. If I had a moment of weakness, then that would be it. Luke would have his show pulled and he would be absolutely finished. That wouldn't be fair to him. I would be the instrument of his ruin. I couldn't look myself in the mirror if that ever happened. My life would be over, because I would have to live with the shame of knowing exactly what I caused with my manipulative ways.

Was this the lesser of two horrible evils? This was my Sophie's Choice, a choice between two unbearable options. One option was to break the heart of the man that I was indelibly in love with, a man that I felt that I would love until I died. There was something so powerful, so raw, about my feelings for him. We had only known one another a relatively short period of time, but he had already claimed me in a way that I never thought that I could be. My heart, my body, my soul – all belonged to him. As crazy as that sounded.

He made me finally believe. In soul mates. In the possibilities of true love. In the possibilities that there was something larger than oneself, and that sometimes sacrifices have to be made for the person that you should be destined to be with. And these sacrifices sometimes meant that you would have to live all your days apart from that person.

Which brought me to my other option. To break the heart of the man whom I was indelibly in love with. Which would happen if I didn't do as Nottingham wished. Because Luke would see his lifelong dream of becoming an artist of note slip through his fingers, and it would be doubtful that he would be able to recover from that. We would be together, but at what cost? At a cost to his career, his livelihood, his dream. How selfish would I be to let that happen?

This was definitely the only option. Break up with Luke, and do it in such a manner that he would be able to get over me quickly. Make him think that I had played him all along, and that I never actually cared about him at all. I had to do it. Any other way would mean that Luke would pine away for me instead of moving on with his life, which is what I wanted him to do. Needed him to do. Yes, I would be absolutely devastated and miserable without him. But I made my bed. I would have to live with the consequences of what I did, while freeing Luke to love again.

I briefly thought about telling Luke everything, so that he wouldn't be too terribly hurt. So that he could see that what I was doing was a necessary thing so that he could achieve his dreams. But, no. I knew that Luke would do one thing if I told him the truth – he would tell Nottingham to go to hell. I knew that boy well enough that I could see exactly what would happen if he knew the truth.

And I couldn't ever let that happen.

A new text was coming in. Luke was sending me a video of a cute little French Bulldog, my absolute favorite breed of dog, yapping, with the translation "I hear you are one sick puppy. Doggone it, get well soon."

I shook my head, wanting to scream out into the heavens. This was what I was going to be giving up. This goofy sense of humor that showed that Luke really got me. He knew just what to say and do to make me feel instantly better.

But there was no feeling better in this case. There couldn't be. Luke could never find the words and right video to make me feel better about what I had to do.

Nottingham called me. I picked up, dreading to talk to him. But I had to. I had to keep him perfectly happy. If I didn't, he would sabotage Luke's career. He had the absolute power to do so. Even after Luke had his show, Nottingham had the power to sabotage him. He also had the power to make Luke into the superstar that he was destined to be. He had all the best connections to make that happen for Luke.

After I had agreed to marry Nottingham, he showed me his plan for Luke, and I was astounded. The *Matthew Jane* was first, of course, and that would be the springboard for Luke to really start making a name for himself. Nottingham also wanted to show Luke at the *Galerie Emmanuel Perrotin* in Paris, for a spring showing. The *Emmanuel* was considered one of the hottest contemporary galleries in that city. The *Dominik Mares* in Prague would be next fall. Another world renowned contemporary art gallery. Nottingham wasn't personally involved with either of these galleries, yet he had the connections to get Luke a showing in each of them.

I knew what Nottingham was doing. He was simply securing his investment, the investment being me. He knew that he had to sweeten the pot, to make sure that I didn't run for the exits when Luke's *Matthew Jane* showing was finished. And sweeten it, he did. Three major showings at three huge contemporary galleries, all in the span of a year? There was no way that Luke wouldn't end up on the A list after that.

"And Dalilah," he said to me, "don't think that you can leave me after Luke's *Matthew Jane* showing. I know you, and I know how devious you are. Trust me, I still have the power to destroy that boy at any point in his career. Even when he makes the A list. And I do say 'when,' not 'if.'"

I shrugged. I knew what he was saying was the truth. I was trapped. Sentenced to a loveless marriage that was actually much worse than merely being considered "love-less." It would be a destructive arrangement with us. Nottingham had the capacity for mental and physical abuse. I knew that.

I knew that, yet I had no choice in the matter. And it really didn't help when I repeated my mantra to myself, over and over again – that I was doing this for Luke. For him. For the man for whom I would walk through fire. Luke would have a wonderful life, filled with accolades and adoration. And, hopefully, he would find a woman to love and give him a family. I truly, truly hoped that Luke could move on without me and that he could be absolutely happy for the rest of his life. He so deserved that. If anybody in this world deserved it, it was him.

"Dalilah," Nottingham's stern voice addressed me through the phone. "Have you told him?"

"Not yet, Blake," I said.

"Tell him tonight. Tonight, Dalilah. Tonight, or our arrangement is off." At that, he simply hung up the phone.

That was how Nottingham rolled. He dispensed with

pleasantries, like "hello," "goodbye," "please," and "thank you." Those words were the ones that the little people used, the ones who actually had a decent bone in their body.

Nottingham was the type of guy that, when somebody kindly opened the door for him, he would just buzz on through without even giving that person a second glance. He was the type of guy who would harangue a waitress for accidentally shorting him a dollar. He would call her stupid, right in front of me, and a cheat. He had more than one waitress in tears because of his behavior.

And I had to sit there and take it like a little wifey. At least, that would be what I would have to do from now on. I couldn't possibly get on Nottingham's bad side now. Not when he held Luke's future in his hands.

I looked forward to the day when, perhaps, Luke was enough of a superstar that he would no longer need Nottingham's largesse. Not that I would ever get back with Luke in that event. That would be too dangerous for him. I would always be paranoid that Nottingham just might have the power to pay a top critic to do to Luke what Henry Jacobs did to me – destroy his confidence to the point where he wouldn't be able to create anything. But, perhaps, I could at least get away from Nottingham one day.

That was my only dream.

Luke was texting me again. "Spaghetti and meatballs tonight and some pool down at the hall?"

I took a deep breath. This was, by far, going to be the very hardest thing that I had ever done in my life. I could think of nothing harder than breaking Luke's heart. I felt my tears rushing down my cheeks. It was starting to feel as if the tears never stopped, but that they were just incessant ever since Nottingham said those fateful words to me in his car – "Luke Roberts. I know about the two of you." Those words echoed in my ears, night and day, day and night.

I texted back.

"We need to talk."

Chapter Two

Luke

I was bouncing off the walls, and had been ever since my dream girl told me that she would be my wife. I had to pinch myself constantly ever since we got engaged right there on the ice skating rink.

I felt a little show-offy, really, as I did my skating moves while she stood there on the ice, trying her hardest not to fall. She was more beautiful to me in that moment than she ever had been, because she finally showed me that she wasn't perfect after all. Yeah, she could probably smoke Fast Eddie Felson at the pool hall if she really tried, and she could win thousands of dollars at the blackjack table without blinking an eye. She had more artistic talent and intelligence in her little finger than 99.9999999% of the population could ever dream of having. And she was astoundingly gorgeous, flawless really.

Not to mention that she was, for whatever reason, hopelessly in love with me. As I was with her. So, yeah, she had good taste on top of everything else.

But, as she stood there on the ice, looking around nervously and looking like she was about to stumble at just any moment, I knew, perhaps for the first time, that she was imperfect. And I also knew, right at that moment, that I was hopelessly, annoyingly, and madly in love with her. As in, there would be no coming back if something ever happened between us, and I lost her. I had passed the point of no return in my feelings for her, which was why I knew, right in that instance, that I had to propose to her.

I really lucked out with the ring, too. A buddy of mine actually owed me a shit ton of money because he was short in one of our weekly poker games. I was a card shark myself when I wanted to be, and I pretty much cleaned up. Liam, the guy who owed me the money, told me that he would hook me up with some really nice jewelry if I ever needed it for a steep discount. Something about a cousin of his owning a jewelry store, so he could get it at cost. At the time, I wasn't having it. I just wanted the $1,000 that he owed me. But, there was no getting blood out of a turnip, and he pretty much got thrown out of our games after that incident.

Well, what do you know? I actually did need his services after all. So, he hooked me up with this amazing ring and sold it to me at cost. And, he was back in our weekly poker games after that. He made good on his part of the bargain, as far as I was concerned. Of course, I did have to pawn my guitar to buy the ring, even though it was so heavily discounted. There was no getting around that. I missed my guitar something fierce, but I knew that I would buy another one soon with all the money that would be rolling in from the *Matthew Jane* showing.

Nottingham informed me that he was going to be pricing my paintings starting at $20,000, which absolutely floored me. Once the gallery took its cut, I would be taking home around $10,000 for every painting that sold, minimum. And some of the paintings were priced at $30,000. I dreamed that I would sell out, which would mean that I would have a tidy sum of money, around $100,000, when everything was said and done.

I could move to the city, hopefully get a nice apartment for myself and Dalilah, and watch the proceeds roll in from subsequent showings that would inevitably come my way after this one was finished. In no time, I would be able to really give Dalilah everything that she ever deserved. That was all that I wanted, too. To make her happy.

Would there be sacrifices? Of course. When I moved to the city and made Dalilah the center of my universe, I probably wouldn't be seeing the guys as much. The weekly poker games would be a thing of the past. That would make me a little sad, because those games were an indispensable part of my life. Even when Dalilah was hanging out here all the time, I had to leave her once a week to go to the games. She was pretty cool about it, too, because, well, she was Dalilah. She was cool about everything.

But the poker games were a small sacrifice, really, for getting everything that I had ever hoped for. A woman to love, who loved me back. And, yeah, the art career taking off was a good thing, too, I had to admit. But being with her was worth more to me than 100 *Matthew Jane* showings. It really was.

That something seemed a little bit off with her texts didn't even faze me. I was that confident of our future together. She wasn't feeling good, and she seemed to have a migraine headache, which, I admit, was unusual for her. She didn't usually get migraines. She also didn't text back

45683968, which was our code for "I love you." Nor did she put little xoxoxoxo at the end. All that was strange, because Dalilah tended to be effusive that way.

But I shrugged my shoulders. She wasn't feeling well, so I had to give her space. As anxious as I was to see her, because I was always anxious to see her, I wasn't going to push her if all that she needed was to go to a dark room and lay down. I had seen that scenario 1,000 times with my mom, who suffered from chronic migraines, so I knew the drill.

Oh, but I was so hyperactive! I didn't know what to do with myself. I wanted so badly to get going. Call the caterers, reserve the hall, find out if I could get a credit card that I could pay off once my show went through, etc., etc., etc. If I thought that Dalilah could be happy just going to City Hall, I would have married her that day. That hour. But I wasn't going to ask that of her. She deserved to have a special day, as all women always wanted when they got married. I remember well when my sister got married. She was a regular Bridezilla, but I also knew how much it meant to her to take her vows in front of everybody that she loved.

So, no, I was going to do the proper thing and make sure that Dalilah and I had a real wedding. Of course, the tradition was that the bride's family would pay for the shindig, and God knew, they had the money. But, oops, I got hasty and never even asked her father for her hand, so I was embarrassed and figured that maybe I could try to pay for it all myself.

But I knew that really wasn't going to happen. Her dad would probably throw the thing at some Hampton's mansion. Which actually wouldn't be that bad, because taking our vows on the beach wouldn't exactly be a form of punishment.

I chuckled as I realized how much my mind was racing. I had to focus. But I couldn't paint at that moment. Usually, my art came when I was calm and could concentrate. When I was wired, songwriting usually was the better way to spend my time. But, I couldn't very well do that until I got another guitar.

So, finally, I just decided to text Dalilah and hope that she would be recovered enough in the evening to maybe want to do some dinner over here and go play some pool. I was truly astounded how good that girl was at pool. I wasn't the only one. She usually attracted a crowd to watch her play, even more of a crowd than usual.

I mean, Dalilah attracted attention wherever she went. She was gorgeous and charismatic. She had the *je ne sais quoi* that attracted people like the *Millennium Falcon* to the Death Star. Well, that was a bad analogy, because the *Falcon* really couldn't help being pulled into the Death Star, seeing as it was caught in a tractor beam. So, yeah, Dalilah always attracted attention, but give her a cue stick and put her around a table, and suddenly there were throngs just watching her, mesmerized. I guess nobody had ever seen a woman run a table like that.

I was a mean pool player myself, but not quite up to her level. So, I had been practicing a bit more. Jake and I went down there when I wasn't working or seeing Dalilah, and we hung out and took our shots. I was getting better, and, yeah, I wanted to show Dalilah my skills. It was embarrassing how much I wanted to show off for her.

I texted Dalilah my message about spaghetti and meatballs and pool, and she texted back four words that seemed ominous. "We need to talk."

I took a deep breath. I didn't like the sound of that. For one thing, it didn't sound like her, at all. She never was that serious, even in her texts. And, once again, there wasn't any kind of emoticon or other niceties that she usually included in her messages.

I was vaguely apprehensive, but I had no idea why. I felt my breath catch as I texted her back. "Sure, when and where?"

"Let me come over," she texted. "I'll be there within an hour."

"See you then." My texts were mirroring hers. Short, staccato, all business. I had no idea why Dalilah would be acting so strangely, and it was making me feel really off all of a sudden.

My mind wouldn't entertain the possibility that perhaps she was getting cold feet. There was just no way. I mean, she and I never had an off moment between us. Whether we were having sex, watching movies, going out, or just sitting together reading, we were truly comfortable with each other. I couldn't imagine that Dalilah would want to get cold feet when we really seemed to get each other so well.

Well, if she is getting cold feet, you'll deal with it. Give her space, and she'll come around. After all, she was only 20 years old. Maybe she had a friend who told her that she was some kind of a nut for committing to somebody when she was so young. Maybe we might have to wait a few years. I mean, that would be cool, as long as we still were together. Did I want to wait? Hell, no, I wanted to be married to her yesterday. Would I wait? Yeah, I would. It probably would be prudent to wait anyhow.

So, yeah. Maybe she just wanted to tell me that she wanted to wait until both of us were going with our careers. Because there was one thing that I knew – Dalilah was going to make it big again. God, that woman was talented. I was astounded by some of her latest works. She wasn't rusty at all. They always say that former athletes have muscle memory, so that, even when they get all blubbery after they quit playing their sport, they could bounce back and get in shape again a lot quicker than somebody who never played sports.

From the looks of things, there was such a thing as artistic memory as well. Dalilah was once in the big leagues in the art world. It might have been years ago, but, once she picked up her art again, she went right back to where she was. A superstar. Everybody was going to want her.

That's probably all it is. She got her voice back, so it was time to try to make a name for herself again. She probably wanted to wait to get established before we got married.

That's all it is, I told myself. That's all it is.

Chapter Three

Dalilah

Nottingham sent me a limo that would take me to Luke's. As much as I wanted to just take the bus and subway like I usually did, Nottingham insisted. So, I acquiesced.

I stared out the window, trying to rehearse what it was that I was going to say. How I was going to say it. One thing I knew, I was going to have play a part. There was no way that I could go over there without getting into some kind of actress mode, because I couldn't get through it.

As it was, I had to stop the limo several times so that I could get out and puke. I felt sorry for the people who had to pick up the trash from those cans, because I left them a mess.

I felt myself shaking all over, and I tried very hard to remember some of the lessons I learned in my various acting courses over the years. My high school offered these courses for people, like myself, who had either tested out of the basic courses or had already completed them. Since I tested out of just about everything, I was able to take fun electives such as acting. I actually got into them. I loved the chance to play somebody else, to really inhabit that person's skin.

I even thought briefly about trying to become an actress once I got to New York and still couldn't get my art muse back. I soon was dissuaded from this, however, when I talked to Scotty's bestie Jack, who lived just a few houses down from Scotty and Nick.

"You have to have the passion for it, girly, not just the looks. And, god knows, you do have the looks."

"You mean I can't make it unless it's something that I really and truly want?"

He snorted. "Honey, it's hard to make it even if you do have the passion for it. If you don't, then forget it. Sorry to disappoint."

I knew that, really. Jack had a lot of problems getting even the smallest part until his breakthrough role in *The Odd Couple*. That play was a smash, and he was on his way. But, before that, it was many, many years of languishing in the chorus, going to auditions and just generally starving until he got his break. And he was passionate about it. It was his only dream in life. It was what he lived and breathed.

For me, I was a dilettante at best when it came to acting. So, I didn't pursue it. But I had learned enough in those classes to do a passable acting job.

So, as I sat there in the limo, I ran through some of my acting exercises in my head. I tried to get my "part" in my head. I was going to play the part of a ruthless bitch who was playing Luke like a cello. I was going to have to come off cold and cruel.

I was going to be playing the part of Nottingham. As ironic as that was, Nottingham was the first person I thought of when I tried to figure out who my character was going to be modeled upon.

I was going to get through this. I was going to get through this, and then, after I left him devastated, I was going to go home and cry like I had never cried before.

The limo made its way to Luke's apartment. As much as I wanted time to just stand still so that I never had to do what I was about to do, the limo made it there way too soon. I looked down at my hand, which was shaking like a leaf. I willed myself not to puke again. I took a mirror out of my purse, and tried to make my face the way that I wanted it. I wanted my eyes to be cold and lifeless. I needed him to not see how I was really feeling.

Because what I was really feeling was beyond devastated. Beyond depressed. Beyond hopeless.

I had to do this, and I had to do it right. I had to do it so that he could move on. I had to make him think that he was wrong about me, dead wrong, so that he could get over me. Rip off that band-aid so that he could start to heal.

Taking a deep breath, I made the dreaded walk up his stairwell. I got to his apartment and knocked on his door.

This was going to be the longest night of my entire life.

Chapter Four

Luke opened the door. I almost melted right then and there. Inside, I was screaming for help. My inner self wanted so badly just to fall into his arms and rip off his clothes and make love with him all night long. Just feel our naked bodies entwined with one another. I was so in love with that guy...I never thought it was possible to feel that strongly for another human being. I never thought that another person could get me on so many levels.

I wondered if I could pull it off. Even if I managed to somehow give the performance of mine or anybody's life, Luke probably would still see through it. He saw my very soul, I was convinced of that.

Still, I had to try.

As cold as I possibly could, I said "hello, Luke. Please have a seat. I need to tell you a few things."

He crinkled up his brows and looked at me quizzically. "You okay, Dalilah?" My heart broke as I looked at his face. He was still so trusting, so open. He definitely wasn't even entertaining the idea that I might be about to break his heart.

That wasn't even on his radar.

"I'm fine," I said curtly. "Please sit down."

He looked at me like he didn't quite know what to do. He kind of had his usual crooked grin on his face, the crooked grin that always made me swoon. He narrowed his eyes, and smiled. "You playing some kind of game, Dalilah? If so, you haven't let me in on it. But, I get it. I'm supposed to pretend that you're somebody else. Maybe some lady who got lost in the rain and now you're here, all lost and alone. Well, I'll play along. I kind of like role-playing, to be honest with you."

I took a deep breath. *Come on, Dalilah, you have to pull this off. You have to break his heart completely. You can't back down. His career depends on this. His very future depends on this.*

"No, Luke. No games. I need to talk to you."

He cocked his head, and, still looking confused, he sat down on the couch. He patted the cushion next to him, his expression confused, yet still hopeful.

I just shook my head. "No, I'm okay right here."

He blinked his eyes at me, and, finally, his expression was starting to look concerned. "I don't understand. What's going on, Dalilah?"

"I'm very sorry, Luke. I can't be with you anymore."

Now he was really starting to look like he was about to either panic or go into shock. "I'm sorry? I don't follow. What are you talking about? Dalilah? What are you talking about?"

"I'm sorry. I carried this all too far. The truth is, I never really wanted to be with you. I think that maybe you knew that about me. That I really need to be with somebody wealthy. My parents brought me up with a certain standard, and my husband is going to have to keep me in those standards."

Now he was really looking confused. He shook his head manically and stood up. "What? What do you mean that you carried this too far? What, was this all a game to you all along?"

"Yes, Luke. It was all a game. That's what I do. Play games. Mind-fucking games. I'm quite good at it, too. But, it went too far. I knew that it went too far when you asked me to marry you. I never wanted it to go that far. And now it's over. Sorry."

Now he was getting agitated. "Oh my fucking God. I can't even believe this. I meant nothing to you? Really? This was all an act?" He looked like he couldn't quite comprehend what I was saying to him. "I don't believe it. I don't believe it. I mean, you're just going to fuck with somebody like that? What kind of a monster are you?"

"I can't help it. I have antisocial personality disorder. You do know what that is, don't you?"

"Yes, I fucking know what that is. It means that you don't have empathy or real feelings. You don't have a fucking conscience. I know all about that. Goddamn it, why does this bullshit keep happening to me?"

For just one second, I almost broke character. I wondered what he meant by that.

Now he was pacing. "Serena. One of my sisters. She has that. Broke my parents' heart so many fucking times. Stole from all of us. Lied to us all. Didn't even fucking go to my mom's funeral. What a fucking waste. Goddamn it, Dalilah, you're good. You're good. I thought that I would know a psychopath when I saw it because I grew up around that. Lived that all my life. You got in under my radar, and that really pisses me off."

My heart broke when he referenced his mom's funeral. I never even got a chance to find out what happened there. He was still raw about it, whatever it was. That was one of the things that I was wanting to do – help him come to terms with that. He was so kind and optimistic, yet I could always sense a certain level of sadness in him, and I knew that it was related to his mom.

Come on, Dalilah, you can't back down now. You're almost home free. I nodded my head a little. "Well, Luke, I don't really care about any of that. I'm a mercenary, really. I go where the money is, and it certainly isn't here."

He narrowed his eyes. "Well, that was below the belt, and if you were a human being, you would know that. But, you're not." He shook his head. "How did I not know? God, how could I be so fucking stupid?" He sat down, and put his head in his hands.

I fought down the urge to go to him. To put my hand on his shoulder and comfort him and tell him everything. Tell him the whole sordid and sorry story and let the chips fall where they may, as my dad would say.

No, Dalilah. No. If you do that, Luke's future is done. Done. Do this, Dalilah. Do it.

So, while he sat there on the couch, his head in his hands, I simply turned around and walked out the door.

I fled down the steps and into the waiting limousine, where I collapsed into a torrent of tears.

When I got home, I took off my clothes and got into bed and cried all night long.

Chapter Five

Luke

Two Weeks Later

My door was knocking. I had no idea who was on the other side, nor did I care. I didn't care about much, actually, even my show, which was coming up in a week and a half. Not that I even had to do anything, because Nottingham was taking care of all of that, but he did want me to make a guest appearance during opening night. It was optional, of course, but he told me that if the patrons and public could meet the artist, my paintings were more likely to sell.

Fuck that. It took all my energy just to go to work, and I was like a zombie there. The rest of the time, I pretty much just slept. Wasn't eating too much, either. That, too, took too much energy. And my workouts were definitely suffering as well.

As for the guys? I didn't answer their calls. No way did I

want to act all cheerful and like nothing was wrong, when everything was clearly wrong.

I hated that I fell so hard for a con artist like that fucking Dalilah. A con artist. How stupid was I? Goddammit, and she was so fucking good, too. She played the part so masterfully, there was just no way that I could have ever seen that she was actually a sociopath who apparently got her rocks off on seducing guys and making them fall madly in love with her, and then pulling the rug out in the most unceremonious and cold way possible. Cold. Cruel. That's what she was. She wasn't who I thought she was at all.

She was Ted Bundy. Charming on the outside, but her façade was just a shell that hid her cold, cruel heart. No, sorry, that wasn't even a good description. Because she, by definition, didn't have a heart. And, yeah, Ted Bundy was probably going a bit too far, because Dalilah wasn't a serial killer, to my knowledge. But, then again, anything was possible.

Dalilah wasn't Ted Bundy, really. She was more like Serena. I had two sisters, one who was the Bridezilla, and she was pretty cool most of the time. Two brothers, Mark and Chris, who were twins and just a little older than me. Both were pretty chill.

And then there was Serena. She was eight years older than me, and she was the most manipulative woman alive. From the start, she would lie to me to get me to do what she wanted. Started with promises that she didn't keep – like she would give me five bucks if I would let her cheat in our card games. Went on to blackmail, as she told me that she would tell awful lies to the girl I was crushing on if I didn't give her my allowance. And that was just the kid's stuff.

Everything out of Serena's mouth was a lie, and we all figured that out pretty early on. She would crash the car, and then blame her boyfriend, who wasn't even driving. She had no problem implicating him, though, even though the forensics of the crash proved that she was the one who drove the car. She got a high powered job at a law firm by pretty much sleeping with everyone in the office, married or no. Serena was married, but had multiple affairs, yet would fly into an absolute rage if her husband even looked at another woman.

Just like Dalilah, Serena was charismatic and beautiful. People let her get away with everything, because nobody could ever imagine that such a woman would be so devious and cunning and heartless. She was able to cheat people ruthlessly, and she used this ability constantly.

And when my mom died, Serena couldn't be bothered to make it to the funeral. She wasn't talking to my mom, anyhow, because my mother had called her out on her bullshit more than once. Serena stole $5000 from my mom by getting access to my mom's bank account, and refused to pay it back. $5000 doesn't seem like a lot, but, for my mother, it was more than she could financially afford. My mom saved all that she could from her part-time job working at the local Wal-Mart, so $5000 to her was a lot of money. And it was in her personal account, as my pop pretty much let my mom spend her Wal-Mart income on anything that she wanted, and my mom loved that sense of independence.

Mom pressed charges against Serena, a move that the rest of the family cheered. It was about time Serena had to pay for the crap that she put us through. And that was that. Serena refused to talk to mom after that, even though she was still a minor and living under the same roof as mom and pop. And she has never, to this day, addressed mom's death whenever we were subjected to seeing her. She acted like none of it even happened. The rest of us were devastated beyond belief, in shock and in worse pain than anybody should ever have to bear. Not Serena. She was busy getting her nails done while we were watching my mom being lowered into the ground.

"I can't go to the funeral," she said, "not with these nail chips. You guys have fun." And she bounced out the door, and didn't come home until the next day. She apparently ran into some guy she knew and couldn't make it back. My pop was so devastated by what happened that he didn't even challenge her.

In fact, my pop was a devastated shell of a man, period, even now. A light went out when my mom was murdered, and he was never the same. Never the same.

The same light went out in me when Dalilah showed her true colors. I shouldn't even compare my devastation to my pop's, though – mom and pop were married 20 years, and had five kids with one another. I had known Dalilah for only a matter of months.

Yet, I felt that I had known her forever.

Turns out, I didn't know her at all. Period. That thought made my insides churn.

The door kept knocking, and I didn't make a move to answer it. Finally, the door got kicked in, and Jake and Henry, two of my best buddies, were bursting into the apartment.

"What the fuck?" I said. "You two douchebags gonna pay for that door?"

"Hey," Jake said. "Look who's calling who douchebags. We gotta game tonight, and we're not taking 'no' for an answer anymore. Now get your candy ass into your shower, because you're ripe, man, and meet us down at Brown Betty in a half hour. A half hour, bro, or we're coming back up. Capice?"

"No, man, I can't make it," I said. "I got the flu, or something, I don't know. I can't shake it. You guys go on without me."

"A half hour, or we're coming back in here with Leo, and he's gonna force your pussy-whipped butt out of this apartment," Henry said.

I sighed. Leo was 250 lbs of solid muscle, and if anybody could force me out of this apartment, it would be him.

"Fuck off," I said. "I'll meet you in a half hour. Try not to pick up on anybody in the meantime, Jake, although I know that it'll be hard."

"Eh, fuck you," Jake said, but he wasn't serious. "See you in a few."

A half hour later, after I took a shower and shaved, I met the guys at Jake's car. They were leaning against the car, Henry smoking a cigarette. They saw me, and we all got into the car without a word.

"Man, when are you gonna quit with those cancer sticks?" I asked Henry.

"I quit," he said, taking another drag and flicking the ash out the window.

"How's that working out for you?" I asked, and Jake started laughing. To my surprise, I actually managed a smile and a chuckle myself.

"Fuck you," Henry said with a smile. To his credit, he actually stubbed the cigarette out in the ashtray, as opposed to throwing the butt out the window. He knew that I would ream his ass if he would do that - because if there was one thing I hated, it was a litterer.

"Sorry to ambush you like that," Jake said. "But we had

no choice. Pauly's in town, and there's no way we weren't going to get everyone together for that."

"Pauly" was Paul Schraeder, who was living on the West Coast, having moved out to San Francisco a year before. He rarely came to visit, but when he did, it was like an event, really. He actually was one of my favorite guys, so I was finding that I was glad that these two clowns forced me out of the house.

"Yeah," Henry said. "And we gotta get your pussy-whipped ass out of that apartment. Man, it's been two weeks. No chick is worth moping for two weeks. You gotta join the living, man. The living. That's where it's at."

I said nothing. Henry couldn't understand that Dalilah wasn't just some chick to me. She was everything.

And now she was gone.

Chapter Six

"Your deal," Pauly was saying to me. "Call it."

"Five card stud," I said, passing out the cards.

I looked at my hand. I had an ace high and nothing else. Still, I put in ten bucks to start things off. In our games, the dealer had the opening bid.

As the other guys were variously throwing in their own chips, or folding, Ralph, a big black guy, was saying "so, you and that hot number are through, huh? What a class act like that was doing with a guy like you in the first place, I don't know."

I glared at him, but I wasn't angry. That was what we did – we busted each other constantly. Par for the course, but it didn't make me feel any better.

Eventually everyone folded, and I collected the kitty. Pauly was dealing next, and he chose Jacks or Better. Fortunately, I had a hand that could open the deal, as I had a couple of Kings, so I was able to make a wager.

"The problem with your situation with Dalilah," Henry was saying, "is the law of supply and demand."

"Come again?" I said.

"Supply and demand. Girls like her are in short supply, so there's a high demand. Guys like you are a dime a dozen, so there's not as much of a demand."

"Hey, fuck you," Jake said to Henry. "Why don't you stop busting him like that? He's got a show coming up where he might really make some bank."

"Hey, it's okay, Jake," I said. "Go on with your theory, Henry."

"Dalilah is a 1943 copper penny," he said.

I nodded, but everyone else looked at him like he had grown another head. "What the fuck does that supposed to mean?" Leo asked.

"In 1943, World War II was going on, and copper was in short supply," I explained. "So they made most of the pennies out of silver. But, by some mistake, there were actually 40 pennies made that year out of copper. Now, those 40 pennies are worth hundreds of thousands of dollars, because there's so few of them."

Henry nodded solemnly. "The boy speaks the truth," he said. "Now, Dalilah is a 1943 copper penny, and you, Luke, are just a regular penny. Yeah, you're a pretty boy, and you're smart, and I guess you have a lot of talent. Although the stuff you do is over my head, I'll admit. But you don't have two nickels to rub together."

"What is it with the coin analogies?" Pauly asked.

"Just sayin'," Henry said. "And, yeah, you got that opportunity at that fancy gallery, and hopefully that's going to go gangbusters for ya. But Dalilah is a rarity. Classy, gorgeous, smart, and mega-bucks. Sorry, but a woman like that is going to be with another 1943 copper penny. She's in short supply, in high demand, and she'll end up with a guy version of her. Just you wait and see."

I tapped my fingers on the table, not really wanting to believe what Henry was saying. But secretly knowing that he was probably right. Even if I made $100,000 at this show, so what? What was that to a woman like her?

Nothing, that's what.

And Henry was bringing up something that was nagging me all along. Perhaps Dalilah wasn't playing me at all, but she just didn't think I was good enough for her? She changed her mind, and decided to put on a cold woman act so that I would forget about her. Would that be worse? She could find another wealthy guy who wasn't a douchebag, but would treat her special. Another 1943 penny, as Henry would put it. Was that worse than her being a sociopath who got off on playing mind-fuck games with men?

I sighed. No, that wouldn't be worse. At least in that other scenario, she could find happiness. And her finding true happiness would actually bring me joy. Because I wanted that for her, even after she so coldly dumped me. I wanted her to be happy. Needed for her to be happy.

And if she were a true sociopath, as she had said, then happiness would be impossible. Sociopaths couldn't feel happiness, as they really couldn't feel anything at all.

The game continued, but I couldn't really concentrate, so I ended up making more than a few mistakes. I was definitely off my game, as my bluffing skills were sub-par, and I was having a difficult time picking up on the non-verbal cues of the guys around me. Usually, I did an excellent job of reading the body language and facial expressions of the other players, which was why I usually was able to clean up at the poker table.

Not on that day. I was just off. So, by the time the game was over, I ended up losing around $500, which, at that time, was a lot of money for me. And, what the hell, who knows? My show might be a complete and utter flop, and $500 might always be a lot of money for me. Nothing in life was guaranteed, and that would include this show.

I threw down my cards on the last hand and glared at Jake, who was looking pretty sheepish next to me. "Thanks, Jake, for dragging me here. Thanks a lot. Now, on top of losing the love of my life, I've also lost $500. Talk about the cherry on top of the sundae."

Jake slapped my back. "But, hey, I got you out of the house. Out of your wallowing for just this one night. You can go back to your pity pot tomorrow. And, look at it this way – now you have something else to mope about. Maybe losing this money will take your mind off her of her."

"Oh, that was your plan all along, huh? Give me a different pain to think about? Good thinking, there," I said, with a roll of my eyes. "Sorry, but that isn't going to work. My heart has been ripped out, and no amount of different pain is going to change that."

Jake was quiet for a few minutes. The other guys were too. They didn't quite know what to say for once.

Finally, Henry broke the silence. "Aw, Luke, cheer up. Dalilah was one of a kind, but guys like us don't belong with girls like her in the first place. Listen, I got five sisters, any one of them would go for a guy like you. Well, maybe not Elaine, she got a husband and all, but she's always looking for side projects, if you know what I mean. But I know that's not up your alley. And Terri, she's pretty easy. You could score with her the first night."

Henry continued to ramble on and on, naming each of his sisters and concluding that none of them would exactly be right for a relationship, but they all would be right for a night or two.

"Sounds like your sisters are real winners," Leo said.

"Hey, fuck you," Henry told Leo. "At least they don't have an old man who's in prison for securities fraud, unlike your sister."

Leo just laughed and shook his head. "True, that."

I just watched the guys busting on each other, not taking part in any of that for once. Jake looked over at me and I could tell that he was feeling badly for bringing me along. He stood up. "Well, guys it's been a good night. I'm gonna take Luke home now, so I'll catch up with all you losers later."

I nodded my head and stood up too. I was relieved to be getting out of there. All I wanted was to get back home and go back to my usual routine of lying on the couch and zoning out. That was still all that I had the energy for.

Henry stood up, too. "Hey, Jake and Luke, it's good that you guys could make it. I'm gonna stick around and get a ride home with Leo."

Jake nodded to everyone, and the two of us went out the door.

After we had been in the car awhile, Jake said "hey, Luke, don't mind that stupid Henry. You're not a regular penny."

I was zoning out and, at first, I didn't know what he was talking about. "Huh? What do you mean?"

"All that talk about Dalilah being so special and you being so ordinary. That's bullshit. You're not ordinary, and you never will be. You got a gift, man. A gift. So, don't listen to idiots who don't understand that. I've seen your work, and I think that you're just as much of a 1943 copper penny as she is. Probably more."

I nodded my head. Jake could be obtuse as anybody, but, when it came right down to it, he usually knew just what to say to me when I really needed to hear something encouraging. "Thanks for saying that, Jake."

And then I was quiet for a few seconds.

"You know what is the worst time of day?" I finally said, as I stared out the window of the beat up Corolla.

"When?"

"The morning, when I first wake up. It's like after my mom died. For the split second when I open my eyes, it's like I had forgotten the pain. Everything seems new for that split second, which makes it all the more hard when I realize, just a few seconds later, that this is my life. This is my life. I had a love and now I don't."

"How do you deal with that?"

"Usually by going back to bed, unless I have to work."

Jake put his hand on my back, and slapped it lightly. "You're grieving. I know that this probably isn't going to help, but, a year from now, when you're rich and famous and you're dating some German supermodel, you won't even remember Dalilah's name."

I nodded my head, but said nothing. As much as Jake was trying to cheer me up, he wasn't at all. I didn't want a German supermodel. I just wanted Dalilah. But, at the same time, I knew that he meant well, so I just played along.

"A German supermodel. Maybe her name is Anke. And she's tall and blond and willowy like Heidi Klum. Man, when I was a kid, I had such a crush on her."

"When you were a kid, she was already like 100 years old."

"Shut up. She was in her forties and still smoking. Ageless. Like Dorian Gray."

"Dorian Gray? Who the hell is that? Some other supermodel?"

I shook my head. "No, he was a guy in one of Dalilah's

favorite books, *The Picture of Dorian Gray.* He was this handsome young guy who was full of himself, so he never wanted to age. He didn't age – his portrait did, though. His portrait also showed all the ugliness that he had inside of himself. He stayed perfectly preserved, while his portrait got older and uglier all the time."

"Sounds like a cool book. I should check that out," Jake said, humoring me. I knew better. He didn't read much, except comic books, and he certainly wasn't going to read something that was written in the 19th Century by an eccentric Irish playwright.

"It was one of Dalilah's favorite books, because it was how she saw many of the people that she knew. Especially the ones that she grew up with. Beautiful and wealthy on the outside, rotting on the inside. But she also would bring up the book when she saw people who never seemed to age – she said that they were like Dorian Gray. Others would joke and say that the youthful-looking people were vampires, but Dalilah was more literary, so she used the Dorian Gray analogy instead."

I sighed. Just one of the things that I loved about her – her fierce intelligence and her ability to call bullshit on just about anybody. There wasn't anything that I could put over on her, and I loved that. She couldn't be bullshitted. She had read just about everything there was to read, so she was also a fascinating font of knowledge. I was well-read, too, so I was able to keep up with her somewhat, but she really just blew me away in that department.

Not that she lorded it over me or anyone else.

"Hey," Jake said. "You gotta forget about her. You gotta show coming up, and you're going to blow everyone away. Think about that. That's your future, there, man. You can't just half-ass this premiere. You gotta be there and kiss the ring and do what you gotta do to make sure that your show sells out and you start getting the commissions you need. You gotta go for it. Never let a chick stand in your way of that. Love might be fleeting, but success ain't, if you play your cards right." And then he chuckled. "Which you didn't tonight, I'll admit."

In spite of myself, I started laughing too. "Yeah, I really sucked tonight at cards, didn't I?"

"Yep. Gave the term 'flop' a whole new meaning," he said, referring to the first three face up cards in Texas Hold'em.

We laughed a little bit more, and Jake said "man, I couldn't believe that you bluffed when Leo had a ladies high full house. When you laid down your shit hand, I almost lost it."

I shook my head. Something like that never would have happened before Dalilah left me. I was normally a better player than that. "Yeah, maybe I need to cool it with the cards until I actually have money to lose. But we can still hang out, of course."

"Goes without saying," he said. "Well, looks like we're here." He pulled up to the curb in front of my apartment. "You gonna be okay?"

"Eventually," I said. "I just need to wallow some more. But, you're right. I at least have to make a guest appearance at my show. Not sure how I'm going to be able to glad-hand everyone there, but I at least have to try."

He slapped my shoulder again. "Hey, you take care, alright? This is your first broken heart. Man, I've had fifty broken hearts. Doesn't even phase me anymore."

I smiled, not telling him that Dalilah was different from any of his short-termers who were, by and large, bimbos. No, Dalilah was truly a 1943 copper penny, while Jake's women were truly regular pennies. I knew that I'd be hard-pressed to find a woman like Dalilah again, which was what made it all the more depressing. "I love you, bro."

"You too," he said, pointing to me as I got out of the car.

Then I went upstairs to my empty apartment and did what I did best – laid down on the couch.

Chapter Seven

Dalilah

I was waiting at the restaurant, nervously sipping my water. I had asked Nick to meet me here, because he was going to be the front line in breaking the news to my father about my impending nuptials to Nottingham. Dad was going to go Defcon 1 when he heard the news, I knew, so I thought that I could try to get Nick as an ally in this whole situation. After all, it was Nick who first told my dad about how much of a creeper Nottingham was. Maybe if I could get him on my side, then my dad might accept the whole thing a little bit better.

Maybe, but probably not. Still, a good word from Nick to my dad might make the whole thing a bit more palatable.

The last thing that I wanted was for my dad or anybody else trying to blow this whole thing up. As heartbreaking as it would be to have to live with a man like Nottingham, it had to be done for Luke. His show was close, and Nottingham had already arranged for some of the top international art critics to be there. Including Henry Jacobs. He was a star-maker, no matter what he did to me. An artist gets a good review from him, and that artist would be on his way.

And Nottingham had been saying ominous things lately. "You have to keep your end of the bargain, Dalilah. If anything interferes with me getting what I want from you, then Luke will be a never-was. And just remember, even after he makes it, I can make him a has-been just as quickly."

I wondered if Nottingham had ever felt guilty about how he manipulated people for his own gain. For the ruth-less way that he used his money and power to bring the little people to heel. I envisioned him as a puppeteer, and I was on the string, dancing.

The only good thing was that we hadn't had sex yet. Nottingham told me that he wanted to "save me" for after we were married, and then he pretty much wanted free reign. He had explained that he had been looking for just the right submissive, and that he thought that I would be just the woman.

I wanted to fight back. I wanted so much just to tell him to go to hell, and I would have. I would have if I didn't know exactly how much devastation he would cause for Luke if I did that.

How did I get so trapped?

I drummed my fingers on the table impatiently, and sipped my water some more. Nick wasn't usually late, but he was this evening, for whatever reason.

Finally, he came through the door and I stood up and he kissed me on the cheek. "Good to see you, Dalilah," he said as he took his seat.

"You too," I said, feeling awkward. It was strange to feel

awkward around this man whom I grew up with and lived with for two years.

In typical Nick fashion, he cut through the bullshit the second he sat down. "So, you wanted to see me. What's up?"

I took a deep breath, taking another sip of my water, and wishing that it were wine. But this was a place where I knew I wouldn't be served, so I didn't even try to order any alcohol. "I, well, Nottingham. I'm going to marry him."

Nick cocked his head a little bit and narrowed his eyes. "Is this some kind of a practical joke? Because it's not funny, Dalilah."

"No, no practical joke," I said. I had been wrestling earlier about what to tell Nick about this unholy union, and decided just to come out with the truth. The truth sounded actually better than anything else that I could think of. "I have to do this."

"Why? You're not pregnant, are you?"

"God forbid. God forbid," I said with a shudder. To bring a child into my ugly relationship with Nottingham would be the last thing that I would want. I already screwed up my own life, and I certainly didn't want to screw up another person. "No, it's not that."

"Well, then, what is it? Because this better be goddamned good."

The waiter came around and we gave our drink orders. Nick asked for a double scotch, and I just settled on iced tea.

"A double scotch, huh? My news isn't that bad."

"You kidding me? You're telling me that you're about to marry a controlling, manipulative dom, and you're telling me that the news isn't that bad?" He shook his head and snorted a little. "Now, out with it, kid. Tell me your whole sorry story, and maybe I can think of a way out of it for you."

"There's no way out," I said, and then launched into the entire story. I told him all about Luke and how Nottingham held Luke's future in his hands. About how I brought all of it on with my manipulative behavior, so now I felt that I had to make the sacrifice and pay the price, so that Luke could achieve his dreams.

Nick listened intently, to his credit. He didn't try to interject.

Finally, after I was done telling him the whole story, Nick shook his head. "Listen, Dalilah, don't think that I'm not sympathetic to this whole bullshit scenario. Because I am. You want to protect the person you love. I get that. Boy, do I get that. I'd do the same if I were in your shoes, and somebody was threatening Scotty like that. In fact, I've done despicable things, all in the name of protecting her. So, yeah, I get where you're coming from."

I took a breath. Nick didn't know that I knew, but I was aware of just what despicable thing he was referring to. And I did consider that to be my ace in the hole, if Nick refused to get on board. As much as I didn't want to use that Ace, I would.

I would do anything to ensure Luke's future.

"Okay, then, you're good? You'll ease my dad into this situation, so that he doesn't blow up too much? I mean, he'll listen to you if you tell him that Nottingham is a good guy after all."

"Hell no, I'm not good. Listen, Dalilah, you can't sacrifice your entire life and happiness like this. Not for anybody. I don't know this Luke guy, but I suppose he must be really somebody special that you would go to these kinds of lengths for him. But I don't know him, so my loyalty isn't to him, it's to you. And if you're going to ruin your life, then I can't be on board with that. Sorry. You're going to have to handle your dad without my blessing."

I bit my lip. I knew that he would say that. I knew Nick too well to think otherwise. So, I had to bring out my Ace.

Taking a deep breath, not wanting to do this, but feeling that it was necessary, I said "I know, Nick. I know what you did 17 years ago."

Nick suddenly got white as a sheet. "What are you talking about?" he asked, his hand suddenly shaking as he brought his glass of scotch to his lips.

"Paul Lucas. He committed suicide. There was no doubt about that. But who forced him?"

Nick's face continued to go pale, and then, just like that, he looked angry. Really angry. "What the fuck? How do you know about that, and are you really going to use that against me? Who are you?"

I fought back tears. "I told you that I would do anything to ensure Luke's future, and I meant that. I need you on my side, and I need you to convince my father that what I'm doing isn't going to ruin my life. Even though we both know that it is."

Nick got quiet for a few minutes. I watched as the anger on his face drained away, and his color returned. Finally, he said softly to me "how do you know about all that?"

"When I was 12, I had given up art, so I was bored. I was bored, so I learned how to hack computers. It was something that was challenging for me. It was like a puzzle or a game. And, well, I came upon the video of you threatening Paul and handing him the gun to kill himself."

Nick shook his head. "That entire file was deleted. Ryan and I cleaned it completely off his computer."

I sighed. "Nothing is ever completely deleted. Yeah, it

wasn't something that I could have just stumbled upon by any means. But I got really, really good at hacking, and I could find files that were long since erased. You could, too. You just have to know where to look."

Nick took a deep breath. "Okay, so, what are you saying, here, Dalilah? Are you telling me, what, that you'll turn me in if I don't give you my blessing on Nottingham? Is that what you're saying?"

I bit my lip, and then decided not to go through with it. I couldn't do that to him – blackmail him like that. Yeah, I probably could have used that video to go to the authorities and get him into trouble. How much trouble, I didn't know, as what he did wasn't exactly murder, so the statute of limitations would have run on the crimes that he did commit. Namely burglary and blackmail. So, truth be told, unless there was a really enterprising prosecutor who might be able to argue that the whole thing really was a homicide, Nick probably wouldn't have been in trouble, even if I did go to the authorities.

Which I never would do, ever. Even if I tried to threaten Nick with going to the authorities, if he called my bluff, then I couldn't go through with it. I loved him too much to ever do something like that to him.

"No, Nick, I wouldn't do that to you," I said, and I saw Nick's tense posture relax considerably as I told him this. "I just wanted you to know that I know the lengths that you went through to protect Scotty, so I hope that you can understand that I would do the same for Luke."

Nick shook his head. "It's not the same. That man was a really, really bad man. He did evil things to Scotty and to a bunch of other girls."

"I know. I saw the video."

42

"Yeah, well, then you know that I had to do what I did. I had to. There was just no way around it."

You keep telling yourself that, Nick. I saw the look on his face, which I read as absolute guilt. I could see that he knew that what he did was wrong, no matter how much of a justification he had given himself all these years.

"Well, look at it this way. Maybe I'm ruining my life, here. But it's my choice and it's my life. Will I be happy with Nottingham? Not a chance. But this is a necessary thing. It's necessary, and I need you to help my father come to terms with it. I mean, he won't ever be entirely happy with this situation. I'm his little girl, and, truth be told, I think that he really wants me with Luke." I looked at my glass. "As do I. God, I'm so in love with that guy, I just can't stand it. He's all I think about. But I can't be with him, and I have to be with Nottingham. Please help my father come to terms with this."

Nick just shook his head. "You're something else, you know that? Well, that was always something that I knew about you – if nothing else, you're very loyal. To a fault. But I still can't do this for you, Dalilah. I'm sorry, I know how much this all means to you, but I can't lie to your dad like that. I've never lied to him before, and I'm not about to start now."

I stared at my food, which had just arrived, feeling very defeated. Everything was against this. What I was going to do with Nottingham – I was going to alienate everyone I cared about. Everyone I loved. And Luke was bound to find out, and he would be even more devastated.

I had created a mess and a trap, and I had no clue how to get out of it.

Chapter Eight

After I had my dinner with Nick, I trudged home, and knew that I had to make the dreaded phone call to my mom and dad. Without Nick to be a buffer between my parents and me, I knew that there was going to be a huge problem when I told them.

Of course, Nottingham couldn't have been less concerned about this. When I told him how much I had dreaded talking to them, he simply said "sorry, Dalilah, it has to be done. It has to be done, because I want you to be my wife before Luke's show."

Considering that there was less than a week and a half before Luke's show, it didn't exactly give me a lot of time to help them come to terms with this. So, I had to make the dreaded phone call to them about meeting me for dinner.

"Mom," I said, calling her.

"Dalilah, what a surprise! What's going on?"

"Um, I need to see you and dad tomorrow night. Can you make it to the city? I'd like to go to dinner with you."

"Sure, Dalilah. Is there something wrong?"

"No," I lied. "Nothing's wrong. Why?"

"Well, you usually don't initiate seeing us, that's all. Of course, we always love to see you. It's just unusual, that's all."

I momentarily thought about telling her just to forget about it. Maybe Nottingham and I could be married in secret and none would be the wiser. But then thought better of it. My secrets and lies were what got me into this mess in the first place. Better not keep them in the dark. "I do need to talk to you guys about something."

"Uh oh. This doesn't sound so good. What's going on?"

"Can't talk about this right now. Please, let's just go to Wolfgang Puck's tomorrow night. I can't tell you what I need to tell you over the phone."

I heard a long silence on the other end.

"Mom?"

"Oh, sorry, Dalilah. I was distracted. You know how much I worry about you. It sounds like what you're going to tell us is going to be not so good."

Not so good. Understatement of the year.

"Just see me tomorrow night, with dad. Thanks." At that, I hung up. I didn't want to hear her try to pry the news out of me on the phone, as she always tried to do.

After I got off the phone, I went and got dressed for my date that evening with Nottingham. I did my usual ritual before I had to see him – I took two shots of Jack Daniels and ate part of a pot cookie. After what had happened with Luke and Nottingham, I became so depressed that I sought help and was able to get a prescription for marijuana. Part of the reason I was able to was because I had really been depressed for years, so the doctor I spoke with had determined that I was suffering from chronic depression and gave me a prescription based upon that.

The pot that I was prescribed wasn't the giggly kind, as I liked to call it, but, rather, was more of a relaxant. Very little bothered me when I ate the cookie, which meant that I was able to get through my dates with Nottingham with a feeling of relaxation, which bordered on euphoria. I didn't know if Nottingham suspected how drunk and high I was when I saw him, but he never said a word about it, so I assumed that he didn't really know.

This was my life. Becoming, once again, comfortably numb with substances, because I was so unhappy. And, of course, my art stopped once again. Depression can sap one's energy and zest for living, and art, for me, required that I had some kind of passion in my body. The kind of passion for life that Luke had invoked in me – that was the stuff that my art was made of. But now, well, I did my nude modeling, and ate my cookies and drank my shots, all while trying to get through dates with Nottingham without killing him.

I had stopped posing for Luke, of course. He had to finish the portrait just through memory, and based upon the photos that he had taken of me early on. Nottingham had kept me abreast of the progress, and assured me that the portrait would be delivered on time. Which would mean that Nottingham would have that portrait around the same time that Luke had his show, which was scheduled for the week of December 15.

Nottingham picked me up at 7, and we were going to be headed to the Union Club, which was where he always liked to take me. I secretly thought that he wanted to take me to this place because he knew how much I hated it. It was a gorgeous club, and served only the very well-heeled, but that was the problem – I craved ordinariness. Playing pool, going bowling, playing blackjack at the casino, hanging out and drinking hot chocolate while listening to music – that was my idea of heaven, if these activities were done with Luke. And, of course, the sex with him was out.Of.This.-World. I couldn't get enough, and neither could he.

I got into Nottingham's limo, and he kissed me lightly on the cheek. I looked at him, feeling nothing at all. Which was actually good, because if I didn't calm myself down with my cookie, I probably would have cut a bitch. The bitch being Nottingham.

"Nice to see you Dalilah," he said.

"And you."

Nottingham looked down at his hands, and I noticed that his thumbs were twiddling. Finally, he looked at me. "I have decided that I want you to attend Luke's show with me."

At that moment, my heart started racing and panic arose in my throat. My pot cookie notwithstanding, this simple sentence from Nottingham induced terror in me. Not to mention the fact that the very idea of going to Luke's show on Nottingham's arm was utterly incomprehensible. It was something that I literally couldn't imagine. "Why? Why would you want to do this to me?"

He put his hand to his chin. "Because, Dalilah, I want to make you suffer. And I can think of no better way of doing that than to make you see Luke whilst you're on my arm. And, I want him to know that you're mine, now, in case he is entertaining any ideas that would contradict that."

At that moment, I wanted to castrate him without anesthesia. I was so angry that no substances I took could keep me calm. I said nothing to him, but looked out the window. I wasn't going to protest, though. I had to bite my tongue about that. If Nottingham wanted to torture Luke and me by having me show up on his arm, then that was what was going to happen.

"Dalilah," he said, jerking my face towards him. "You're going to do this." And then he changed the subject. "Your parents. When are you going to tell them?"

"Tomorrow night. It's already set."

"Good. You do know, though, that, even if they don't approve, this wedding is going to happen. Right?"

I nodded my head and said nothing. "Right."

He nodded back and went back to looking out the window.

For the rest of the evening, I sulked and hardly said a word. Not that he cared. On the contrary, I swear that he got a perverse sense of pleasure in seeing me squirm. He did all the talking, and I pretty much answered "yes," or "no," and really didn't say much more.

This was probably the longest night of my life. Except, of course, for the night that I broke Luke's heart.

Chapter Nine

The next night was my dinner with my parents. I dreaded this almost as much as I dreaded seeing Luke at his show. After Nottingham dropped me off at my apartment after our dinner, I laid awake all night, filled with anxiety and dread for having to see Luke while I was with Nottingham. I felt that such an appearance was going to be rubbing salt in both of our wounds. I could never move on from my feelings for him, but I really, really wanted and needed for him to move on from his feelings for me. And seeing him was just going to reopen that wound and pour rubbing alcohol on it.

So, I thought about sending a text message to him. I felt that I had to warn him that I would be coming and that I would be with Nottingham, who no doubt would be busy introducing me to everyone as his wife. That would be completely unfair to just blindside Luke like that.

My heart in my throat, I was going to text him. But then thought better of it. If I warned him, then he probably wouldn't come to his own show. If he didn't come to his show, then it probably wouldn't be a hit. Nottingham had invited hundreds of luminaries to the premiere, most of whom had RSVP'd yes. Celebrities, politicians, critics, patrons, art A-listers – all would be coming to the premiere, and Luke would have to at least be there to meet everybody. If he didn't, well, then he would be missing out on a huge opportunity.

The next trick would be to make sure that he wasn't completely thrown off his game by seeing me there. If he was going to truly be able to mix and mingle and meet important people, then seeing me there with Nottingham would no doubt put a total damper on his spirits and motivation. I somehow would have to hide from him as much as possible, which was going to be tricky at best.

I wrestled with what to do for that entire afternoon. I was caught between wanting to warn him, and take the chance that he didn't show to his own premiere, and blindsiding him, which would certainly cause him anxiety, such that he might not want to meet anybody. I had no idea which option I should take, so I just decided that blindsiding him might be the safest choice.

My parents arrived to take me to dinner at 6 PM, and our reservations were at 7. I opened the door for them, and my mom and dad both enveloped me in a hug.

As my dad held me in his arms, I felt safe. Like when I was a small child. I found myself wanting to go back to that time, when I was young and helpless. Before I started making crappy decisions about my life. I wanted to start all over again, so that I could do things differently.

In my alternative universe, where I could start anew, I would have the lessons learned in this universe to draw upon, so that I wouldn't make the same mistakes. I never would have started seeing Nottingham, as I would know that Nottingham would have given Luke a show without my intervention. So Luke and I would still be together and happy and planning our wedding. In a couple of years or so, we would start a family. A hip, jazzy family living in the Upper West Side. I would take our daughter to the park every day, and both of us would have sizzling art careers.

"Dalilah, honey, what's wrong?" my dad was saying. "Why are you crying?"

I didn't even realize that I was crying. But, sure enough, I lifted my head and saw that my dad's shirt was completely soaked. "Oh, dad, I'm so sorry. I got a mascara stain on your shirt. Do you happen to have an extra one around?"

"No, Dalilah, but I do have a t-shirt under this shirt." At that, he took off his shirt, and wadded it up into a ball.

"I guess Wolfgang Puck's is out, huh?" I said.

"Why don't we order pizza in? And maybe you can pour us a couple of glasses of wine. You look like you need it," my father said.

I nodded my head and smiled. It wasn't every day that parents encouraged their under-aged daughter to drink alcohol, but I was almost 21. And, really, my father, having spent years in Europe, had an almost European sensibility when it came to drinking wine. He usually let me have a glass here and there, from the time I was 13. As long as I didn't abuse it in his presence, all was good.

So, my parents took a seat on my couch, and I sat on the beanbag on the floor. We ordered a mushroom pizza from the pizzeria down the street and I poured them a glass of wine, and got one for myself.

While we waited for the pizza guy, my mom, not wanting to beat around the bush, said "okay, Dalilah, you needed to tell us something important. We're here. I've been on pins and needles ever since getting off the phone with you. Please tell us, finally, what is going on."

I took a deep breath and sipped my wine. I had earlier wrestled with what to tell them, but, as with Nick, I decided that honesty would be the best policy. There wasn't much, or anything, that they could do to stop my marriage to Nottingham, so there was no reason to lie.

"Okay. Okay. Uh, um…."

Mom and dad were looking at me with bewildered and concerned expressions. I looked at them, and had a difficult time finding my words. I mean, how does a daughter tell her parents that she is going to willingly fuck up her entire life? How does a daughter tell her parents that she is going to embark into a relationship that will definitely be destructive and devastating? Their first instinct was to protect me at all costs. And now I was about to tell them that they wouldn't be able to protect me, because I was going to go forward with what I had to do. They couldn't stop me.

Honestly, if I was going to tell them that I had pancreatic cancer and I only had three months to live, I think that I would have had an easier time of it. I felt at an absolute loss for words.

Dad looked very serious. "What is it, baby girl? You can tell us anything. Anything at all. We'll deal with it, as a family. Just tell us."

I breathed in through my nose, out through my mouth. Finally, I just blurted it out. "I'm getting married."

After I said that, my parents looked even more confused. "But, Dalilah," my mom said. "If you're marrying Luke, then you should be happy. He seems like a great guy for you. But you don't look happy at all. You look terrified."

My dad was just staring at me. I could almost see his wheels turning. One thing about my dad, he was sharp. In intelligence, I was clearly my father's daughter. "Yes, Dalilah, you do look terrified. Which makes me think that you're not marrying Luke at all. If you were, you would be happy. But you're clearly not."

I took another sip of my wine. I couldn't meet either of their eyes. "I'm not marrying Luke." I finally was able to look at them, and my mom still looked befuddled, my dad looked like he almost understood. "I'm marrying Nottingham. And I'm marrying him almost immediately."

My mother's face registered shock, and my dad looked like he was about to blow a gasket. I had never seen him angry in my life. He was such a cool, laid-back guy. So gentle and caring. But he looked as if he was about to blow steam out of his ears.

Finally, mom said "I don't understand. You're marrying the man who is into BDSM? Who Nick calls 'that cold bastard?' Why would you do that to yourself? It's not for love. It couldn't be for love. So why? What are you thinking, Dalilah?"

My father was narrowing his eyes. "He's blackmailing you. The bastard is blackmailing you."

I nodded my head. "Yes, mom and dad. He's blackmailing me. But I brought it on to myself."

My dad was pacing, and I started to get concerned. I remembered that my dad was in on the forced suicide of Paul Lucas. He planned it right alongside Nick. He had to have, because it was on my dad's computer that I found the incriminating video. And, before he ever knew my mom, it was my understanding that he hung out with drug dealers and other rough sorts.

In other words, my dad certainly was no pushover. I wondered what he would be capable of.

"Dalilah, you can't do this. You can't mess up your life

like this," he said. He stopped short of telling me that he forbade me to do it, because he knew that wouldn't stop me. I had always been a girl who had her own mind, and I pretty much did what I wanted, even before I was an adult. Now that I was an adult, I certainly wasn't going to be forbidden to do anything. He knew this, so he didn't even try to say that he absolutely was going to stop me.

"Dad, sit down," I said. I looked over at my mom, and she was crying. "Oh, crap," I said, seeing her. "Please quit crying, mom. Please."

"I can't help it, Dalilah. You seem to have your mind made up about this, and your life is going to be completely ruined if you go through with this. How can I just stand by and watch you do this to yourself? How?"

"I don't know, but it has to be done."

Finally, my dad stopped pacing and sat back down on my couch. "Okay, Dalilah, tell us the entire story. Tell us what is going on. Maybe we can help."

"No, you can't. You can't. I got trapped. I got trapped and there's no way out. And it was all through my own doing, too. All of it. I have to marry him, or else Luke's future is in jeopardy."

My dad, sharp as a tack, said "Oh, I get it. I get it. That bastard is threatening to sabotage Luke if you don't do this. And he's just powerful and well-connected enough to succeed, too."

"Yes," I said, grateful that I didn't have to tell him everything. "He said that he not only would pull Luke's show if I didn't marry him, but that he also would ensure that he wouldn't get another show in this city. You don't understand, dad. Luke was ready to give up and go work for his dad in Maine. He was so discouraged, and getting this show made him so happy. This is his life. Luke's life."

"Dalilah, it's your life, too," my father said. "You have to also think of yourself, here. It's awful that Luke would lose the one thing that he has dreamed about and worked for his entire life, because of the caprice of one man. But it will be even worse for you to enter into a destructive, love-less relationship out of some misguided sense of loyalty and obligation. I'll bet that Luke would much rather have you by his side, even if he is struggling, then to have all the money and fame in the world, with nobody to share it with."

"Dad, I love you, and you always give great advice. But, in this case, I have to do this. I have to. Listen, I caused this. Me. Nottingham became so infuriated with the fact that I was using him that he did this. He made the ultimatum, because of my actions. If I just would have left well enough alone, then Luke would have still had his show, and I would be marrying him, not Nottingham."

"Do you really believe that?" my father said. "You're one of the smartest people on this planet, but I can't believe that you're still so naïve."

"Naïve about what?"

"A man like that, who is that obsessed with you, would have pulled Luke's show regardless of whether or not you were using him," dad said. "Just because he's jealous. Just you dating Luke would be enough for a guy like him to do that. So, you can't feel guilty about this. If you're doing this out of a sense of guilt about your actions, just stop. Just stop, because no matter what you did, the outcome would have been the same. That's what men like Nottingham do. They use people as their pawns, because life is one big chess game to them. In this case, his pawns are named Dalilah and Luke."

"Be that as it may, I have to do all I can to ensure Luke's

future. So, I'm doing this. I'm going through with it. And neither of you can stop me."

My mom continued to cry, and my father continued to look angry. "Why is Luke's future more important than your own?" he asked.

"Because I love him. I love him, and I'm willing to make any sacrifice for him. Just like you saved mom from being shot by deflecting that gunman's attention onto you, I'm doing the same thing. Taking the bullet for Luke. I'm figuratively taking a bullet for Luke."

The anger drained away from my father's face, because he finally understood. He finally understood my need to sacrifice myself for Luke. "Dalilah, this is all very noble of you. It is. And you're right. I would take a bullet for you or your mother even now. In a heartbeat. Without even thinking about it. But Luke's life isn't in danger, here."

"No, it's not. But his future is. His dream is. You take away a man's dream and a man's livelihood, then what does he have left? Think about that. I mean, we can still be together if I don't marry Nottingham, but he'll just be broken down. Defeated. I can prevent that, just by…"

"Doing what Nottingham wants, when he wants," my father said "Is that you what you want for yourself? What about your dreams of having a family and a husband that you love? What about your dreams of being a working artist again? What about you?"

"Again, dad, it's my sacrifice. You just said yourself that you would sacrifice for the ones that you love. I will, too."

"Yes, but you hardly know this boy," my mom was saying. She finally had quit crying and was now ready to beat me down as much as my dad was. "You hardly know him, and.."

"Oh, really? Really? That's all you got? That I haven't

known him that long? What difference does it make how long I've known him? All that matters is that I am truly in love with him, and I'll do anything for him. Anything at all."

My dad didn't try to bring up that point, about my not knowing Luke long enough to want to make a sacrifice like this. He knew better, having fallen in love with my mom at first sight. And, if you're in love with somebody, then you're in love with somebody. No matter if you've known him for 50 hours or 50 years, love is love.

"Dalilah, your mom and I understand your position. We really do. But you have to rethink this and not go into this blindly or in haste. And maybe he's bluffing. Perhaps you should see. Maybe if you don't marry him, he'll still give Luke his show and help guide his career," my dad said. But I looked at his face, and saw that he didn't really believe his own words.

"Do you really believe that, dad? You just said yourself that Luke and I are both pawns in his sick game. Do you really believe that he'll just be Luke's fairy godfather, even if Luke and I are together?"

To this, my father had no words. After a few minutes, he finally just said "no. No, I don't really believe that."

I just took a deep breath. "Okay, so, I'm doing this. I'm doing this, and it has to be done next week, before Luke's show. For obvious reasons, Nottingham needs to seal the deal before Luke's premiere date."

My mom and dad both just looked defeated. They both knew the reality of the situation – once my mind was made up, there was pretty much no changing it. It had always been that way, as I was always very willful and independent.

"I hate this, Dalilah," my dad said. "I hate this, and I don't approve of this. And that man will not be welcome in

ANNIE JOCOBY

our house. We draw the line there. He won't be welcome in this family, or in our lives. Ever. Are we clear about that?"

"Of course," I said. "I'll just have to come and see you without him. And spend holidays with you and not him."

And then my mother, of all people, surprised me. "After Luke's show, if he's a hit, you can just divorce Nottingham. You can divorce him, because you won't need him anymore. Right?"

In spite of myself, I smiled at my mother suddenly being so devious. "If only. But, no, Nottingham will always have the power to put Luke right back to where he was before. A man that powerful can turn all the major benefactors and galleries against Luke at any time. He can make Luke, but he can also break him. I don't think that you understand that kind of influence he has on the people in the New York City art scene. So, no. Unless I want to ensure that Luke gets blackballed, just as he's taking off, I can't divorce Nottingham and marry Luke, even after his debut is a hit."

Now my mom and dad were looking as resigned as I felt. I secretly wished that my dad could bad-ass the whole situation like he helped Nick do with that Paul Lucas pervert all those years ago. Maybe my dad could hire a hit man or even do the deed himself.

Come on, Dalilah, you know that's not going to happen. Nor do you really want it to. It's just your dark fantasy.

My father shook his head. "You're going to do what you're going to do. But I won't support you, and I don't think that your mother will either."

"No, I don't support you, either," my mom said. "We still love you. You'll always be our little girl. But there's no way we're going to give our blessing to this."

"Well, as long as you don't disown me, I guess all isn't

Secrets & Lies

lost," I said, only half-joking. "I love you both, and I'm so sorry I let you down like this."

"You didn't let us down," dad said. "You got caught in a bad situation with a devious, obsessive and powerful man. I want you to think about this decision long and hard, though. Think about the commitment that you're about to make. About the life you're going to have. Think about that, Dalilah. That's all we ask."

I smiled. The entire thing was really a *fait accompli*, as my mind was made up long before mom and dad heard the news. They didn't accept it, of course. What parent would? But I was going to go through with it anyhow.

Maybe my dad was right. Maybe my actions didn't actually lead to this situation, and Nottingham would have played the same stunt no matter what my actions were. He probably would have, seeing as he was so obsessed with me. Perhaps I was always destined to be his pawn, and Luke as well.

No matter. Fate was hurtling me down this path, and I was going to meet it. I was going to meet it with my head held high, knowing that Luke would finally achieve his dream through my actions.

That was really good enough for me.

Chapter Ten

It wasn't a week after I told my parents about marrying Nottingham that he and I ended up at City Hall, after getting our marriage license. I didn't bother to dress for occasion, of course, choosing to wear jeans and a t-shirt with the message *I'd tell you to go to hell, but I live there, and I don't want to see you every day*. Surprisingly, Nottingham said little about my attire. The one thing he did say was "I know you're trying to get a rise out of me, Dalilah, so I'm just going to treat you like a child and ignore your bait. But I will say this – you're being disrespectful to this judge. I see that you have a sweater in your purse, so please put it on when we go up to take our vows."

Nottingham was right. I had a sweater tucked in my enormous Coach bag, which was one of Alaina's hand-me-downs. I really didn't want to disrespect the court, either, but, at the same time, I wanted to rebel against this arrangement in any way that I could.

We sat on the wooden bench outside the courtroom. People were streaming in and out. Most of them were young, like me, but they were marrying people who were just as young. They looked excited and in love, and I envied them. They probably saw Nottingham and me, and would never have put us together. After all, I was wearing jeans, a snarky t-shirt and scuffed-up Doc Marten boots. In my arms was my leather bomber jacket. Meanwhile, right next to me, was Nottingham – three-piece suit, hair perfectly in place, with shoes buffed to a perfect sheen. His trench coat and hat were with his assistant, who discreetly sat on the other end of the hall, checking his text messages.

Everyone else who came in and out fit together. Tattooed boys were with tattooed girls. A boy in a wife-beater and baggy jeans was with a girl dressed in a similar manner. Another guy who was dressed in a suit was with a girl in a simple white dress. All the other couples coor-dinated.

Not Nottingham and me. We couldn't look more disparate if we tried. Well, actually, that wasn't true – I deliberately made sure that I looked the way that I looked, because I wanted to send a message to Nottingham that this entire situation was under protest. He was actually lucky that I didn't color my hair blue and get a nose piercing and a neck tattoo for the occasion. So, yeah, maybe we could have looked more disparate if I really would have gone out of my way to do so.

I glanced over at Nottingham, who looked like he was rapidly losing patience with the whole thing. He checked his watch. "When are they going to call us in? I have a meeting at 3."

I raised my eyebrow. "Maybe you shouldn't have sched-uled a meeting on your wedding day. Just a thought."

He glared at me. "Unlike you, I have to work for a living. I have a company that depends upon me. Your life is nothing but a cabaret. You get high and you lay on couches for people. My life is just a little bit more complicated than that."

Oh, so he does know about my getting high. I mentally gave him points for not being as stupid as he came across. "Well, I'm sure that business can wait. After all, you're marrying the girl of your dreams, aren't you? I would think that this occasion would be the cause for taking off at least one day from the office."

He smirked, but said nothing. He was learning to ignore my snark, much to my dismay.

Finally, our names were called. I took a deep breath, willing my feet to go towards the door. Nottingham grabbed my hand, as my other hand reached into my purse for my black sweater. I pulled the sweater over my head, and we approached the bench.

I felt sick as the judge matter-of-factly asked us questions. He asked each of us if we took one another as our lawfully wedded spouse. Both of us said "I do." I tried very hard not to puke on the floor after I said these two words. The two words that were going to irrevocably change my life. I was strangely calm, though, having come to terms with this unholy arrangement and having done my grieving beforehand. Plus, I had an entire pot cookie right before I got to the courthouse, so I was pretty out of it. The judge apparently didn't know this, however, because he would have had to stop the ceremony if he did. One couldn't be incoherent with a mind-altering substance and be married.

Short, sweet – the ceremony was over before I really knew what was happening. The judge pronounced us husband and wife, and we both thanked him and left. As I walked out of the courtroom, I looked at the next couple in line. They were sitting closely together, holding hands and giggling. They both looked giddy. Young and idealistic, like how I felt when Luke asked me to marry him. They had their whole lives ahead of them, and I was so jealous of them I wanted to die.

That should be me. I should be with Luke, giggling and holding hands and joking around. I should have a face that was completely lit up, and a man next to me whom I adore. My entire life should be ahead of me, filled with love and support and lots of great sex. It wasn't fair.

It just wasn't fair.

Chapter Eleven

Luke

It was the day of my premiere. I was beside myself with absolute worry. Panic, even. I was going to be meeting all of these important people, and I really didn't know what I was going to say to any of them. I was just happy that I was finally able to get motivated enough to actually make an appearance and kiss the ring, as Jake had put it. My heart said not to go, but my head said that I had to. I had to if I wanted to make my show a success.

My brain had to overrule my heart every time. After all, this was what had worked for my entire life. This was what I had dreamed about ever since I was a little boy. I dreamed about this moment in time, when everybody would be coming to see my work. When people finally started to notice me. I composed my art for myself, of course, but I really also wanted others to share in it. It wasn't selfish to want this kind of an opportunity. It was necessary. Without financial backing and attention, I would always toil in obscurity and, let's face it, probably would have ended up back in Maine with my pop. I still would paint, draw and sculpt, of course, but it would have been merely a hobby for me.

But this show would be my way of actually making a living doing what I loved. There could be nothing better in the world than to be able to do that. To have people pay money for the privilege of having my paintings on their wall – that was something that I never thought would happen anytime soon. But, tonight, it would be.

Of course, I tried to put Dalilah out of my mind, just for the one night. It had been almost a month since she pulled the rug out from under me, and I had been wallowing ever since. I still hung out with Jake, of course, but I didn't go to the poker games. I was as good as my word with him – I needed to lay off the games until I got my head together, because I literally couldn't afford to play as badly as I was. But, other than my nights out with Jake, and my shifts at the bar, I was a hermit. I needed to feel my grief. To own it. Just like after my mother had died.

There were moments when I wanted to die. Brief moments, though, because I immediately pulled myself out of that thinking. What was it they said? That suicide was a permanent solution to a temporary problem? Or something like that. And I didn't really want to die. It was just that the pain had gotten so bad, so acute, that I thought about putting myself out of my misery.

But grieving goes in spurts. It was always like a roller coaster, and I had good days and bad days. On the bad days, I would be on my couch, not doing a single thing. The thoughts of Dalilah would become obsessive on these days, so that every single cell in my body seemed like they were filled with some kind of lead. My body felt heavy, and my depression was deep.

On the good days, though, life was bearable. Not great, but bearable. I would actually be able to leave the apartment and grab a bite down at Joey's Diner, knowing that Joey, with his boisterous personality, would never fail to cheer me up. Other days, I would sit on the sidewalk next to Freddy, my homeless friend, and the two of us would shoot the shit. Sad to say, but Freddy would make me feel better about my life, because he had some real problems. One day I actually felt energetic enough to volunteer at the homeless shelter where Freddy got most of his meals. Giving back made me feel better, and being around the homeless made me appreciate anew how much I had and how much I was given.

I would think that I had turned a corner, but then, the next day, my depression would be back, worse than ever. And it was funny – whatever mood I would be in on any given day was the mood that I, at that time, thought would be permanent. On the good days, I thought that I was over my grieving, and that I could move on with my life. On my bad days, I thought that my extreme despair and depression were here to stay. Of course, neither of these thoughts were ever true, because my emotions changed on a dime.

Which brought me to my premiere night. Thankfully, it happened on one of my good days, so I felt reasonably ready to show up and try to meet as many people as possible. Nottingham had taken care of all the publicity and the rest of the details, so that all that I really had to do was show up. Even that was optional, but I felt that it was something that was really necessary.

I was even looking forward to the evening just a bit. There was going to be an open bar and hors d'oeuvres, which was going to include all kinds of little gourmet bites. If nothing else, I was looking forward to getting some free food and drinks, although I wasn't going to get hammered by any means. I just wanted to drink enough to take the edge off, because I had to be charming if I was going to impress these big shots who were going to be there.

Jake called me right before I was getting ready to leave. "Hey," he said. "Just wanted to wish you good luck, man. I know that you're gonna take names, but I wanted to call and tell you that I'm behind you. You got this, buddy. You got this."

I smiled. Good ol' Jake. I could always count on him to have my back, no matter what. "Thanks for calling," I said. "I'll hit you up later and let you know how it goes."

"Break a leg, dude," he said.

"Later."

At that, I looked in the mirror one last time. My hair was behaving a little bit, and I was dressed as nicely as possible – I was wearing the pants from the suit that Dalilah's father gave me, with leather shoes that weren't too worn, and a purple button down with my collar open. I wanted to look dressy, yet casual, which was why I didn't go the entire suit and tie route. Then I went down to meet the cab that I had called for the evening.

My anticipation was high as the cab drove off the curb and towards my future.

Chapter Twelve

Dalilah

Luke's premiere was upon me, and I had tried mightily to get out of going. I tried every excuse that I could think of, but Nottingham simply said "you're going. I want everybody to meet my new wife. And you're going to behave yourself, too. I'm sick and tired of your rebelliousness. You're going to wear that cocktail dress that I bought for you, you're going to be gracious to everyone I introduce you to, and you're going to smile politely at everyone there. Do I make myself clear?"

"Crystal," I said. I was terrified about being there, though. How could I do this to Luke? I hated Nottingham more than I had ever hated him, right at that moment, for making me do this. By this time, he was well aware of how much I loved Luke. He and I shared a bed after we were married, and I submitted to him, just like he told me I would have to do. I hated that. I hated for him to touch me, period, so the sex games were insufferable. The only good thing was that he had lain off of the beating, unlike the first night that he met me, because the cocktail gown that he had bought for me was backless, and it wouldn't do for me to have any kind of marks on my body when I was going to meet his fancy friends.

But, because Nottingham and I shared a bed, he knew how much I was in love with Luke. Because I dreamed about Luke every night, and Nottingham told me every morning how much I talked in my sleep.

"And the only thing you talk about, Dalilah, is him."

"Sorry," I said. "I'll try to control what I dream about from now on."

"Sarcastic little bitch. I'm very happy that you have to see him at his premiere. I'm very pleased that he's going to see you with me, and he's going to know that you belong to me now. I can't wait to see the look on his face when I go up to him and introduce you as my wife."

I immediately regretted my insolence to Nottingham. Because, right at that moment, I wanted to beg him not to make me go through with this. I couldn't do this to Luke, I just couldn't.

But I had to. It was going to break my heart into a million pieces, but I had to do this. Nottingham had made it clear that I had no choice.

As I laid in the bathtub, trying to psyche myself up for what it was that I was going to have to do, my mind drifted to my "honeymoon" with Nottingham. He actually had taken off of work the weekend after we were married – much to my chagrin, as I preferred it when he worked 18-hour days, for obvious reasons – and we went to his beach house in the Bahamas. It was a typical billionaire beach house – all glass and marble, with a stone façade. It was easily 6000 square feet, and was equipped with everything –

indoor and outdoor pool, several hot tubs, a game room, a movie theatre, etc., etc. It was situated right on the beach.

It actually turned out to be not that great of a honeymoon for him, but a nice one for me. Something was blowing up back at his job, and he spent most of the weekend on the phone and on the computer, trying to straighten everything out. Which meant that I spent that weekend virtually alone, and took advantage of that.

I ended up swimming in the ocean much of the time. Which was nice, really, except for that one day. That one day when I almost lost my life. And I realized that perhaps I really wanted to die after all.

Chapter Thirteen

It happened on the second day that we were there. Nottingham was on the phone, screaming in Italian at some poor sap, and I informed him that I was going to be down at the beach if he needed me.

"Whatever," he said to me. "Have fun," he said in a tone of voice that made me know that he really didn't want me to have fun at all. "I have to talk to Antonio about this crisis."

I gathered that "Antonio" referred to somebody who was part of the Italian subsidiary of Nottingham Enterprises.

I shrugged, got on my suit, put on a ton of sunscreen, and headed down to the secluded beach. I laid down my towel, erected an umbrella, and just listened to the waves. Back home, it was 20 degrees, but here it was 80 and sunny.

I closed my eyes, and imagined that I was on my honeymoon with Luke. What would we be doing right now? Probably having sex on every piece of furniture in the house. But maybe not. Maybe we'd be teasing each other over a game of backgammon. Or perhaps we would each be reading a book, him sitting on the couch, me with my head on his lap. We both would probably get a lot of painting done, too. We would swim in the ocean together, maybe, him carrying me playfully while kissing me passionately.

I breathed in the daydream, trying to feel it. Trying to put myself into the dream so that it seemed like a reality. Sometimes I was able to do this, and it made me feel really happy for just those few stolen moments.

But, today, just thinking about being with Luke made me feel nothing but depressed. Because I wanted so badly to be with him, and I couldn't. I couldn't, and that was the reality. My fantasy was never going to become a reality, so I had to stop dreaming and start trying to figure out how I was going to survive life the way that it was for me.

I went down to the water, the waves washing over me. I went further and further out, as I tried to get to an area that was somewhat calmer. I was an excellent swimmer, so I really wasn't too worried when I realized, suddenly, that I couldn't touch anymore.

I tried to swim to shore, but I realized that I was caught in a rip tide. It was a powerful one, too, and, even though I tried to swim horizontally towards the shore, it seemed that I got further and further out. The shore looked like it was a hundred miles away, and I felt a sense of panic welling up in my throat.

Was this it? Was this how it was going to go? I was just going to sink into oblivion out here, all alone? The tide was pushing me further and further back, and it seemed as if all was lost.

And I...accepted it. An overwhelming sense of peace washed over me, as I realized that I was welcoming it. I said a little prayer that Luke and everyone who loved me would eventually be okay, and I floated on my back and looked to the heavens. I didn't even try to fight anymore. I just let the waves push me further and further back.

Of course, I didn't actually drown. I eventually found that I was out of the rip-tide, so I was able to ride the waves back to shore, as I swam furiously. By the time I got to shore, I was exhausted and my heart was pounding out of my chest. It took me about an hour to truly recover from that near-death experience, as my entire body was trembling and I was near tears.

I almost died. If I wasn't as strong of a swimmer as I was, I would have drowned. I had no idea how I got out of that rip-tide, and this was, by far, the scariest experience that I had ever had.

Finally, the shock of what just happened wore off, and I laid down on the beach and bawled more than I had ever bawled. It was partly out of relief that I made it out of the ocean alive. But it was also that my emotions and grief over my life finally caught up to me, right at that moment, and the tears simply couldn't stop. I laid down on my blanket, under my umbrella, for hours, just holding myself and crying. Rocking back and forth, sobbing, and barely being able to catch my breath.

I finally trudged back into the house when the sun started to set, and Nottingham was still screaming at somebody, in French this time. I was fluent in French, Italian, Spanish and German, so I understood every word he said. And what he was saying to this poor lackey on the other end of the phone wasn't pretty.

He didn't even acknowledge me as I walked past him on the way to the bedroom. I got changed into my clothes and laid down on the bed, and immediately fell asleep.

Chapter Fourteen

So, as I laid in the bathtub, dreading what was ahead, my mind had drifted to that day at the beach. I mean, once I got out of the situation, I was relieved. But while I was in it – when I actually thought that I would die – there was almost a sense of peace. When I had a chance to process all of my emotions, I started to feel concerned that I almost welcomed the prospect of slipping beneath those waves and never resurfacing. I had no idea what waited for me after death, if anything did at all, but no matter – I realized, in that moment, that dying was something that I really was looking forward to.

Because I had no idea how I could live a lifetime in the situation that I was in. Nottingham was abusive, cold, cruel and vindictive. My father was right – the world was his chessboard, and the people in it were his to manipulate to try to get his checkmate. Luke and I were but pawns in his game, and the game was what he really delighted in. As long as he could see me squirm, and make sure that Luke was sufficiently humiliated and depressed, Nottingham was going to be happy. As happy as a man like him could ever be.

I took the sponge and filled it with water, and squeezed it over my body. My toes were pruning a little bit, which was when I realized that I had been in the tub for longer than I had thought.

In a few minutes, Nottingham was pounding on the door. "You have to get out of there right now, because we're leaving in less than an hour."

I tried to will away my tears, which were threatening, because seeing Luke at the premiere was going to be something that was going to be incomprehensible. No doubt, Nottingham was going to make a show of going right up to him and introducing me as his wife. And Luke would immediately be thrown off his game. I was starting to question my original decision to not text him to warn him, but, then again, it might still be the right decision – at least Luke would be at the party tonight. If I told him what was going to go down, he no doubt wouldn't be.

I grabbed my pot cookie and ate the entire thing. Within ten minutes, I felt myself relaxing. I then got out of the tub, and went into the bedroom, where there was a backless black cocktail dress waiting for me, along with a pair of high-heeled stilettos. I got dressed, and put my hair up and a little bit of makeup. I grabbed my clutch and went downstairs, where Nottingham was waiting for me in a tux.

I took his arm, and he led me into the limousine, and we took off. We took off to where Luke was, and I knew, for a fact, that I was going to break his heart anew. Even moreso than ever. Inside, I wanted to puke and scream and cry. But I tried to show no emotion outside. I, once again, was going to have to play a part that evening. The part of the charming wife. And I was going to have to somehow shut off my feelings for Luke. That was going to be next to impossible.

I had no idea what was going to happen that evening, but I had a feeling that whatever it was, it wasn't going to be good.

Chapter Fifteen

Luke

I walked into the premiere, feeling nervous and excited. I had actually psyched myself up for this, and I was astounded at how many people were milling about. Granted, I wasn't the only one who was showing – there were two other artists as well – but I still felt more than flattered to see several different people at each one of my paintings just admiring them.

I went over to one of my paintings and just kinda stood behind the people who were looking at it. I tried to absorb what the general buzz was.

"So, what do you think about this?" a tall and lanky man, dressed in khakis and a suit jacket with patches on his elbows, was asking a petite woman with perfectly coiffed brown hair.

She cocked her head a little to the side. "I'm not sure. I love the use of the light and the brush strokes are superb. I'm just trying to get the message." The painting that they were referring to was that of a dreadlocked man playing a violin. "It seems to be a perfect blending of something that is classical and timeless with something that is urban and modern. And the expression on that musician's face is devastating. The eyes just draw you in."

I felt myself beaming as I listened to the two talk some more about my painting. The tall man had a different interpretation. He saw it as more of a commentary on our times – that perhaps "the artist" was trying to convey a yearning for a simpler time, which would be why the eyes of the musician looked so dark and depressed.

I walked over to another one of my paintings, that of a ballerina. There were about five people gathered around this one, silently looking at it. Finally, one said "I think that I'm in love with this painting. It speaks to me somehow." She looked carefully at the price, and saw that it was selling for $22,000. She nodded slowly, and said to her companion. "What do you think? Wouldn't this look awesome in the den?"

I held my breath. Her companion put his arm around her and said "I think you're right. I love the colors on this one and there's something about those eyes that really draw you in. I've never heard of this Luke Roberts, but it looks like he has a great future."

When I heard that they were going to buy the painting, I felt overjoyed, for the first time since Dalilah told me goodbye. I didn't think that it was possible to feel happy again, but, somehow, just knowing that these two strangers wanted my art on their walls, and they were willing to spend over $20,000 to accomplish this, was a feeling unlike any other.

At that, the woman immediately started looking at the companion painting to this one. It was very similar to the one that she was wanting to buy, but, instead of one ballet dancer, it was two – a male and a female. She stood in front of it and nodded. "I love this one, too. Look at the detail. The sinews, the facial expression, the use of light. It's reminiscent of Robert Krogle and Melinda Morrison. Not to mention Monet."

Her companion nodded and said "let's get them both."

I started breathing faster. I just got here, and the premiere was only a few hours old, and I already sold two paintings at $22,000 apiece. Which would mean that I already would be leaving with at least $22,000, assuming that these two actually did buy these paintings.

I looked over and saw Henry Jacobs himself looking at one of my paintings of a jazz musician. He was studying it carefully, and then went over to another of mine and studied that as well.

I hated that man, because of what he did to Dalilah. At the same time, he was a star-maker. I wrestled with conflicting feelings as I saw him go to one of my paintings after another, and silently prayed that he didn't find them wanting. Right next to him was another art critic, Elaine Bush, who was well-known for her extremely popular blog. She, too, was a star-maker, especially for the younger patrons who got much of their information on-line. Jacobs was more of the old-guard, as he was the lead critic for the New York Times, and Bush was the new-guard. A good word from one of them would put me onto the A-list. A good word from both of them would put my career into the stratosphere.

I took a deep breath, knowing that I probably shouldn't go up and talk to them. I didn't quite know the etiquette of that situation, but something told me that if I went up and introduced myself that might be seen as intrusive. They probably wanted to look at my paintings and review them without my input.

It was just as well, because I was feeling hungry and in need of a glass of wine. I was getting butterflies and feeling like the entire experience was surreal. I mean, people – important people and unknowns alike – were looking at my work! And at least two of these people were wanting to buy! Inside, I was feeling so giddy that I had to calm down a little bit, so I headed to the bar. On the way, I passed by a string quartet who were playing strains of Bach.

While I walked to the bar, I grabbed some hors d'oeuvres off of a waitress who was walking around. The hors d'oeuvres were delicious – there was warm camembert with wild mushroom fricassee; mini tarte-flambees; salmon tartare with caviar; beef tartare; and chicken liver patee. I had to admit that I was expecting summer sausage and cheddar cheese, with maybe some mini hot dogs and some crab rangoon and egg rolls. The appetizers here, though, were well thought out, delicious and gourmet.

The open bar was just as high dollar. All of the liquors were premium – there was Ketel One vodka, Glenfiddich scotch, imported tequila, and Tanqueray gin. These were all some of the better liquors, and there wasn't anything behind the bar that I would consider to be cheap. The wine, too, was some of the better stuff – they were all Italian imports and I recognized that most of the bottles retailed for $100 or more.

I'm impressed. Somebody spent some good money on this shindig. As I looked around the crowd, I suddenly understood why. There was a prominent Broadway director chatting with a United States Senator in one corner. In another, I recognized some top models canoodling with some very wealthy-looking men. Everywhere, people were laughing and drinking and walking around looking at the paintings.

I took a deep breath, and went right up to one of the rich guys. I held out my hand to him. "Hi, my name is Luke Roberts, and I'm…"

At that, the guy got a huge smile on his face, and grabbed me in a hug. "Oh, my God," he said in a very thick German accent. "You've made my wife so happy! She just made me buy three of your paintings, and she wanted me to find the artist immediately because she wants more. What good fortune that you came up to me to introduce yourself!"

I felt a little overwhelmed by the effusiveness of the guy, so I just stood there and nodded, at a loss for words. "Well, uh," I finally said, "here's my card, and…"

"Give me about fifty of your cards," he said, slapping my back. "My wife is already in love with your work, and she has lots of friends who are just as into art as she is."

I felt a little embarrassed. I had only brought about 70 cards, but I took out a big stack and he passed them to some of the people in his group. Then he put his arm around me, and guided me over to a tall blonde woman who was dressed in a red dress and strappy gold shoes. "This is Luke Roberts," he said.

"Oh, my," she said, putting her hand out for me to shake. "I love your work. Where have you been all my life?" She evidently was tipsy, because she was swaying just a little. "Your art is so compelling. There's something about them that is just so tragic, yet so deliriously happy at the same time. I can almost see your subjects' thoughts, they're so real."

I found myself struggling for words. This was a little too much, too soon. I mean, I'm the blue-collar son of a fisherman. My friends were all working labor jobs, with the exception of Jake, who just got a job in an automotive factory. And, suddenly, I was talking to a tycoon and his wife, and they were introducing me to even more of their fancy friends.

They were asking me questions about how I composed my art, and how I got my inspiration. They were interested in how long I had been painting, and what my family was like. I couldn't believe how friendly and gregarious these people were, and I found myself relaxing and trying to enjoy the ride.

I finally extricated myself from the group, and went up to some more people and introduced myself. I was feeling emboldened, confident and happy after the previous group was so effusive over my work. This group also knew who I was, and were more than happy to talk to me. They, too, peppered me with questions, and the whole group ended up taking a selfie.

I went around to various groups for another hour or so, and everyone was friendly and interested in me. I also went around and listened to what people were saying about some of my other paintings, and I heard effusive praise from just about everyone. So far, it seemed that six of my paintings had sold, which meant that only four were left unsold. I calculated the haul in my head, and realized that, even if another painting didn't sell that night, I would still end up with at least $70,000. The gallery would take 50%, and I would take the rest.

I was on my way!

Chapter Sixteen

Dalilah

Nottingham and I arrived at Luke's premiere, and I felt like I was going to pass out. There had to be some way that I could give him the slip so that I could get out of there as soon as possible. It might not be as difficult as I thought, because, after all, Nottingham hardly ever noticed me. He was always so busy running his company that I was an afterthought, which, really, was a great thing for me. I was pleasantly surprised - I thought that I would have to deal with being around Nottingham much more than I had to in reality. But, he was working 18-hour days, so I was left alone most of the time, and I was so happy about that.

The horrible thing was the sex, which he demanded just about every night. There weren't beatings anymore, which was a blessing, but he was always rough. It was clear that he was very angry with me, and he tried to take it out on me as much as he could without leaving a mark.

We arrived at the gallery, and he took my hand and the

two of us made our way into the entrance. I looked around and immediately saw Luke. I felt my heart pounding out of its chest. He looked so handsome. He was wearing dress slacks and a purple button-down shirt that was open at the collar. He was standing in the middle of a group of people, holding court, and they were hanging onto every word that he said. I recognized some of the people that he was talking to, because I had seen them at the Union Club more than once. So, I knew that these people were wealthy, and the fact that they were so interested in Luke gave me hope, and my heart soared.

I surreptitiously stood behind a sculpture, and watched him from afar for awhile. Nottingham was nowhere to be seen, having abandoned me as soon as we got into the doors. I knew that I wouldn't be alone the entire night, though, because Nottingham had warned me that he wanted me to be on his arm that night. But, right at moment, Nottingham had left me, presumably because he was going to get something to eat and drink. So, I was able to just watch Luke. I watched him go from one group to another, and each of these groups embraced him more than the last.

I walked over to his paintings, and saw that six of them already were sold. I felt tears coming to my eyes, knowing that Luke was finally on his way for sure. Prior to this evening, there was always a question. Sometimes these large premieres fall flat, and the artist is lucky to sell one or two. I didn't think that Luke would fall flat, of course, not at all. But there was a small chance that he would. However, as I watched Luke making his way around the gallery and I saw the people admiring his paintings, I knew. I knew that he was a hit, and that it was only a matter of time until he became a well-known name.

I sighed. My sacrifice was worth it. It was 100% worth it. It made the prospect of being with Nottingham almost bearable. I couldn't be happier for Luke. My life was still shit, of course, but he was getting what he wanted, and my heart absolutely soared.

Just then, Nottingham yanked my arm. "Come on, Dalilah, let's go and talk to Luke. He needs to know that you're with me, just in case he gets an idea in his head otherwise."

Oh, God, no. No. I was so happy, and now, once again, I was full of dread. I didn't know how I could possibly go through with this.

I soon was going to find out.

Chapter Seventeen

Luke

I was in the middle of a group of wealthy Italians, when I heard Nottingham's voice. It was always just vaguely familiar to me, as I rarely talked to him, but I was starting to recognize it.

"Oh, and this is the man of the hour," he said. "I see you're talking to my Italian friends. Giorgio, what do you think of this fine young man?"

"He's exquisite," Giorgio said to Nottingham. "Where did you find him?"

"I hired him to paint the woman who is now my wife." And then he looked me right in the eye, as he casually jerked Dalilah over to the group. "Giorgio, Nino, Maria, Giada – I'd like you to meet my wife, Dalilah Nottingham."

All at once, I felt that I was in the middle of a nightmare. Prior to this moment, the entire evening felt like a wonderful dream. But, just like that, it turned on a dime, and I wanted the floor to swallow me whole.

I felt a little bit in a state of shock as the Italians fussed over her, and embraced her in big hugs. I stepped out of the group, and I watched her. She didn't meet my eyes. I felt my breaths coming faster and faster, and my heart started pounding. It was like it suddenly hit me that she was there, and, worse than that, she was apparently Nottingham's wife.

Nottingham's wife. That was it. That was why she dumped me. Her words rang in my ears. *I'm a mercenary. I go where the money is, and it certainly isn't here.* She also told me that she wanted somebody wealthy. Which Nottingham certainly was. It was just as I had suspected.

I wasn't good enough for her after all. She wanted to live the life of a wife of a billionaire, instead of being with a dirt-poor artist. Well, I wasn't going to be so dirt poor anymore, but I wasn't good enough still. I would never be good enough. I just wished that she would've been honest with me. Instead of giving me some story about how she lived to mind-fuck men, she should have just said that she was going to marry a billionaire and that I just wasn't good enough.

And, just like that, my confidence was shot to pieces. Who was I to believe that I would ever fit in with these people? I would never be one of them. I would always be like some kind of pet for them. They were nice to me, and very friendly, but I would never truly be accepted by them. Just like Dalilah would never truly accept me. She pretended that she would, and that she loved me. But she didn't. She couldn't have loved me. It was all a big lie.

She had been slumming. Seeing how the other half lived. And she simply got tired of it. She simply got tired of it, and she reverted to type. It was always her destiny to be the wife of a bastard like that Nottingham. Just like Henry had said, a guy like me didn't belong with a girl like her. I didn't belong in her world, and I didn't belong with her.

I tried to slink away, but Giorgio didn't let me. "Luke, did you get a chance to meet Blake's new wife?" he asked me, apparently forgetting that Nottingham had told the group that he had met me because I was hired to paint a portrait of her.

"Yes," I said, looking at her. She was looking down at the floor, and I noticed that her hand was shaking wildly. But she didn't meet my eyes. "As Mr. Nottingham said, he hired me to paint, uh, Mrs. Nottingham, and that's, uh, that's uh…" I lost my words. "If you would excuse me, I have to, uh, I have to, um…" At that, I rapidly walked away from the group.

I went outside into the cold night air. It was the middle of December, and it was freezing outside. My breath was visible in the air. I shoved my hands in my pockets, and I put my head down. I tried to calm my racing heart, and I took several deep breaths because I felt tears start. I couldn't cry, though. At least, I couldn't let anybody see me cry.

You have to get through this, Luke. You have to hold your head high. You can't let her win. I was devastated, and I knew that, once I was home, I was going to feel this betrayal to my very core. I had no idea if I could recover from this, ever. But I had to get through the party. If I didn't, then Dalilah would win.

She played me like a bass violin, that was for sure. And I kicked myself for being so fucking stupid.

Hold your head high, Luke. Hold it high, and don't let yourself feel your devastation until later on tonight.

After about a half hour of trying to get my composure out in the cold air, I went back inside. I made a bee-line for the bar, and ordered a scotch and water. Somebody came up to me, and introduced himself. "You're Luke Roberts," he said. "Somebody pointed you out to me. Your work is incredible."

I looked at the guy and just nodded my head. Suddenly, it didn't matter that there was somebody else who wanted to tell me how good I was. Earlier in the evening, I would be basking in the praise and feeling over the moon that somebody liked me. But seeing Dalilah with Nottingham – I felt like a balloon that completely deflated. "Thank you," I said.

"Listen, I have a gallery down the street," he said, giving me his card. "It's not a large one, but we work with some established artists. I would love to feature you in some of our upcoming shows."

I forced a smile. It didn't matter. Nothing mattered anymore. Dalilah was married to somebody else, and that fact was just sinking in. "Thank you," I said, giving him my card. "That would be great." I turned my head, and felt tears coming to my eyes again.

Dalilah was married to somebody else.

She never loved me.

I felt like such a fool.

"Well," the guy said, "I just wanted to let you know how talented you are."

I nodded my head, knowing that I was being rude. This guy obviously wanted to talk to me more about my art, but I couldn't find the words anymore. I felt like telling him that he didn't matter. This gallery didn't matter. The money I would be hauling in that night didn't matter. There was nothing that mattered.

The guy, seeing that I wasn't engaging him in conversation, awkwardly turned around and disappeared into the crowd.

I doubted that I would hear from him. An opportunity

that was going to slip through my fingers because of Dalilah.

And, just like that, my feelings changed again. Dalilah. Who did she think that she was, coming here? Rubbing salt in the wound? Why couldn't she just leave well enough alone? She knew how much this premiere meant to me. Why would she sabotage it like this for me? She had to have known that if she appeared here that I would be devastated. She had to have known that seeing her here would ruin my entire evening.

I had let her in on every feeling I had for her. She knew just how I felt. And I started to feel hatred for her for doing this to me. It wasn't enough that she pulled the rug out from under me. Devastated me beyond measure. No, that wasn't enough. She had to come here and fuck with me some more. She wasn't satisfied with simply stabbing me in the heart once. She had to do it again and again and again.

My blood pressure went through the roof. She was standing in the middle of a crowd, holding court like she always did, and I felt like going over there and ripping off her beautiful face. She never even looked my way, even once.

I finished my scotch, and ordered another. I tried to make my body language less open, because I suddenly felt very anti-social.

Shake it off, Roberts. Shake it off.

After two more drinks, I finally got my liquid courage. I was going to confront that two-timing, lying….woman. I shook my head. I still couldn't bring myself to call her a name, no matter what she did to me. No matter what she continued to do to me. I was angry with her, beyond angry. I never once thought that she would be capable of such duplicity.

But I still loved her so much that my heart literally started to hurt. I felt a pain in my chest that radiated and grew as I approached her. So, no, I couldn't call her a name, even in my head. I had far too much respect and love for her.

My feelings for her weren't reciprocated, and probably never were, but no matter. How I felt for her was how I felt for her, and I couldn't help it. I wanted so badly to be as cold and cruel as she was. I wanted to stoop to her level.

But I couldn't.

I loved her so much I couldn't stand it.

Finally, I got to her group. I stood right next to her. I breathed in her scent. It was vaguely floral, yet musky. She looked so beautiful…for just a split second, I forgot her betrayal. Her cruelty. I forgot how angry I was with her, and all that I wanted to do was to breathe her in. To drink in her essence and her soul, and capture it somehow, so that I could take something of her home with me.

Don't back down, now, Luke. Don't back down.

I put my hand on her shoulder, and she jumped a little. And, in her eyes, I saw the old Dalilah. I might have been imagining it, but I saw love, hope and passion in her eyes.

I shook my head. I was obviously seeing what I wanted to see.

We stood there, just looking at each other, and Nottingham was standing off to the side, giving her a look that was unmistakably a warning.

But she didn't see him. She was too busy looking at me.

We stood there, just looking at each other. I didn't notice what the little group was doing, but I would imagine that they were wondering just what was going on.

Dalilah didn't look like the cold, cruel person who dumped me, and who came here to rub in her new marriage. She looked, in her eyes, like the woman who I fell in love with. Who fell in love with me. I felt like I was getting lost in her, just like I always did before.

I had no idea how long we stood there, just staring at each other wordlessly. What I do know is that, too soon, Nottingham was jerking Dalilah's arm harshly, and her eyes broke away from mine. "Come, Dalilah, we need to go over and talk to Heinrich and his wife," he said, gesturing to the German man whom I spoke with earlier. "They're prominent investors in this gallery, so we need to make sure that we talk to them."

She nodded her head at him, and, as he jerked her towards Heinrich, she was looking back at me. In her eyes, I think that I saw regret and sorrow. A few seconds later, Nottingham and Dalilah had disappeared into the crowd.

I watched her until she disappeared, and then I smiled at the Giorgio and the group. "Well, I hope you guys have a good time tonight. I'm going to go and get a drink at the bar. I hope you don't mind."

"Not at all," Giorgio said. "We hope to see you around the party later on. Do not be a stranger," he said, in his thick Italian accent.

I nodded, and said "I won't. I'll try to catch up to you guys later."

At that, I tried to get to the bar, but, by then, it was too crowded. So, I ended up outside again. Because it was so cold outside, there wasn't anybody else hanging around. I could, thankfully, be alone.

I tried not to think about the cold, as I stood there and thought about the night and seeing Dalilah. It was so weird. In her eyes, she was the Dalilah whom I loved. The Dalilah who loved me. She looked like she was full of regrets, passion and love. I could feel it from her. It emanated from her very aura.

Yet, she was married to Nottingham. And she was throwing that up in my face by being here. She didn't even care enough to warn me that she would be there with him. Her actions belied her eyes – her actions told me that she didn't give a crap about me. And she never did. How could she? She was married to somebody else, and she married him within a few weeks of breaking up with me.

She must have been seeing him all along. That was the only thing that would make any kind of sense. After all, you don't just marry a man after having dated him for a matter of weeks. No, she must have been with Nottingham at the same time that she was with me.

My heart hurt so much. My brain was completely confused, too. I knew what I saw in her eyes a few seconds ago. So, I really didn't know what to think.

I had no idea who to ask, either. I needed somebody's opinion on the matter. But whose? Jake, God love him, was more clueless than anybody about the female gender. He would be of no help if I were to ask what he thought.

Then I thought that maybe, just maybe, I should go ahead and talk to her parents. I had nothing to lose by doing so. Dalilah and I were already completely kaput, and she was married to somebody else. But maybe they might know what happened.

All that I knew was that I needed answers. This entire situation was killing me. Prior to seeing her at the premiere, I was confused enough. I had no closure. All that I knew was that I was with Dalilah, and then, just like that, for no reason at all, I wasn't with her anymore. We went from engaged to nothing at all so quickly, I really had no way of processing any of it.

I had tried to forget about it. As much as I was obsessed with what went wrong, I also tried very hard to forget that she and I were no longer together. And that she apparently never loved me.

But now, at long last, I needed answers.

There was no way that I could ever move on with my life unless I got them.

Chapter Eighteen

Dalilah

After seeing Luke, I was pulled and jerked all over the gallery, as Nottingham made sure that I spoke with as many people as possible. I had to talk to one group after another, and all that I wanted to do was to find Luke and talk to him. Congratulate him on a massively successful launch. Tell him how much I was completely, head over heels, in love with him. Tell him that I wanted so badly to run away from Nottingham and just go and be with him forever.

It was so hard for me to actually engage in conversation with anybody, especially after I saw Luke. I had no idea that seeing him would be so heart-rending. I mean, I knew that it would be, but the magnitude of the heartbreak after seeing him was something that I really wasn't prepared for.

I tuned everyone out. I ignored Nottingham, who clearly was giving me a warning throughout the night. I knew what he expected from me – that I was going to be the charming wife. I was going to make scintillating conversation with everyone, and they would all converse amongst themselves, after we left, about how witty and intelligent I was.

But, as with everything else, I didn't cooperate. I barely answered the questions that were asked of me. My brain wasn't engaged with these people. It was engaged with Luke, wherever he was.

So, the conversations with me and Nottingham's friends went something like this....

"This Luke Roberts painted a portrait of my wife, and it was just delivered today by courier. It's a beautiful, sensuous portrait that really captures my gorgeous wife's essence. You really should come and see it sometime." Nottingham.

"What was it like to pose for this portrait?" somebody would ask.

But I wouldn't answer. My eyes were searching the room, and I barely even knew that a person was addressing me. Nottingham would then jump in with something like "she really enjoyed herself. She's very in demand for her modeling, of course, for obvious reasons," he would say with a knowing chuckle. I was vaguely aware that he could turn on the charm for his fancy friends, and I felt more resentful than ever.

And so it went, throughout the evening.

I couldn't think about engaging in conversation with Nottingham's friends, because I was too busy thinking about how successful this launch seemed to be for Luke. There were two other artists featured, both of whom were major names, but it seemed that Luke was the talk of the party. Everywhere I went, I heard people talking about him. I heard snippets of conversation, and people were saying that Luke was "brilliant," "a rare talent," "a hidden gem," and "an up and comer." Another group was talking about

Luke's premiere was being a "sleeper." A woman in this group was saying "I wasn't expecting much from an unknown artist, but I was so surprised with how mature his work is. And he's really young, too."

And that was the general sentiment of the night. Luke was a hit. He was a major hit, and he was soon going to be on the A-list. There was no doubt about this.

In the back of my mind, I was thinking about how much Nottingham wasn't even necessary to Luke anymore. As much as I was afraid to leave Nottingham after this premiere, I had a glimmer of hope. Maybe I could go ahead and leave Nottingham, and be with Luke. It seemed that he would be able to make a name for himself, Nottingham or no. After all, Nottingham might try to black-ball him, but, judging by the comments of the patrons, he was going to be hot. And galleries always wanted to work with hot artists. There was only so much that Nottingham would be able to do to convince galleries not to work with him.

And the thought that maybe, just maybe, I could get out of my situation with Nottingham occupied my thoughts for much of the night. I was so distracted that I finally just had to excuse myself, on the pretense that I needed to use the restroom.

What I really needed was a breath of fresh air. So, I went outside.

And, to my surprise, there was Luke. All by himself. He wasn't wearing a coat, yet he didn't look like he was overly cold. He was staring off into the distance, looking at the brightly-lit New York City skyline. He wasn't making a move.

I stealthily stood there, ruminating on what to do. I really wanted to go up and talk to him, but I didn't know if

I had the words to say. My mind wasn't made up on what I wanted to do with Nottingham. As much as I wanted just to leave him, I was still afraid to. Because, as much as I was thinking that Nottingham probably wouldn't be able to touch Luke, now that he was such a hit, I wasn't entirely sure. I certainly didn't want Luke to see his momentum stopped, which is what would happen if Nottingham was at all successful in convincing gallery owners not to work with him. And this was exactly what would happen if I left Nottingham – he would badmouth Luke to everyone, and, considering the fact that Nottingham knew everyone who was anyone in the art world, that could be devastating to him.

I finally decided just to surreptitiously go back inside, before Luke could turn around and see me. Because I knew that if I was outside, and alone with him, I would have broken down. I would have broken down, and started crying or worse. I might have even kissed him passionately, simply because I felt a need to do so. I wanted so much for my skin to be in contact with his. My lips were longing to be on his. It was such an overwhelming feeling for me – that I had to be with him, close to him, touching him – I knew that I had to leave. If I stayed, and talked to him, I would have given away just how I felt. And that wouldn't be good.

I had to decide if I wanted to take the risk of leaving Nottingham. And I hadn't had the chance to really think that through, yet. It couldn't be something that I did with haste and without thinking. I had to weigh the pros and cons, and maybe talk to some gallery owners about whether or not they wanted to feature Luke in the future. Nottingham had his thumbs in many pies, when it came to the art world, and his influence was diffuse. So, I had to do my research on what the consequences would be if I left him. Especially if I left him and reunited with Luke.

I quietly opened the door, and went back inside. The place suddenly seemed stuffy to me, insufferable. It was too warm, and there were too many people. I was feeling claustrophobic, like I really had to go home.

I tried to find Nottingham, but he was nowhere to be found. So, I called a cab.

The cab came and picked me up. "Where to?" he asked me.

I started to give my address, and then, out of nowhere, I did something else.

I gave Luke's address.

There was something inside of me, some voice that was loudly telling me that I needed to go to him. It was as if there was something that was compelling me to go to his apartment. I still had a key to his place, too, so my plan was to go to his place and let myself in.

And wait for him to come home.

Chapter Nineteen

Luke

The night wore on. I tried mightily to put on my game face for everyone. I was astounded on how sought-after I was at my premiere. I wasn't, at all, prepared for this. I figured that I would be received politely, and that maybe one or two of my paintings would sell. I certainly wasn't prepared for people to really want to talk to me, and that my paintings would be sold out by the end of the evening.

Which was actually what happened. It was crazy how well things were going for me. I had wealthy patrons trying to make appointments with me, because they wanted me to do commissioned works for them. Gallery owners were trying to line up future shows with me. I even heard critics talking about my show, and it sounded like they would give me a positive review. Including Henry Jacobs and Elaine Bush.

The entire thing felt surreal. And, if it weren't for the fact that Dalilah had come and ruined me, emotionally, I would have had to say that the night would go down as one of the best of my life.

It wouldn't be known as *the* best night of my life, though, not by a long shot. The day at the skating rink, where I asked Dalilah to marry me – that was, by far, the best day of my life. Any night that I spent with Dalilah would have been considered better than that premiere night, in fact.

But, for a non-Dalilah night, the premiere night would be, definitely, the best of my life.

I finally left the party at around midnight. It was still raging, but I was tired and just a little bit drunk. Not bad, though – I made sure that I wasn't incoherent, because I still had to schmooze. But I had drunk a few scotches after seeing Dalilah, just because I had to get my mind off of her. Seeing her threw me so badly, that I had to do something to take the edge off. So I drank a few scotches, just enough that I was able to engage with the crowd without feeling depressed about seeing Dalilah.

I got a cab, and headed home.

I was finally able to think, and process, about the evening, as I sat in the back of a cab. It was definitely a night of highs and lows. The highs were all the people who apparently loved me. The low, of course, was seeing Dalilah.

How could she be married to somebody else? How could she do that to me? How could she rub it in like that? What would compel her to come to my premiere and try to sabotage it by bringing her new husband with her?

I just couldn't believe that I was so wrong about her. I was normally so good about reading people, and I just was so wrong about her. I fell so in love with her. So completely, head over heels, in love with her.

And she didn't even have enough respect for me to not

flaunt her new husband to me at my own premiere. What kind of a person was she? An awful person. A truly terrible person.

Yet she was still a person who I was completely, head over heels, in love with.

I finally got home, and trudged on up. I was starting to come down from the high of the night. Dalilah not-with-standing, the night was something that was out of a dream. There was no doubt that I would be in demand after my premiere. No doubt at all. I had already lined up appoint-ments with many wealthy people for commissions, and already gotten firm offers for showings.

I opened the door, and almost fell down in surprise.

Dalilah was sitting there on my couch.

Chapter Twenty

Dalilah

Luke was finally at his apartment. I was sitting there on his couch, waiting for him, and, when he came through the door, it looked like he could have been knocked over with a feather.

But now that he was there, I found that I didn't have words for him. I had already started to question what it was that I was doing there. After all, earlier in the evening, I was determined not to make a move until I could do so safely. Only after I knew that Nottingham wouldn't be able to poison the well against Luke did I want to go ahead and try to be with him again.

Yet, I couldn't not come to his apartment. There was something, unseen and unknown, that was pulling me to his place. But, now that I was face to face with him, I didn't really know what to say.

So, we just stood there, looking at one another, wordlessly.

Finally, Luke spoke. "Dalilah, I. What are you doing here?"

I took a deep breath. "I felt bad, Luke. I blindsided you like that. That wasn't right of me."

He nodded. "No, it wasn't. An understatement." He shoved his hands in his pockets. It was suddenly an awkward moment between the two of us. Neither of us, apparently, knew what it was that we were supposed to say to one another.

"Well, I needed to apologize to you," I said. "I should have at least, uh, warned you that I was going to be there."

"Oh, okay. I suppose that you feel that you didn't need to warn me that you were married to Nottingham. I certainly would have appreciated the heads-up about that one."

I was quiet for a few seconds. I was struggling on how to explain that to Luke. "Yes, Luke. I know. I really should have warned you about Nottingham as well."

He nodded. "Okay, then. You apologized. So, let me call you a cab and you can leave and get back to him. I'm quite sure that you snuck over here without his knowledge, and he seems to be the type of guy who wouldn't take kindly to that sort of behavior. You need to get out of here."

I knew that he was right. There was going to be hell to pay when I got home to Nottingham. I had no idea how he was going to react when he found that he couldn't find me at the gallery anymore. And then to come home and see that I wasn't there, either...I was actually afraid to go back to him at that point.

Very afraid.

I stood up, and took Luke's hand. He looked at me, a questioning look in his eyes. I started talking, and it seemed, once again, that I couldn't control myself. Just like when I was compelled to go to his apartment in the first place, when I started to talk, it was if I couldn't stop myself.

"Luke, I, well, I can't live with myself. Knowing what I did to you. I just, well, I haven't been able to live with myself. I love you, Luke. I think that I have been in love with you since that first night when you came over. You remember that night? We listened to *The Dead Kennedys* and you beat me in that card game. And you kissed me. You kissed me, and nothing has been the same since."

I wasn't looking at him when I was talking. Rather, I was looking down at the floor. I didn't want to see him reject me. And I knew that he would. Of course, he would. After all that I did to him? He would, no doubt, reject me.

And if he didn't reject me? What then? I couldn't leave Nottingham. Not until I knew, for a fact, that he wasn't going to be able to destroy Luke.

You didn't think this through, Dalilah. Once again, you're making stupid decisions that are, no doubt, going to have ugly repercussions.

Finally, I looked up. He was looking at me, and not talking. It was as if he was astounded at what I was saying. Trying to process it. He was not only not speaking, at all, but he also wasn't making a single move. It was as if he suddenly became a statue. Like that game that I used to play when I was a kid, where the other kid would have to become a statue if he was tagged.

"Luke," I said. "Please, say something. Anything."

He shook his head. "I don't know what to say, Dalilah. I mean, you come here, and you tell me that you are in love with me, still. And, you know what? I believe you. I believe you, 100%, when you tell me this. Because I see it in your eyes. I see how much you love me. I thought that I saw it in your eyes back at the gallery, but, at that time, I thought that I was just imagining things. Now I know that I'm not."

I took a deep breath. "Well, you need to know that you're not crazy. I'm still in love with you. I want to be with you so much, you just can't imagine it."

He cocked his head. "Okay, then, I don't understand. Why are you married to Nottingham? Why did you break up with me? Why, Dalilah? Why would you do something like that?"

I looked at him, wavering. Not knowing what to say. I was going to have to come up with something, and it couldn't be the truth. Because the truth would mean that Luke would rightfully go over and tell Nottingham to kiss his ass. I knew Luke well enough to know exactly how he would react if he knew the truth.

Finally, I said "I'm doing this for my friend, Nick. He's my father's best friend. I lived with him for a couple of years, and I owe him quite a lot."

Luke gave me a look like he had zero understanding about what I was talking about. Indeed, as the words came out of my mouth, I, myself, had no idea what I was talking about. It was just the first thing that popped into my head.

"Nick. I don't think that I know him. But tell me what you're talking about. Why would you marry Nottingham, and how does that help your friend? Help me understand, here, Dalilah, please. I need to move on, and I really need answers, here."

I started to panic just a little. I was weaving a web here, and I had to figure out how to get out of it. What could I say that would appease Luke, to where he wasn't going to want to kick either Nottingham's or Nick's ass? If I told him that Nick tried to force me into this, for whatever reason, then Luke would probably read Nick the riot act. If I told him that Nottingham was blackmailing me, and this somehow involved Nick, then Luke would want to kick Nottingham's ass.

Finally, I thought about the marriages of convenience that occurred between powerful people, marriages that somehow secured each of the parties. "It's a marriage of convenience," I began. "Nottingham is one of Nick's firm's biggest clients. Nick is the managing partner of one of the largest architecture firms in town – O'Hara, White and Stroker. And Nottingham is worth millions to him."

"Okay," he said. "Go on."

"Well, I just thought that I should try to secure Nottingham's patronage of Nick's firm. That's all. Losing his business would be devastating for Nick, and, well, he was making noises that maybe he would leave Nick's firm to go with somebody else, and I married him to secure his continued patronage."

He nodded his head, like he understood. "I don't know what to say, Dalilah. I'm still kinda in shock that you're here at all, and now you're telling me that you married Nottingham for some kind of altruistic reason. That you somehow want to sacrifice yourself and your own happiness so that Nick's firm won't lose Nottingham's business. I mean, I can almost understand why you would do that, but, come on, Dalilah. You shouldn't have to fall on your sword, no matter how much this Nick has done for you."

Oh, if you only understood exactly why I'm falling on this sword. I'm doing it for you, Luke. Only for you. The irony of Luke thinking that I was sacrificing myself for Nick wasn't lost on me.

"You don't understand," I said. "Nick took me in when

I was totally lost. He didn't have to do that. He has three kids of his own at home. Then I went to stay with him, and I was a surly 16-year-old. I think that I gave him and his wife more than my share of grief. I found an opportunity to repay him for all that he did for me, and I took it. I took it, and believe me, I regret that. Because it means that I can't be with you. But I did want you to know how much I love you. I never want you to think differently."

Luke just looked at me, perplexed. I looked down at the ground, not wanting to meet his eyes. I was playing with fire, just being in Luke's apartment, and I knew it. I think that he knew it, too.

Finally, after what seemed to be an eternity, he spoke. "I don't know what to say, Dalilah. I mean, for whatever reason you married that man, you are married to him. Not to me. To him. So, you need to leave my apartment right now."

I felt tears coming to my eyes. "Luke, I-"

Now he was pacing the floor. "I'm sorry, Dalilah, this whole thing is just starting to sink in for me. You're not the woman that I thought you were if you're going to treat marriage like some kind of game. You don't marry a person to repay him, you marry a person because you love him. That's it. There's no other reason. But you – you give marriage a bad name, really. Marriages of convenience happen in other countries, and they happened in historical times. And I guess that they still happen now, in this country. But I don't agree with them. Especially if said marriage of convenience is to a rich asshole like Nottingham."

I went up to him, and I just kissed him. I put my arms around the back of his neck, and drew him to me. I could feel him breathing heavily, and I was shaking all over. But it felt so right to do that. I had this need to feel my lips on his, to taste him. To physically feel him, skin to skin. I longed to strip off his clothes and feel his nakedness and his warm skin on mine, and never leave his bed, ever. He enveloped me in his strong arms, as his lips gently glided with mine. I felt myself getting completely lost in his touch, just like I always did before.

After a few seconds, though, he pushed me away. "What the hell, Dalilah? I mean, really. You think I don't have an ounce of self-respect, do you? What, you're not getting it from Nottingham, so you're going to get it from me? Get out, Dalilah. I'm serious. Out. Now."

"Luke, please," I said. "Please don't send me away. I made a mistake. A bad mistake. Please. I love you. I love you, Luke. Not him. You. It has always been you. Only you. Please."

Here I was, pleading again, but, instead of pleading with Nottingham not to pull Luke's show, I was pleading with Luke himself.

Pleading with him to love me.

He seemed to waver. In his eyes, I saw so much pain and love and forgiveness. I saw into his heart and into his soul, so I knew the truth. No matter what he might say to me, I knew that he loved me just as much as I loved him.

This knowledge was cold comfort, though, when he said "I'm sorry, Dalilah. But you have to leave. You're married to somebody else. I don't know about you, but in my neck of the woods, it means something to be married to somebody else. It means that you made a commitment, and you need to see that through. And that commitment that you made wasn't to me. It was supposed to be, but it wasn't. It was to Nottingham. So, to him, you must give all your love. Not to me."

His words stung me beyond belief. Yes, I deserved this,

really. In his eyes, I just married Nottingham willy-nilly without giving any regard to Luke, or to my commitment to him. Or my absolute, undying love for him. If he only knew the truth, then I knew that I could stay. He might even help me find a way out of my trap.

But he couldn't know the truth. He couldn't, because he needed to be safe. His career was going to take off, so to have Nottingham sabotage that, as Nottingham surely would if I stayed with Luke, would be devastating to me. Everything that I did, everything that I sacrificed, would be for naught.

I couldn't let that happen.

Now his arms were crossed. I still saw the hurt and love in his eyes, but he was assuming a defensive posture.

I didn't move a muscle. I even tried to control my breathing. It was as if I thought, I believed, that if I stood perfectly still, maybe he would just let me stay. I looked down at the floor, because I didn't want to see his expression when he decided, once again, to try to make me leave.

I couldn't leave. I felt like my feet were rooted into the floor.

"Dalilah," he said, softly. "I love you. I'm completely in love with you. But how I feel about you, and how you apparently feel about me, isn't the important thing here. The most important thing here is that you made a commitment. Why you did it really isn't relevant, either. The fact is, you made vows with somebody else. And, unless you want to tell me that you're perfectly fine with making a complete mockery of the very idea of marriage, then those vows that you took with Nottingham should mean something. Otherwise, you're no better than my sister, Serena."

I felt tears coming down my cheeks. But I couldn't leave. I just couldn't. It was as if I were in a dream, one where my legs were made of lead, and they won't move. "Serena. Tell me more about her."

He shrugged his shoulders. "What is there to tell? She cheats on her husband right and left, and doesn't even care that she's doing it. That's not how a marriage should be. That's not how it's supposed to go. I get that you don't love that guy, but you married him. For whatever reason, you married him. Now you have to go to him. If you're the woman who I think you are, then you will leave this apartment and never come back. Because the Dalilah I know has integrity."

His words were like daggers. I had gotten myself into a position where he was going to think less of me. I couldn't have that. Not that I blamed him, at all – all that he could see was that I married somebody else, for the wrong reasons. He didn't have the truth about what, exactly, the wrong reasons were. He only knew that I was married to Nottingham, a man that I didn't love.

"Okay," I finally said. "I'll leave."

"I'll call you a cab," he said, taking out his phone and dialing. He got off the phone and said to me "he'll be here in five minutes."

I nodded my head. I accomplished exactly zero in coming here. Luke still had no desire to be with me, and, if anything, I did further damage – he thought that I had come here to have my cake and eat it, too, essentially. That I came here to have sex with him, while being married to somebody else. I hated the fact that he possibly thought that about me.

He didn't meet my eyes, but he motioned to the door. I went through it, and looked back at him. I so wanted to tell him the truth. I never, ever wanted to leave him. But I had to.

I had to.

After a few moments where I just stood out in the hallway, pleading with him with my eyes, I finally just turned around and went down the stairway and into the waiting cab.

Chapter Twenty-One

Luke

Fuck, that was the hardest thing that I ever did. Throwing Dalilah out took all my will. My heart was so fighting my head in that situation. My heart, and my soul, were begging her to stay. Not to return to him. To divorce him and be my wife, yesterday.

My head, though, was what finally won out. Dalilah was married. Who really cared why she was married? The fact of the matter was, she took vows, those vows weren't with me, and that was that.

Call me a hopeless romantic, but marriage is supposed to mean something. Too often, in this society, it didn't mean a damn thing. But, for me, it did. Dalilah's place was with her husband, not with me. I got that she married him for reasons other than love, but she made her bed, goddammit.

She made her bed.

God, but seeing her here in this apartment…the memories came back so vividly. For a few brief moments, before my head took over, it was really as if she had never left. She was back in my apartment, and it took everything I had not to strip off her clothes and make love to her all night long. To wake up with her in my arms in the morning – that would be my idea of heaven.

It occurred to me that I would gladly trade every bit of praise and success I had at my premiere for her. If there was a genie who had the ability to give me one or the other – either I became an art A-lister, or I got to be with Dalilah forever – there wouldn't be any hesitation. I would choose being with her. Every.time.

I laid down on the couch, feeling confused. More confused than ever. On the one hand, it seemed that I had finally arrived. The one thing that I have worked for my entire life, the sparkling debut where everybody sat up and took notice, finally happened for me. My premiere couldn't go any better than it did. It really couldn't.

So I really should be ecstatic. Bouncing off the walls.

But I wasn't. I couldn't be. Not when I couldn't have Dalilah. This entire evening was therefore muted at best. I never thought that achieving a lifelong dream could seem so…unimportant. Insignificant. All because of Dalilah. She wounded me so deeply by dumping me. And then twisted in the knife by showing up at my show. And then somehow managed to make it even worse by showing up here to profess her love for me, while being married to somebody else.

I wasn't going to have that bullshit. I had to find a way to move on.

It will come in time, I told myself.

Just give it time.

In the meantime, though, the pain in my heart was more than I thought that I could bear.

Chapter Twenty-Two

Dalilah

As I headed home in the cab, I was so sad about my whole situation with Luke that I didn't even feel fearful about going home to Nottingham. Truth be told, I should have been scared, but I wasn't. Luke occupied almost all my thoughts as I stared out the window of the cab.

I tore out his heart, that much was clear. It was in his eyes, and it was in his body language. He loved me as much as I loved him. I couldn't stand knowing this, while having to be apart from him.

So, my mind was only on him as I trudged out of the cab, and took the elevator to the top floor. I got my keys out when I got to the door of the penthouse suite. I unlocked the door and opened it.

I took a deep breath. Nottingham was nowhere to be seen, and the place was dark.

And then I heard it. A woman's laughter and ecstatic squeal, and Nottingham groaning.

Oh, good Lord. Really? I shook my head, and went over to the bar and poured myself a stiff scotch. I learned to drink neat scotch from my dad, as that was always his drink of choice. I poured the drink and put on the television. As much as I wanted to flee the scene, I thought it prudent to stay put. Besides, I really had no place to go at that point.

I listened to the two of them going at it for a few minutes more, and then the woman emerged from the bedroom, completely naked.

Nice boob job. Wonder who did them?

She smiled and came over to me. "Blake heard you come in. He wanted me to come out here and see if you would like to join us."

I shook my head. "No, really, be my guest. You just go on ahead. Don't mind me."

"Okay, then," she said, heading back to the bedroom.

To my dismay, though, she came back out in about five minutes. This time, however, she was fully clothed and had her purse on her arm. "Well, I guess I'll be going. It's nice to meet you Mrs. Nottingham."

I groaned inwardly as she addressed me by my married name. I hated that I was married to him, and I really hated when others reminded me of that fact.

She left, and then Nottingham himself appeared outside the door. He cocked his head at me silently, and then came over and sat next to me. "Dalilah," he said. "How nice of you to make a guest appearance here at home."

I raised an eyebrow. I wasn't expecting this reception. I wasn't even sure what this reception was.

Then, just like that, he hit me across the face. Hard.

I looked at him, and his face had definitely changed from just a few seconds before. He now had fury in his eyes.

He shook his head. "You fucking whore. You humiliated me tonight. You refused to talk to any of my friends there at the party, and then you just up and disappeared. Up and disappeared. And don't think that I don't know just where you went. I can smell him on you."

It was then that I realized that I *did* have Luke's scent on me. His cologne was mingling with my own perfume. I inhaled, and instantly felt comforted. Just smelling the scent that was so familiar for me was something that enveloped me like a warm security blanket.

"Nottingham," I said, defiantly. "I said that I would marry you. I said that I would be your quote unquote 'sex slave.' I never promised to love you."

"No," he said. "But you did promise never to see him again. You've broken your promise. And now you're going to pay."

My heart quickened. I had no idea what he meant by that.

He grabbed my wrists and jerked me over to a railing that separated the living room from the kitchen. In one stroke, before I had a chance to react, he handcuffed both of my hands, so that I was secured to the iron bars. I squeezed my eyes shut, and tried, hard, to tamp down the fear of what was about to happen to me.

I was helpless and scared to death.

He spread my legs open wide, and took his belt and wrapped it around one of my legs. He then pulled on the belt, hard, so that it broke my skin. I cried out in pain and fear, and I soon felt the belt on my bare back. My dress was backless, so he didn't bother to remove it, as he gave me lash after lash.

And then he kicked me, hard, on my side. "You're a

fucking whore, and a fucking waste of breath and energy," he was saying, as he kicked me, hard, again and again. "I won't be humiliated by you or by anybody. Do you understand me?"

I felt that he was in a blind rage at that point, as I felt his powerful kicks on my sides and my back, again and again. Tears were streaming down my face, and I was crying out. But the more I screamed and cried, the more he beat and kicked me.

At one point, I was actually afraid for my life. I felt that if Nottingham was truly in a frenzy of rage that he might go too far and beat me to death. While I was helplessly bound to the iron railing. I felt my breath coming faster and faster, until I was almost in a state of panic.

I didn't want to die here. I couldn't die here. I desperately tried to free my hands, but the handcuffs were on too tightly.

I had to fight. I had to stay alive.

I saw my purse to the side of my head. My elegant little Prada clutch was beckoning me. My phone was inside that purse. If I could just get to it and dial 911…

I managed to jerk my head just enough that I could almost put the purse in my mouth. By then, by some miracle, Nottingham had actually stopped assaulting me, and I could hear him in the next room, pouring himself a drink. He was muttering to himself about how I was a worthless slut, and how he was going to teach me a lesson, even more of a lesson than what he was already showing me.

I finally did get that purse in my mouth, and I nudged it open. Thank god this was a purse that was secured by springs, not a zipper or a snap. The phone spilled out onto the floor, and I used my nose to dial Emergency.

"911, what's your emergency?" a friendly voice said to me on the other end of the line.

"Please come. Hurry. I'm in trouble," I whispered. "Hurry."

"An officer will be on his way," she said. "In the meantime, please keep calm," she said. "An officer will be there in less than five minutes."

I put down my head, feeling terrified that Nottingham would return to me before an officer could get there. If he came in and saw what I was doing, there was just no telling how he would react. He might finish the job.

My adrenaline was such that I wasn't feeling the sting of where he lashed me, or the pain of where he kicked me. All I could feel was the fear that he was going to kill me, and the anxiety that an officer wouldn't get there quickly enough.

I could hear my own heartbeat in my ears, and I squeezed my eyes tightly shut. I tried mightily to think of something that comforted me, anything at all. I felt that I was on the verge of having some sort of cardiac arrest, as my chest was tightening on my left side. Squeezing, and a pain was radiating down my arm.

I realized that I was hyperventilating, and my next fear was that I was about to pass out.

Finally, after what seemed like years, an officer was at the door. He knocked and announced "open up. This is the police."

"Bitch!" Nottingham shouted at me. "You fucking cunt, how could you do that?" And then he went to the door.

"May I help you?" Nottingham said in a voice that wasn't his usual cold, cruel cadence, but, rather, was rather charming. Kind of like the voice I heard him use with his friends at the party.

"We've received a phone call about a disturbance. Do you mind if we come in and look around?"

I prayed silently that Nottingham would let them. Because, if Nottingham said "no," then the officers would have to leave and come back with a search warrant.

By the time they would come back to me, it would already be too late. I knew that.

"I'm very sorry," Nottingham said, as my heart sunk into my shoes. "But you cannot come in."

"Okay, sir, then good evening. We will be back after we obtain the proper warrant to enter the premises. Your refusal to let us in the door, coupled with the 911 call that came from within this apartment, will give us probable cause to search the premises."

NO! NO! You can't just leave me here! I knew that Nottingham was capable of anything. I cried out, so that maybe the officer would hear me, but, apparently, he was already gone. I heard the door shut and Nottingham came over to me.

"Okay, you little bitch," he said, unfastening my hand-cuffs. "You get the fuck out of here. And you leave here with only the clothes on your back. Do you understand me?"

What? He was letting me go? My heart soared beyond belief. I was going to leave with my life?

I got on my feet, feeling very unsteady.

"You have to get out of here before that officer gets back with a search warrant," he said. "Which means that you need to get the fuck out of here right now."

I nodded my head, clutching my purse to my breasts. I ran out the door, and got the elevator and made it out to the street.

It was freezing out, and I didn't have a coat. But I didn't

even think about that. All that I could think about was that I was free from that monster.

I called a cab, and did what came instinctively for me. I didn't ask the cab to take me to the hospital.

I asked the cab to take me straight over to Luke.

Chapter Twenty-Three

I got to Luke's apartment, and crawled gingerly out of the cab. By that time, the adrenaline was wearing off, and I was feeling the searing pain of where Nottingham savagely beat me. I barely made it up the stairs, but, somehow, through sheer force of will, I did.

I knocked on Luke's door. I knew that it was really, really late. Or really, really early. It depended on how you looked at it – but it was around 5 AM by this time.

Luke seemed to be awake, though, thank God, because I soon heard him rustling around inside the apartment.

He opened the door, and his eyes got wide in shock. "Oh my God," he said. "Oh my God. Dalilah, oh my God," he said, helping me into his place. He sat me gingerly down on his couch. "Dalilah, what happened to you?"

I just shook my head, and, all at once, I finally was able to access my emotions about that entire evening, and about my life for the last few weeks. I started sobbing, hard, so hard that I couldn't speak at all.

"Luke, Luke, Luke, I'm so sorry," I finally said when I found my voice. "I'm so sorry, Luke. Please forgive me," I said, over and over and over again.

He was kneeling over me, an ice pack in his hand. "Dalilah, honey, I have to get you to a hospital. I don't know what happened to you, but I really need to make sure that you get treatment."

I shook my head violently. I was afraid for my life at that point. I was terrified that Nottingham had the connections to have me wiped off the face of the earth, without his hands ever getting dirty. "No, Luke, please. Please. He'll kill me, and maybe you too. Please, Luke. Don't make me go to the hospital."

"Who?" Luke demanded, his eyes narrowing. "Nottingham? I swear to fucking God, I'll kill him with my bare hands." Luke's normally laid-back demeanor suddenly got stiff, and his eyes looked determined.

I laid there, completely confused, and not really sure what to say to him. Everything just happened so fast – I had to figure out my bearings and how I wanted everything to go.

I mean, there was one thing that was abundantly clear in my mind after Nottingham's abuse. I couldn't stay with him any longer. Not that he would even have me back after what happened, but, if he did, I wouldn't go back. He had crossed the line from sex games to abuse. And, after seeing the look in his eyes – I knew that he was absolutely capable of anything. For all I knew, he could have killed me.

And Nottingham was just the kind of guy who could get away with murder, quite literally. Maybe he already had. Who knows? A guy like that, with those cold, cold eyes and cruel demeanor...he had no soul, no conscience. And extremely violent tendencies. Yet, he was extremely intelligent and well-connected. Not to mention loaded. He was the perfect storm, really, and I wouldn't be surprised if he was like Patrick Bateman, who was the main character in the book *American Psycho*. Bateman was a wealthy yuppie who was also a vicious serial killer.

Yes, if there was one thing that I had learned in my life, it was that wealthy people could pretty much get away with anything. They always surrounded themselves with yes-men and people who depend upon them for their livelihood. Not to mention the people who fall over themselves trying to please them, mainly because they want to be associated with somebody with wealth and prestige.

After all, Nick, my father's best friend, basically got away with murder. Of course, there was a good reason for that one. Paul Lucas was a particularly low form of scumbag, and, like Nottingham, he was pretty much capable of anything. If there was anybody in this world who got what was coming to him, it was Paul.

I looked at Luke, at those beautiful eyes, which were so full of love and concern, and I knew that I had to keep on lying. I didn't want Luke to endanger himself, which is what would happen if he decided to go and take care of Nottingham. And I knew that he would do that. He would do something to Nottingham if he knew that Nottingham did this to me. And that would surely endanger him.

I couldn't have that.

I shook my head. "No, Luke, I, was, uh…" And then I started crying again. What was I going to say to him? That I was mugged? Assaulted on the street? And then what? He was going to make me go to the police station to make a report. There would be a sketch artist and a line-up and all kinds of investigation. To chase a phantom.

When I started thinking about how all my secrets and lies were finally catching up to me, I almost broke down right then and there.

Luke was sitting by the side of the couch, putting an ice bag all over me. He gently dabbed some antibiotic ointment on my cuts as well. All the while, he was stroking my hair and speaking to me in a low voice.

"Dalilah, just relax. You can tell me what happened after you calm down a little bit. Please, just take some deep breaths. And I'm here, Dalilah. I'm right here. I'm not going anywhere. I love you, Dalilah."

He had tears in his eyes, too. He shook his head. "This is my fault," he said.

I had no idea what he was talking about. What was his fault? That Nottingham was a violent psycho? How was that Luke's fault? So, I just looked at him. I tried to find my words, but, somehow, none were coming out.

"Luke, please, don't blame yourself. I don't even know what you think that you did wrong, to be honest."

"I made you leave. God, that was so stupid of me. I should have let you stay here, at least for the night. What was I thinking?"

"No, Luke, I was the one who wasn't thinking. I shouldn't have come to your place earlier. I should've known better than that. Now, I feel that I have put you in the middle of a drama that you should never be a part of. This is my drama, and my mess. I should be the one who is feeling terrible for involving you in it."

Luke was still stroking my hair gently, and he got up and got some water for me and some aspirin. "Here, Dalilah, drink this down. You look like you're in a lot of pain. And I really, really want to take you to the hospital. I think that you need to go and be examined. You might have some type of internal injury."

I winced as he examined my bruises on my side. "No, I won't go. I won't. I'm okay, Luke, really. Superficial wounds. Please don't worry about me too much. I'm going to be just fine."

Luke sighed. "Dalilah, I don't think that I can take no for an answer, here. You need to get to the hospital."

I started to feel slightly panicked at the prospect. What was I going to tell the doctors who would examine me? I was scared to death to implicate Nottingham. He could very well hire somebody to wipe me off the face of the earth. Luke, too.

I shook my head again, more forcefully this time. "No. No means no. I won't go anywhere. If you try to make me, then I'll call a cab and leave right now." I got out my cell phone for effect.

Luke just shook his head, and kissed me lightly on my forehead. "That's my Dalilah. Stubborn as anything. I love that about you, but it frustrates me as well." He put his arm around me protectively. "I hope that you change your mind, but I won't push it."

"Thanks. I appreciate that."

He sat there, putting a cool compress on my injuries. I winced in pain while he was taking care of me, but I also couldn't help but think that there was no place else that I would have rather been right at that moment. I felt so incredibly safe and comfortable there with him, especially in contrast to how I felt when I was with Nottingham. Nottingham always had me on edge, and I felt incredibly unsafe with him.

But, with Luke, I just felt like I was home.

And I never, ever wanted to leave.

Ever.

"Well, Dalilah, do you think that you can sleep a little bit? You look really tired."

I didn't know if I could, as I was in so much pain. But, I closed my eyes anyhow. And, to my surprise, I soon felt myself drifting off…

Chapter Twenty-Four

Luke

Dalilah had just passed out on my couch, thank God, and I had to think fast about what was next. She refused to let me take her to the hospital.

I knew why.

She was afraid of him.

And, knowing Nottingham, she probably thought that he was capable of anything. Not that I blamed her. I always got the feeling that there was something clearly wrong with that man. The way that he stared, his demeanor...if he had really pale skin, I might have thought him a vampire or something else that was less than human. He seemed not to have a soul.

He was void. Even more than Serena, who also was void. Yet, there was always something that I could sense underneath his cold exterior. And that was that he had the capability of great cruelty.

Dalilah didn't say as much, but I was reasonably certain

that he did this to her. Which enraged me beyond measure on one hand, yet made me feel completely guilty on the other.

I shouldn't have made her leave. I should've listened to her more when she was over here, pleading with me. Instead, I sent her away. I was so angry with her for throwing her marriage in my face, and for marrying somebody else in the first place. Not to mention the fact that I never got over the way that she so cruelly dumped me.

Even so, I really wanted her to stay there with me. It took every fiber of my being to turn her away. But turn her away I did. And, by doing that, I was sending her straight into the dragon's lair.

I really didn't think that I would ever get over that feeling. That I was supposed to protect the woman that I loved, and, instead of providing this protection, I did the opposite. I sent her into a dangerous place. A place where she apparently got beaten and whipped.

It was then that I noticed it. Very faint scars on her back. I traced my fingers lightly, wondering why I never noticed them before. But they were unmistakable.

I wondered what had happened. These scars weren't fresh. They were probably from months earlier.

I shook my head. Dalilah was still pretty much a mystery to me. I loved her more than I thought that I ever could love a woman, but there obviously were things that she was hiding from me. Like the fact that she was with Nottingham. Or where it was she got the earlier injuries on her back. Those were just two mysteries that begged to be answered, and there might be even more.

I stroked her hair while she lay on my couch asleep. And then I got on the phone with Jake, who was my 420 connection. I wondered if he had access to any Oxycodone or any other kind of painkiller. Because Dalilah might not be feeling the pain right at that moment, but she soon would, and I knew that she was going to end up thinking that she got run over by a truck.

"Hey," Jake said. "Luke, my boy. How did it go?"

"Great," I said. "Listen, I can't talk about that right now. You got any access to Percocet or Oxy or anything like that?"

"No man. I got some Tylenol 3, though."

"That'll have to do. Can you bring it over right now?"

"Sure. Anything you need to tell me?"

"No. I mean, there is, but, no. Sorry, bro, I can't let you in on this right now. It's a pretty bad situation and the person who needs the stuff is pretty scared. Not sure how much I can tell you. Sorry about that."

"Not a prob. I'll be there in about fifteen."

"Later. Thanks."

Tylenol 3. Well, it was better than nothing. After all, it had codeine in it, which was a pretty good painkiller. I actually was impressed with Tylenol 3 when I had an ear infection and my eardrums burst. Unimaginable pain. When the doctor prescribed Tyenol 3 for me after that, I almost went down his throat. Goddamn it, I was in severe pain, and the doc prescribes Tylenol? But it was prescription strength and was surprisingly effective.

I went back over to Dalilah and stroked her hair, while I waited for Jake to show up with the promised Tylenol. "Dalilah, a woman of so many secrets. I wish that you would open up to me. What are you so afraid of?" I wanted so much for there to be no secrets between Dalilah and me, yet there seemed to be so many of them. Such an ocean there seemed to be between us, right at that second.

I just sat there with Dalilah, staring at her and kissing

her forehead. She was still in her evening gown, but her shoes were off. Yet she seemed comfortable lying there, for she was sleeping soundly.

I wanted to help her, but I had no idea how. I didn't even know where it was that I would start. Because I had no idea what the problem was. I mean, this whole story about her friend Nick, and how she married Nottingham to help Nick out – that just sounded like bullshit to me. I knew of that firm - O'Hara, White and Stroker – and that firm wouldn't even miss Nottingham's money, even if the account was worth millions. The firm was one of the biggest in the world. I just couldn't imagine Dalilah sacrificing her very life and happiness so that a wealthy architectural firm could keep ahold of a few million more.

No, that made zero sense to me.

Yet, she clearly married Nottingham for a reason. But what was it? What would be compelling enough for her to do something like that?

I pondered this as I answered the buzzer. Jake was downstairs waiting for me. "Be right down," I said, and then went out the door and down the stairs to meet him.

"Hey," he said. "Here's the stuff."

"Cool. How much do I owe you?"

Jake shrugged. "Nothing, bro. On me."

"Right," I said, and then took out the money I brought with me, which was $50, and stuffed it into his coat pocket. It was a kind of a weird dance we always did, just because it was always uncomfortable doing business with a friend. Jake always tried to say that the 420 was on him, and I always stuffed the money into his pockets over his protests. But we both knew that Jake really wanted the money, he was just too much of a cool guy to act like it.

"Hey, thanks," he said. "Looks like there's going to be a lot more where that came from."

"Yeah," I said, feeling in a hurry to get back up to Dalilah. I didn't want her to wake up and think that I ditched her. "Listen, thanks for this, buddy. I'll call you later and give you the scoop on last night. Thanks again."

He nodded his head and turned around and then got to his car and waved at me. "Take care, man. Get a beer later on?"

I shook my head. "Not today. I got some things I gotta take care of. But later on this week, huh?"

"Sure. Later."

At that, I took the package and walked back into the apartment. And lucky that I went back in when I did, because Dalilah was stirring. She groaned a little and positioned herself better on my couch. I got a blanket and pillow for her, and made her more comfortable.

And just sat there and stared at her, willing her to wake up and tell me what was really going on.

Chapter Twenty-Five

As it turned out, I sat there and waited for her to become conscious for several more hours. She seemed to be really exhausted, so I didn't wake her. But she finally woke up with a start around 2 in the afternoon.

She cried out, and immediately sat up. I went over to her, and held her while she breathed heavily in my arms. Her hand was clutching my arm so tightly, I thought that was going to leave a mark. She looked at me as if she really didn't know who I was for a split second. Her eyes were wide with absolute terror.

But then, gradually, she seemed to focus more on her surroundings and her entire face and body became relaxed again. "Oh, thank God," she said. "Thank God I'm here. And not there. With him." She visibly shuddered. "God forbid I was there with him. God forbid."

I took a deep breath. "How are you feeling?"

"Like I've been run over by a truck." She winced in obvious pain, and gingerly got off of the couch. "I'll be right back," she said, getting up to use the bathroom.

That settled it for me. Dalilah obviously was woken up from a nightmare, and she very clearly referenced the fact that she was relieved that she wasn't in Nottingham's place anymore. If there was any doubt as to exactly who did this to her, there wasn't anymore.

And, just like that, I wanted to go over and strangle that cold, cruel man with my bare hands. But I had to conceal my absolute fury. Dalilah didn't need my hostility right then. All that she needed was my love. And my painkillers.

She came back over to the couch after having made a glass of water for herself and one for me. She handed the water to me as she sipped hers. "What time is it?" she asked, squinting.

"It's a little after two. You've been out for about eight hours." I handed her a Tylenol. "Here, take this. It will kill your pain."

"What is it?"

"Just a Tylenol 3 with codeine," I said. "It does the trick, though."

"Thanks," she said, drinking her water and swallowing the pill. She laid back down and stared at the ceiling.

"I'm so sorry, Dalilah, but I should have offered you a change of clothing earlier. Anyhow, here is a t-shirt and pair of boxers you can change into."

She looked at me a bit strangely and took the clothes. "Thanks. Uh, Luke, I mean, I know that you saw my back."

"Yes," I said. "You can tell me what happened in due time." I wanted to push her for more information, but I didn't want to press too hard. I also wanted to ask her about the scars that I just noticed. They were very faint, but I could still see them.

"I will," she said. "Thanks for the clothes." At that, she

got up and went into my bathroom and came back out in a few minutes, dressed in my t-shirt and boxers.

She looked beautiful dressed in my clothes. She was always beautiful, of course, but dressed in my t-shirt and shorts, she looked more like the Dalilah I fell in love with. The Dalilah in the expensive evening gown certainly turned heads at the party, but that just wasn't her.

This seemed so much more natural. So much more right. Like old times – the two of us just hanging around the house together.

Of course, we weren't just hanging around the house together anymore, like old times. She was married and recovering from being beaten, presumably by the man she was married to. And she had a lost look in her eyes. There was so much sadness in those beautiful eyes now that I almost was brought to tears.

Things were strained between us. Awkward. She had a difficult time meeting my eyes, and I felt like I didn't really have words to say to her. I hated that there seemed to be a barrier between us, yet I also knew that she was dealing with a lot right at that moment.

"Dalilah," I began.

"Shhhh," she said, putting her finger to my mouth. "Please, Luke, let's not talk about anything important right now. I don't want to talk about what happened to me or why I married that monster or any of that. I'm not ready to."

And then her eyes brightened, and she forced a smile. "What I want to talk about is your phenomenal reception last night. You must be bouncing off the walls."

I felt uncomfortable discussing that with her, because it seemed inappropriate. She was having major problems right at that moment, and I didn't want to change the subject. "Yes," I said. "I guess it went well."

"You guess? You do know that you had the entire place abuzz last night, including that old fart Henry Jacobs. I still hate him, but, at the same time, I'm dying for him to give you a rocking review in the paper. After last night…" And then she seemed to catch herself, for she didn't finish that sentence.

"After last night, what?" I asked her gently.

She shook her head. "I don't know. It seems that you're going to do very well for yourself after what I saw last night." And then she swallowed hard. "That is…"

I cocked my head. She was hiding something from me, I could tell. There was something about the cautious way she was talking about my future prospects that made me think that she knew something that I clearly didn't.

I brushed her hair away from her face a little and kissed her on her forehead. "What's on your mind, Dalilah? There's something that you're not telling me."

She shook her head. "No, really, it's nothing. The painkiller is starting to kick in, I guess, because I'm feeling pretty light-headed right now. But my pain is subsiding quite a bit, so there's that."

"Just lay back down," I said. "And rest. You don't have anywhere to go, and you need to heal. So that should be your first priority – getting better. Stronger. We can talk about what's troubling you a little later. Right now, just get some sleep."

She nodded her head, and closed her eyes. "I love you, Luke."

"I love you, too."

Chapter Twenty-Six

Days went by, and Dalilah stayed at my place. On the second day of Dalilah's stay, I actually was able to get ahold of her best friend, Alaina, and have her bring a bag of Dalilah's things. She obliged, and I went through the same routine with her that I did with Jake. In that I met her downstairs, outside the building, and refused to let her see Dalilah. This was at Dalilah's request, of course, but that didn't make it any easier.

For Alaina wasn't like Jake. She wasn't going to go away easily or quietly. She wanted answers, and she was going to pester me until she got them.

"Here's a week's worth of Dalilah's clothes. Her toothbrush and shampoo and stuff, too," she said, bringing out a huge bag out of her car and handing the things to me.

"Thanks," I said, taking the things. "Well, uh, I'd like to pay you for your time."

"Nothing doing," she said. "I need you to tell me what's going on with Dalilah. She won't return my phone calls, and she's been neither returning my calls nor at her apartment for weeks now. Now, here you are, mysteriously asking me to bring over some of her things and, even more mysteriously, telling me that I can't see my own best friend. Well, I'm not leaving until I get a chance to see her."

Alaina stood on the sidewalk, her hands on her slender hips. She was about 5'5", and probably a buck fifteen on a good day, yet she tried hard to make herself seem larger than her actual physical stature.

"Alaina, I'm really so sorry. But Dalilah gave me specific instructions. I wish that I could tell you something, and I would like for you to see her. But I have to respect her wishes."

I looked at Alaina's face and saw that my words were not having the desired effect. She looked like she was genuinely going to stand out in the cold until she could see her friend. "Listen, Luke," she said. "I don't know who died and made you Dalilah's keeper, but I know her, and I know that she really wants to see me. Now, you're gonna take me up in that apartment so that I can see her for myself, or..."

I drew a breath. I felt badly for Alaina. She was only trying to look out for Dalilah, I knew, but no matter. Dalilah wanted to see nobody she knew until her bruises were healed, and that was that.

I was surprised, though, that Alaina hadn't talked to Dalilah in so long. That could have only meant that Dalilah kept the truth about her marriage to Nottingham from her best friend.

That whole thing was getting curiouser and curiouser to me. I was no closer to getting a confession out of Dalilah about the true reason why she married that creeper than I was when she first came to my door after the party. For that matter, she hadn't yet talked about her beating. I could only presume that it was Nottingham who did that to her, but I still wasn't 100% sure.

"Alaina, please," I said. "I know that you're concerned for Dalilah. But you have to respect her wishes. I'm sure that she'll give you a call soon enough, and hopefully she'll talk to you about what is going on. I can't force her to see you, though."

Alaina looked like she was about to cry. "I've known that girl since we were like four years old. We've gone through everything together. She's known you for like a minute, and, suddenly, I'm left out in the cold and you're the one who's like her gatekeeper. That's not fair. In fact, that's bullshit. Now, I want to see her, and I want to see her right now."

"I'm very sorry, Alaina," I said. "I wish that Dalilah felt differently. I really do. But-"

"But nothing. I'm not taking no for an answer, here."

I opened my mouth, but no words came out. I had no idea what to say. What lie to tell her to make her go away. She was determined, that was for sure.

Finally, I just said "Alaina, thanks for the clothes and stuff. I'll take this up to her and make sure that she calls you as soon as possible." And, at that, I walked back into the building, trying to block out the sounds of Alaina yelling about her rights and how ungrateful Dalilah was for all that she did for her.

"And don't think that I'm coming to your wedding, either," she was shouting. "I didn't know that she was marrying a douchebag."

I shut the door behind me and carried the things up the steps. Dalilah was waiting for me on the couch. By that time, her bruises were showing, and she was wearing a pair of dark sunglasses to cover up the shiner on her eye.

"Thanks for doing that, Luke," she said from her position on the couch. She was dressed in one of my t-shirts and a pair of my sweats, and her hair was piled on top of her head.

I put her things down on top of my table, and went over to her. "How are you doing?" I asked, stroking her hair. Next to her, on the coffee table, were the remnants of the breakfast I had made for her – leftover scrambled eggs, toast and hash browns. I picked up the tray of food and took it into the kitchen.

"I'm okay," she said, but I knew that she really wasn't. She really started feeling her pain about a day after all of this went down, and she was hazy from the painkillers ever since. And she was very quiet. So unlike herself. She really seemed to be lost and confused, and I worried about her night and day.

I sat down next to her and said "Alaina. She says that you haven't talked to her for awhile. She knows nothing of your marriage to Nottingham. I don't want to press you, but I wondered why you never confided in her about what's going on."

Dalilah sighed. "Because she never would have let me live it down. Alaina would bug me and harass me about marrying Nottingham, and I just didn't want to hear it. My mind was made up, and I was going to do it, so I really didn't need her whining to me about it."

I looked at my hands for a few minutes. "You ever gonna tell me the real story about Nottingham and why you married him?"

"I did tell you the real story," she said. "Maybe it was misguided, but I felt that I was repaying a debt to Nick for being so cool to me. For taking me in when he didn't really have to. I'm very loyal that way."

I bit my lip. I wanted to tell her to quit lying and spill it, whatever it was. I couldn't stand that she was sitting there and bullshitting me right to my face.

But I didn't press her. I knew that somehow, someway, the story was going to come out.

Chapter Twenty-Seven

Later on, when Dalilah was sleeping, I decided to check my phone. It had been a few days since my premiere, and I figured that at least a few of the people I met the other night would be calling me. Not that this was important right at that moment – the most important thing was helping Dalilah. But I was also excited to see who might be interested in giving me a showing or commission. It seemed that, on my premiere night, everybody I met was really interested in me.

Several days earlier, I had called about twenty of the people who were interested in me. Not one of them had called me back. I had also sent out about fifty emails, and none of those were returned, either.

I sighed. I thought that things went really well with my premiere, but, apparently, I was wrong. I guess that my work was forgettable after all. I'm not going to lie, I was disappointed, because everybody had seemed so enthusiastic.

Well, give it some time. They're all busy people. Really busy people. They'll get in touch. Or at least get their assistant to get in touch.

Then I realized that it was Sunday. Maybe there would be a review in the paper. That would certainly get things going. So, I checked on Dalilah, who was sleeping soundly on my couch. I left a note for her that I was going to the corner store to pick up a paper, and then left.

I approached the store and picked up a paper and bought it. I took it up to my apartment, and sifted through it. The paper was big, although it wasn't as big as it was in its heyday. It had gone through the same transition as most newspapers and magazines, trying to adjust to the realities of the Internet, but it managed to weather the storm. It was, once again, the top newspaper in the country, and was still very influential and widely-read.

My heart pounding, I found the Arts Section, and saw that Henry Jacobs did a review of my show. I felt my heart quickening and my hands were shaking, as I read.

I read the review, and kept looking for my name. The review was of the showing at the *Matthew Jane*, alright, but it was entirely about the other two artists.

I read the article two more times, before I realized that I had been entirely cut out of the review. It was as if I didn't exist.

I blinked my eyes. *Was the whole show a dream?* I started to feel that I was in an episode of *The Twilight Zone*.

I feared a bad review. What I never feared was no review at all. That was probably the worst thing possible, considering – any publicity is good publicity, so if there was a bad review, at least people would know your name. But to completely be ignored – that was devastating.

It was bad enough that Elaine Bush had already done the same on her blog. She had reviewed the other two artists and not me. That was disappointing for sure. But now Henry Jacobs also acted like I didn't exist, and that the show at the *Matthew Jane* featured the other two artists and not me.

Combined with the silent phone and silent email, I suddenly started to feel that I was back to square one.

Well, that was a huge setback, really. But Dalilah was back, so I was still happy, much happier than I had felt in a long, long time.

Chapter Twenty-Eight

I had been waiting for Dalilah to get to a point where I felt that she was on the mend, before I went over to confront Nottingham. I was reasonably sure that he was the one who beat her, and, ever since she showed up at my door, I had been looking for an opportunity to go over and kick his ass.

There was no way that I was going to let him get away with doing what he did. But I felt that I had to hang close to the apartment, because Dalilah was needing constant care and I felt that I had to look after her. I even took some time off of work, as I had a vacation coming to me, and I pretty much stayed by her side 24/7.

Finally, though, after about three days of her being at my place, she seemed to come out of her funk. She was up and around, her bruises were healing, and she had weaned herself off of the painkillers. She still seemed lost, sad and afraid, but she was, little by little, getting to be herself again.

It was time to make my move....

So, one morning, I told Dalilah that I was going to my studio for a little while. I had no idea what to tell her about where I was going, because I knew that if she thought for one second that I was going to see Nottingham, she would have done everything in her power to stop me.

"Okay, Luke," she said. She looked hurt that I would leave her. "I understand. I mean, you must be stir crazy staying here with me 24/7. You need an outlet, so, please, go to your studio and do some work. I'll be right here."

"Thanks for understanding," I said, and then went over to her. I held her hand. "I love you, Dalilah. We haven't really talked about anything that we need to talk about, but, hopefully that will come with time. I need you to open up to me, though. We need to clear the air, because there are just too many secrets with you. And, I'll be honest, I have no idea where we stand. For obvious reasons."

She nodded her head, but said nothing. "Hurry back," she said softly. "I miss you already." She bowed her head a little, and my heart absolutely broke.

But I had to do this. I just couldn't let that worm get away with doing this to her. I wished that I could go to the cops, but I knew that wasn't possible. Dalilah would have to get involved, and it seemed that was something that she wasn't willing to do. It seemed as if she was afraid of him.

I wasn't afraid of him, though. How tough was he, if he would do that to a woman? That was just cowardice.

I finally arrived at his office building. I went to his suite, and announced my arrival to the receptionist. I hoped against hope that Nottingham was in his office, but I knew that it was a long-shot at best.

"I'm sorry," said the bored blonde receptionist, who was the same one as the first time I was there at the office, complete with the same fuck-me pumps as before and virtually the same tight-sweater. "What did you say your name was?"

"Luke Roberts," I said.

"Just a second," she said, and called on the phone. She looked at me. "He'll be right with you."

I couldn't believe my luck. I sat down and tried to calm myself, but that was impossible. I could feel my anger rising as I sat there.

After about fifteen minutes, blondie took me back to Nottingham's office, and shut the door behind her. I stood by the closed door for a few minutes, just staring at him. For his part, he stared right back without a word.

Finally, he spoke. "May I help you?"

"Yeah, you can," I said. "I need you to stand up."

He gave me a look like *yeah, right.* But, he did stand up. I guess he was curious about why I would want that.

I went over to him, and, in a very quick move, I punched him hard in the face. I shocked him, apparently, so I gave him an upper cut to his gut. He doubled up in pain.

"How does that feel?" I asked him. "You're going to beat up on an innocent woman? You're a fucking coward. How brave do you feel now that you're faced with somebody who can actually fight back?"

Nottingham said nothing, but just straightened up. I was still crouched down, ready to strike. I had been in more than a few brawls in my life, so I knew that I could take this cold prick, even if he did decide to fight back.

Which he didn't. Of course. He couldn't very well get in a brawl at work. Might end up messing up his hair. So, he simply called the police, and then looked at me. "You might as well wait here," he said. "You're going to get arrested for assault no matter if you leave right now or not."

"That's cool," I said. "I had to do something, though. She won't do anything, because she's apparently scared to death of you. I will tell you this. Men who do that shit to women are cowards, plain and fucking simple. I feel sorry for you that you're such a wimp that you have to take your aggressions out on somebody who's quite a bit smaller than you. If I gave you just 1% of the pain that you gave her, then that will give me some kind of satisfaction."

"I don't know what you're talking about," he said. "Who is afraid of me, and what did I do to this mystery woman?"

"You know," I said. "Very well. She's just now recovering from the pain. I'm taking good care of her, though, rest assured."

"You are?" he said. "You won't be for long, as you will soon be incarcerated."

"I don't think so," I said. "Detained maybe, but not incarcerated. Because I'm not going to prison, no matter what you might think. No jury would convict me when they find out what you did to deserve the beat-down."

"Tomato tomahto," he said. "You will be behind bars soon, that's all that I'm saying."

This was such a weird conversation. He was remarkably unruffled by assault. In fact, he seemed rather amused by it, which enraged me all the more.

I was going to get to him, and I had to do it fast. "Well, make no mistake, she's with me, now. And I'm going to protect her from you. She might be married to you, but she won't be for long, and she'll soon be my wife, not yours."

I thought that I saw his cold eyes show a flash of anger, but only a flash. It went through his eyes so quickly, though, it was easily mistaken for something else. Still, it gave me some kind of comfort that maybe, just maybe, I got a rise out of this inhuman monster.

He waved his hand at me, and I turned around to see two uniformed police officers standing at the door. They cuffed my hands behind my back, and I didn't struggle at all. I looked back at Nottingham to show him that I wasn't broken, but he was already at work on some kind of project, and he didn't even raise his eyes at me.

I soon was down on the street, and shoved in the back of a squad car as I headed down to the county jail. Not that this would be my first time in jail, of course. Like most guys from my neighborhood, I had done a couple of stints when I was younger. Just juvenile stuff, graffiti and minor shop-lifting.

This, time, though, I felt that I could go to jail with my head held high, knowing that what I did to go to this cell was one that was justified and right. I had to do something to stand up for the woman I loved. As ineffective as it was, at least it was something.

Chapter Twenty-Nine

Dalilah

I was on pins and needles, waiting for Luke to return. He said that he had gone off to his studio to do some work, but I had my suspicions about that. He was acting awfully strangely, and I prayed that he didn't go and see Nottingham. I had no idea how Nottingham would react. Something told me that he probably wouldn't take too kindly to seeing Luke.

I already knew that Luke was being blackballed. He didn't say as much, but, when he thought that I was sleeping, I was really trying to listen to what he was doing. I hated being nosy like that, and I really just wanted to have open communication with him again, like we used to. But I just couldn't tell him the truth. I was trying to think of a million and one ways that somehow he wouldn't end up making things worse with Nottingham by confronting him, but I knew that wasn't possible.

All of this was why I was still covering up what really happened, and why I was kicking myself, internally, every day, for putting Luke in the middle of the drama. He didn't belong in the middle of the drama. It wasn't fair to him, yet I had a feeling that he was paying for all of my sins anyhow. Which was why I was anxiously listening in whenever he called some of the contacts that he met at the premiere. I heard him make call after call, and I knew that these people weren't calling him back.

My heart broke for him. If I could change everything about what I did the night of his premiere, I would have. If I could have gone back in time, I would have behaved myself at the premiere and would have silently gone back with Nottingham. I would have kept my feelings and heart-break to myself, and I never would have let Luke in on how I was really feeling.

But I didn't. I went with my heart and my emotions, instead of my head, and I involved Luke in all of this. And now look. Just as I thought, his career was over as soon as it began. He had the most stellar premiere imaginable. Everyone was talking about him. Now, once again, it seemed that he couldn't get arrested.

I was so naïve to ever think that Nottingham's tentacles wouldn't reach, because they clearly did. And, really, it made a lot of sense that Nottingham would be successful in killing Luke's career. After all, Nottingham was the main person who arranged the entire party. All of those people at that premiere were connected to him in some way. And Nottingham was extremely established in the art world. He knew everybody that was anybody, and everybody else as well. If he wanted to stop Luke's momentum, then he had the power to do so.

He killed Luke's career in its proverbial cradle, and I felt like screaming in frustration. Everything I did – marrying that awful man, letting him touch me sexually night after night – was for nothing. Luke was a nobody once again.

It wasn't right. One man should not have so much power, but just because something shouldn't happen doesn't mean that it wouldn't. And I had been around wealthy individuals enough in my life to know that not all rich individuals use their wealth and power for good. I knew lots of good, moral people who just happened to have a lot of money. I also knew people like Nottingham – people who lived to manipulate the world and all the people in it. They used their power and wealth to ensure that things happened to benefit them alone. And they had no compunction about ruining the lives of innocent people.

Luke was nothing but a lowly bug for Nottingham to step on. Just to punish me. Nottingham, as far as I knew, had no beef with Luke himself. But hurting Luke would be the best way to hurt me, and Nottingham knew this. He knew this, and he used this knowledge perfectly.

I was on pins and needles and would be until Luke walked through that door. I should have gone with my gut feeling and tried to stop him from leaving. I tried to call him several times, but apparently his phone was turned off, which made me all the more nervous.

The hours clicked by so slowly. I thought about going down to his studio, but thought better of it. I was completely sure that he really wasn't there and I didn't want to waste the trip. And I wanted to be home when he got back. I wouldn't feel safe and secure until that happened.

By 7 PM that night, I was in a state of tizzy. I had no idea what I should do. Calling Nottingham would be pointless. Beyond pointless. There was no way he would give me any information. I even thought about calling Jake, but felt foolish for doing so. But Luke had been gone the entire day, and he said that he would only be gone for a few hours at the most. To make matters worse, his phone was still turned off, for I got his voice mail as soon as I called him.

My imagination started to go wild. What if something happened to him? He confronted Nottingham and Nottingham went ape-shit and really hurt him? He could be in the hospital or worse.

So, I started to call hospitals. I felt foolish as I called one hospital after another, asking about him. I looked on the Internet for the local news to see if there was anything on there. Maybe there was a hit and run and Luke was badly hurt? Or maybe he really did end up at his studio and he got robbed? I felt just a little bit relieved when I saw nothing on the news that would indicate that something major had happened to him.

I knew that I was getting just a little bit obsessed, but I had to make sure that I knew that he was safe.

I paced the floor, feeling helpless.

Finally, at 9 PM, I broke down and called Jake.

"Hello? This is Dalilah," I said to Jake when he answered the phone.

"Oh, hi, Dalilah," he said, a little bit strangely. Jake was always very friendly with me, but when he answered the phone, he already sounded evasive. "Listen, I can't talk right now," he said. "I'm so sorry."

"Jake, please, I'm sorry to bother you, but I'm looking for Luke. Have you seen him or talked to him?"

"Uh, no," he said, but I knew that he was lying. "Gotta go." And, at that, he hung up.

Crap. Jake clearly was hiding something. I knew that as sure as I knew my name.

I sat back down on the couch and put my head in my hands.

If something happened to Luke because of me....

Chapter Thirty

Luke

Going to jail sucked, to say the least. I was in the joint for about seven hours, in an unheated cell, before they processed me. After that, I got my phone call, and I immediately decided to call Jake. No way was I going to call Dalilah. Yeah, I did this to defend her honor and to give that slime-bag just a taste of what he gave to her, but, still, I was embarrassed. In the end, I was really brawling like the blue-collar boy I was.

"Jake, man, I'm in jail."

"Be right there. How much bail?"

"10,000/10%," I said, which meant that Jake only had to come up with $1,000 to get me out. "You know I'm good for it."

"No question. See you in a few."

He showed up after about a half hour and bailed me out.

As we drove back to my place, he said "hey, I forgot to

tell you. Dalilah called me looking for you. She called when I was on my way to get you."

"Crap. What did you tell her?"

"Nothing. Not my place. But you should probably call her," he said.

As much as I dreaded that, I knew that he was right. I still had no idea what I would tell her. I wasn't anxious to let her know about my Nottingham beat-down. I would imagine that she probably wouldn't take too kindly to that, considering how much she was still trying to hide the fact that it was Nottingham who did that to her.

I dialed her number, and she picked up immediately. "Luke," she said. She sounded a little out of breath, like she had been panicking.

"Hi, honey," I said. "Um, I'm so sorry that I didn't call you."

"You went to see Nottingham, didn't you?"

"Uh," I said. There was no hiding anything from her, or so it seemed.

"You did. Well, thank God you're okay. You don't know what that man is capable of. I can't tell you how worried I've been."

I felt badly for worrying her so much.

"I'll be home really soon," I said. "I love you."

"Oh, I love you, too," she said. "Hurry home."

"I'm on my way."

"So," Jake said, when I hung up the phone. "You mind telling me what happened?"

I tugged on my ear and looked out the window word-lessly. I had no idea what to tell him. I couldn't really spill out what had happened, because I wasn't at all sure, still, that Dalilah wanted anybody to know about Nottingham's beating her. So, I just shrugged my shoulders. "Got in a fight. You know the drill."

"Doesn't sound like you," Jake said. "I mean, not lately. It's been years since you've been involved in a beat-down. Somebody must have really pissed you off."

"Don't want to talk about it. What I do want to talk to you about is paying you back. I actually did quite well at my show the other night, very well, so I should be getting the money from that any day now."

"Yeah. You never did tell me how things went."

"Well, the show went better than I ever could have hoped. I mean, I was the man of the hour. Everybody seemed really excited about my work, and every one of those paintings sold out that night. Every one. Of course, now, for some odd reason, I can't get arrested again." And then I had to laugh. "Oh, wait…"

Jake laughed too and shook his head. "Bad metaphor to use, my friend. But what do you mean when you say that you can't get arrested?"

"Nobody is returning my calls. Ah, but then again, it is right before the holidays. Still, I would have thought that I would get some bites. I mean, people were seeking me out. Making me offers. Going on and on about how they loved my work. It's just weird, man, that I can't get a one of them to return my phone calls or e-mails."

"Give it time. Like you said, it's the holiday season. You might be dry until the new year. By the way, your 21st birthday is coming up soon. The 28th, right?"

"Yep. About time I can actually legally do what I've been doing for years, huh?"

"True that. Gotta take you out and get good and schnockered."

I nodded. I actually didn't know what I wanted to do on

my 21st birthday. Probably celebrate with Dalilah, if she happened to be in a celebratory mood.

We arrived at my place a few minutes later. I punched Jake lightly on the arm. "Thanks, bro. I'm gonna hit you up with that money as soon as I get paid."

"I know you're good for it. Besides, you've done the same for me many a time."

I nodded my head. "Later."

Then went up to the apartment.

Chapter Thirty-One

Dalilah

Luke was almost home, I guess, and I was pacing the floor. Everything was flooding back to me. The past few weeks of torment and heartbreak. Of submitting sexually, night after night, to a man that I loathed. Of wanting to almost die, I was so depressed and hopeless.

And for what? So that Luke can go and fuck everything up in one day? If there was any chance at all that he might be able to salvage something out of his amazing debut, he just flushed it down the drain in one fell swoop.

As I waited for him to come home, I found myself getting irrationally angrier and angrier. Of course, Luke didn't know what I did for him to make his dreams come true, so, really, I shouldn't have been as angry as I was. No matter. There was no way that I could have talked myself out of the way that I was feeling right at that moment.

Finally, he turned the doorknob and came into the

apartment. I stood there, my arms crossed, and he immediately looked puzzled.

"Hi, Dalilah," he said. "What's going on?"

I took a deep breath. "You saw Nottingham. Didn't I get it across to you that I didn't want you doing that?"

He looked chastened. "You did. But Dalilah, I had to defend your honor. He can't get away with doing what he did to you."

"Oh? Defend my honor? Exactly what did you accomplish by seeing him? I'm sure that he's really scared now." I couldn't keep the sarcasm out of my voice. "Luke, don't you know? Can't you see? You're a bug to him. An ant. Nothing but a nuisance to him, but he can crush you without even thinking twice. And he will. Trust me, he will."

"I'm not scared of him," Luke said. "And I felt that I had to do something to defend you. It wasn't much, but at least he knows now that you and I are together, so that's satisfaction enough. I wounded him when I told him that, let me tell you."

I just looked at him, trying very hard to keep my mouth shut before something came out of it that shouldn't. Something that I could never take back. "Luke," I said, trying to choose my words carefully. "You're an intelligent guy. But you're also incredibly naïve. You do know that everybody who was at your premiere was there because Nottingham invited them, don't you? Every single one. You don't know the power that man has. He has your future in his hands. Why would you fuck that up?"

He shook his head. "Dalilah, it's going to be okay. I had a great premiere, and I'm sure that I can make that into a great career. And, if nothing happens, then nothing happens. At least I know now that I have the potential to make it. If nothing else, that premiere gave me confidence in myself. If I have to start from square one, then I have to start from square one."

I paced the floor some more. How could he be so casual about all of this? If there was ever a chance for me to somehow smooth things out with Nottingham, just enough so that he wouldn't blackball Luke, that chance went out the window when Luke decided to confront Nottingham behind my back.

Finally, I took a deep breath. "Okay, so you confronted him. What did you say? What did he say?"

He looked down at the floor. "I told him that you and I are together, and that he can't get away with beating you that way. I think that I called him a coward, too. Because he is. Anybody who does something like that is a coward, and he's no exception."

"I see," I said. "And you just talked to him, right?"

"Well, no," he said. "I punched him twice. Once in the face and once in the gut."

I got quiet. *I knew it. I knew it.* I immediately kicked myself for ever putting Luke into the middle of the Nottingham drama.

I shook my head.

Luke walked towards me, putting his arms out, but I pushed him away. "Don't touch me," I said, shaking my head. "I'm so angry right now...I think that I need to not be here right now."

"Dalilah, I'm sorry. I felt that I...."

"Had to do something. I know. As ineffectual as it is. You might have felt that you've gotten some sort of revenge by going over and doing that, but I'm here to tell you that you've managed to make a bad situation worse. I can't believe that you can't see that."

"Well, I didn't think that he should get away with it."

"Luke," I began. "Don't you see? He *is* getting away with it. And he's going to get away with it. You going over there and doing that did nothing. Well, no, it did something. I would imagine that you were in jail when I was trying to call you. And, I would imagine that he's going to press charges. So, congratulations! You managed to get into a situation where you're going to have to spend the money you made from your show on a lawyer. And you'll be lucky if you don't go to prison for this. And forget about getting more work. I hope that it's worth it."

Luke looked embarrassed. I felt badly for him. He was really from a different world from me. In his world, bad people got what was coming to them, and brawling was one way to make sure that they got their just desserts. He had no idea how people like Nottingham operated.

I did.

Then, it just came out of my mouth. Before I could stop to even think about it.

"Luke, I just can't believe you. I mean, I fucking married that guy so that…."

I stopped myself, and took a deep breath. I saw his face, which registered shock, horror and bewilderment. But I knew that he knew what I was getting at.

Oh, God. Stupid Dalilah. Stupid, stupid, stupid.

I put my hand over my mouth.

"Finish your sentence. You married him because what?"

"Nothing. That's not important right now. Hey, you punched Nottingham, the damage is done. Let's go down to your bar and get a beer, huh?"

"No. Finish what you were saying, Dalilah. Finish it."

"Nothing. I told you already…"

"No, you didn't. You lied to me. Now, tell me the truth about your marriage to him. Right here. Right now."

I started shaking my head, and I felt tears streaming down my face. "Please, Luke, let's not do this. Please...."

"Do what? Oh, god, Dalilah, let me finish your thought for you. Because you obviously can't be straight with me."

As I shook my head and the tears flowed, he said "you married him so that he would give me a show. I'm such a fucking loser, in your eyes, that I couldn't do it on my own. You had to intervene. Is that what you were about to say?"

"No, no, no," I said. "No, Luke. I didn't marry him to give you a show. He was going to give you a show anyhow. Really. Honestly. He told me that when..."

"He told you that? When did he tell you that?"

Was it time? Was it time to come clean with what I did for him? Everything?

"Luke, please, I want to talk to you about this, but not until you're calm. You're obviously pissed right now, and this conversation is just going to inflame everything even more."

"No, Dalilah, we're going to talk about this now. When did he tell you that he was going to give me a show, and why is it that you never said a word to me about this?"

"Sit down," I said, taking a seat on the couch, and patting the seat behind me. "Sit down, and be calm, and I'll tell you everything."

"Everything. That somehow sounds really bad." He refused to sit next to me. He stood in front of me, his arms crossed in front of him.

I shook my head. "No, not bad. I mean, well, it's kinda bad. But I did everything for you."

At that, he finally sat down next to me, and stared at me. The color was draining from his face, and he already looked defeated.

And I knew that, after I told him my story, he was going to be even more defeated.

There was no way around that.

Chapter Thirty-Two

I sat there and just looked at him for a few minutes. I was so nervous, because I didn't know how the whole dirty truth would affect our relationship. It really could go either way. Either he would love me more for doing that for him. Or, he could feel resentful towards me for interfering. He might see it as a sign that I didn't believe in him. Which, of course, wasn't the case at all. I did believe in him. 100%. But I knew that he didn't believe in himself.

Finally, I began. "Luke, bear in mind that I've been in love with you since that night you came over. Since the second that you kissed me, I've been absolutely lost in you."

"I've been in love with you since I laid eyes on you on that bus. As crazy as that sounds. But, go on."

"Well, I was concerned. You were so discouraged about your career. And I thought that you were ready to go back to Maine, and I'd lose you for sure."

"Dalilah, I might have talked a good game, but I had more faith in myself than that. I was only talking when I said that. I never would give up on my dream."

"Well, I thought that you were. I thought that you were going to give up, and I wanted to make sure that you didn't."

"So, what? You kissed Nottingham's ass so that he would give me a show?"

I took a deep breath. "I did a bit more than that. I, well, I dated Nottingham. I went out with him. I made him believe that I was into him." The words were coming out, and it was almost a relief. Coming clean was feeling liberating. "I assure you, though, that we never had sex."

Luke looked astounded. "So, you cheated on me. But, hey, it was for a good cause, though." He shook his head. "I mean, maybe we weren't exclusive, but I thought that we were. Stupid me."

"We *were* exclusive. I mean, I went out with Nottingham, but we were literally just hanging out. No physical contact. I promise."

"Dalilah," he said. "No offense, but with all your secrets and lies, I don't know what to believe. How can I possibly trust you?"

"Luke, please. I did it for you."

"Thanks," he said. "I mean, it's condescending as hell, but your heart was in the right place. Too bad you really thought that I was too much of a fucking loser to actually make it on my own."

"That's just it, Luke. Nottingham told me that he was interested in giving you a show before I even brought anything up about you. I admit, I dated him because I wanted to butter him up so that he would give you a show, but I didn't even need to do that. He would have given you a show even without my meddling."

He shook his head. "I don't believe you. You've been lying to me all this time. Not to mention keeping secrets from me. And you've done it so well. So, I don't believe you. I think that you're the only reason why I ever got that show in the first place, and that really makes me feel like shit. The last thing that I wanted to hear was that I only got a major showing because my girlfriend was dating the gallery owner."

"Please, Luke, you have to believe me. He wanted to show you anyhow. I didn't even have to say a thing to him. *He* brought it up to *me*." Which wasn't entirely true. I mean, I did bring up Luke to Nottingham, but Nottingham still had informed me that he already was thinking seriously of showing Luke when I brought up the subject. So, I was only half-lying there.

"Okay," he said, but he looked skeptical. "But go on. You're stalling. Why did you marry that creeper?"

"Well, he found out about us. And he threatened to pull your show and ruin you if I didn't do what he wanted. So, I did. I couldn't see you get your show pulled. You would've been devastated and so discouraged."

He nodded his head. "So, you did that for me. You married him for me. To help me."

I took his hand, and tried to look him in the eye. But he refused to look at me. "I did that for you. Only for you."

He was quiet, so quiet. He still refused to look at me.

"Luke," I said. "Talk to me. What's going on in your head?"

"I don't know," he said. "I mean, that's….that was some kind of sacrifice. It's…well, it's something that I never thought was possible. That another person could be so self-less as that, to do something like that. And I love you more than ever for doing that."

"Okay," I said. I sensed an undercurrent of tension,

which belied his sweet words. It seemed that he wasn't at all happy that I did that for him.

He hung his head, and crossed his hands in front of him.

He was quiet, so quiet, for what seemed like forever.

Finally, he looked at me. "Dalilah. I thought that you believed in me more than that. And I thought that you knew me better than that." He shook his head. "I just don't know what to say."

I felt the tears coming again. "I do believe in you, Luke. I do. That's why I did that."

"No. That's not why you did that. You did that because you *didn't* believe in me. You didn't have faith in my ability to find an audience, so you just tried to leapfrog me over. Manipulating people to get what you want is never the right thing to do, Dalilah. Even if you think differently."

By then, I was shaking all over. This conversation wasn't going well, to say the least, and I was scared to death about what he was about to say to me. "Luke, please, it was the wrong thing for the right reasons. Looking back, it was the stupidest thing that I could possibly do, but I really just wanted you to have your moment in the sun. Not just a moment, either. I wanted you to soar like you deserve to. You're too talented – "

"I know, I know. Too talented to be broke. But don't you see? I want to make it on my own, not because the gallery owner is obsessed with my girlfriend. And breaking up with me just so that I could have a successful premiere? God, Dalilah, you really don't know me at all if you ever, for one second, thought that doing that is the right thing to do. For even a split second. It should have never even crossed your mind. Give me you, and I'm happy. But becoming an A-lister without you?" He shook his head. "Not a good trade-off. Not a good trade-off at all."

I sighed. "I know, Luke. I just really wanted you to be successful."

"At what price? Think about that. Think about the price that was paid, not just by you, but by me as well. I lost you, and nothing in this world could be more devastating than that. Was it all worth it?"

I shook my head. "No. Nothing could be worth it. I thought that it would be, but it turned out to really not be."

"Yeah," he said. "And, well, here we are, back to status quo. I'm broke again, or at least I will be once I pay Uncle Sam and hire a lawyer to get me out of my assault charge. I don't think that I'm going to be able to parlay my successful premiere into anything now, so I'm just as much of a nobody as I was before all this happened. And, I think, at least I hope, that you and I are back together. So, you did all that to get us right back to where we were before."

I smiled. "Ironic, huh?"

"Yeah," he said with a smile. "Ironic. Eh, well, looks like it's back to the grindstone with me. But that's okay. There is one good thing that came out of you doing what you did."

"What was that?"

"Well, how people treated me the night of my premiere really gave me confidence. It's not going to be as easy as I thought that it was going to be to get a leg up in the art community, after my awesome premiere, but I now know that people really do like my work. So, that helps. And, who knows? Maybe there'll be a few people who aren't totally up Nottingham's ass, and they might be willing to work with me after all. Anything's possible."

I let out my breath. It seemed that the tension between us had passed. My secrets were out in the open, and I wasn't lying anymore. In all, it felt like a huge weight was lifted off of me. For the first time since Nottingham threatened me with pulling Luke's show, I felt like I could breathe.

Luke put his hand under my shirt, and stroked my back. "Okay, Dalilah, everything seems to be coming out in the open. Now, please answer me this. I noticed the scars on your back. They're very faint, though. Do you need to tell me anything about that?"

I hung my head. "Oh, well. That. Yeah. Um…."

He was looking at me, his beautiful eyes soft and loving.

I took a deeper breath. "God, well. Now, you have to know that this happened before you and I got together for real."

"Go on," he said.

"I had a drinking problem before I met you. I was so directionless and aimless and I was just so frustrated with my life. I think that maybe I was also majorly depressed. I couldn't feel. I was numb. And I was looking for something, anything, to wake me up. And I got drunk one night and…"

He was still looking at me, and I was afraid that he was going to judge me. Still, I soldiered on.

"I got drunk one night, and Nottingham was there, and we went back to his place. And, well, it turns out that he's into BDSM, and he beat me while he had sex with me."

He nodded. "Well, I'm a little bit shocked. I had no idea that you were into that. No judgment, though. And, you and I weren't together at that time, so…."

"Right," I said. "We weren't. I mean, I had met you, but only that first time when I had modeled for you. I liked you, I knew that. But at that time, I wasn't even thinking about you and I having a romance."

"So," he said. "Is that, is that….is that something that you like? I mean, is that a secret fantasy of yours?"

I shrugged my shoulders. "I guess. I mean, you and I

have never been rough with each other, and I love having sex with you. I think that maybe I just wanted to do it at that time because I wanted to be woken up. It was like pouring ice cold water on my face."

He looked down.

"Why do you ask?" I said to him. "Is that, is that something that you'd be into?"

"No. I mean, I don't want to hurt you or anything like that. But maybe bondage would be something that would be kinda cool."

I smiled and laughed a little. "That can be arranged."

Chapter Thirty-Three

I smiled at Luke, wanting very badly for him to make love to me. It had been so long, way too long, and all that I wanted was to have him inside of me. He kissed me, longingly, on the mouth, and I started to melt. I could feel my insides doing somersaults. It was such a different experience with Luke than it was with Nottingham. With Nottingham, I put up with it. I hated it, really, but I went into a different kind of reality, one where I really wasn't there with Nottingham at all. I usually tried to imagine that I was with Luke.

Luke put his hand underneath my shirt, and caressed my breast. "Are you sure that you're up to this, Dalilah?" he asked me. "I don't want to hurt you."

I knew that he was trying to be sensitive, but I was feeling better and stronger. Nottingham's beating seemed to be light-years away, really. Like a distant memory. All that I could see that I was there, safe, with Luke, and that Nottingham wouldn't be able to hurt me again. All my secrets were out in the open, and I wasn't lying to Luke anymore. In short, I felt free, and I wanted to express this by being with Luke. Making love with him.

"Oh, of course, Luke, I'm more than up to this. I don't want you to be rough, of course, but I would love a little bondage. That would be something that I could really get into."

His touch was so gentle, like he was afraid that I would break if he got at all rough with me. I felt the goosebumps on the places where his fingers lightly brushed over my skin. The electricity of his actions was coursing through my veins, and my blood was pumping hard. I laid down, and spread my legs open wide. He brought my top off over my head, and then took off his belt, and lightly wrapped it around my wrists and then bound my wrists to the arm of the futon. Then he had a bandana, and tied that around my eyes.

I anticipated what he would do with great excitement, as opposed to the trepidation that I always felt with Nottingham. His hands were all over my body now, as he slowly brought down my shorts and underwear. I sighed as his tongue stroked inside of me, gently, lightly. He used little force, but it felt amazing. To say the very least. He kissed the inside of my thighs, and started licking and caressing my belly.

"Oh, God, Dalilah, I never thought that I would see you like this again," he said, as he worked his way to my nipples. He lightly bit and sucked each one, while a finger made its way to my clit and then inside of me. He swirled his finger inside of me while he hungrily sucked my breasts. I started breathing faster and faster, and I felt an orgasm starting in my clit region and spreading throughout my body. I cried out and arched my back, as Luke's hands went around me, and he started to suck and bite my neck.

ANNIE JOCOBY

He kissed my lips gently, his skin lightly brushing over mine. I shivered as he pulled down his pants and slowly entered me. I instantly cried out again, because my second orgasm was even more powerful than the first. He pressed a little more inside of me, and, inch by inch, I felt an over-whelming sensation of passion and love.

This was how it was supposed to be, making love with somebody. This was how it was supposed to feel. Amazing and loving, not dirty and wrong. I almost felt like this was cleansing me, getting the stench of Nottingham and what he did to me all those nights off of me.

"Don't stop, please don't stop," I said to Luke, and he slowed down his thrusting more. He had his arms on either side of my neck, and his mouth was tantalizing my own. Butterfly kisses, and deep, longing kisses alternated. He kissed my forehead and my cheeks, and then back to my mouth. Sometimes he seemed like he wanted to hungrily devour me, and, other times, he was as gentle as a feather. I inhaled, simply wanting to capture the moment, like a photograph. Wanting to capture him, bottle him, and keep him with me always. His warm skin and soft scent of after-shave and cologne were filling my senses, and I realized that there was no place else in the world that I would rather be.

Luke then got some lotion, and started to rub it all over my body. The lotion got warmer the more he stroked it on my skin. He gently put some of the lotion on my breasts and neck, and the radiating heat from his hands, coupled with the heat of the liquid, made me burn with desire.

My hands were still bound behind me on the couch, but he took off the bandana, and I looked into his eyes. "I wanted to see you, Dalilah," he said. "I wanted to see you when I come." And, at that, he groaned a little, and collapsed on top of me.

I laid there, with my arms wrapped around him. I kissed the top of his head, which was lying between my breasts. Both of us were breathless and sweating, and I, for one, had never felt better or more alive in my life.

Finally, Luke got up to get us both a glass of water, and I drank it silently. "What's on your mind?" he asked me.

"Well, remember when you said that you were afraid that we'd never be together like this again? Like you never would see me naked? I felt the same way about you. All those nights that I was with him, all that I could think about was you. I despaired so much, you wouldn't believe it." I hesitated. "I even found that I perhaps wanted to die. I had such guilt and shame over hurting you, and I missed you so much. On top of that, I was literally wed to a man who was cruel and indifferent. I was so desperate that, when I almost drowned in the ocean, I almost welcomed it."

Luke looked horrified. "What do you mean, you almost drowned?"

"Nottingham has this beach house in the Bahamas, and we went there after we…you know…" I couldn't bring myself to say the words. Finally, though, I did. "We went there after we got married." I shivered. "And I went swimming. I'm a very strong swimmer. I try to swim a lot of laps on days when I don't run. Anyhow, I got out to far and I was caught in a rip tide. I know that even strong swimmers drown in such circumstances, and I thought that I would too. And I felt a sense of peace coming over me. A sense of welcome. I think that I was just so desperate that my life was going to be this horrible thing, wed to this horrible person, that, frankly, death seemed to be a preferable alternative."

Luke stroked my hair, smoothing it back. "How do you feel now?"

"Happy, to say the least. Joyful. Like a 1,000 lb weight

has been lifted off of me. Like I can breathe. That was one thing, when I was with Nottingham – I couldn't breathe. I felt like I was suffocating all the time. My legs felt like lead, all the time. All the time. It was the worst feeling in the entire world, really. Knowing that I pushed the knife into you, yet feeling the acute sting of that same knife pushing into me every second of every day."

Luke smiled, and lay down behind me. He put his arm around my waist, and snuggled close. "I'm completely happy, too. The circumstances aren't ideal, by any means, just because, well, you're technically still married. But I really do think that we can make this work, just as soon as you get a quickie divorce. There's nothing holding that up, either. It's not like you guys were together for years and had lots of property and children together. So, it'll hopefully be a slam-dunk, and you and I can get right back to planning our own wedding."

I put aside my own feelings that I might have ruined him, career-wise, by leaving Nottingham so soon, and turned around and kissed him. He responded, physically, and entered me again. I sighed. It seemed that nothing had ever happened between us. Those weeks apart never happened. They were like some kind of bad dream that disappeared into the ether, like smoke or fog. How could I have left him like that? That was so wrong of me, no matter the reason. Luke was absolutely right about that. I thought, I really and truly thought, that I was doing the right thing in leaving him like that, but I knew, in my heart, that I was really doing the absolute wrong thing for both of us.

This went on for awhile, both of us exploring each other's bodies with our tongues and fingers. I got on top of him, and rode him, and he got on top of me and thrusted in and out eagerly. As the night wore on, we started to get more rough and passionate with each other. It was as if, the more we made love, the further away our separation seemed. Where the beginning of the night was tentative, tender and sweet, the end of the night ended with more animalistic, wild, passionate fucking.

As the night ran into dawn, and Luke and I were still going at it, there was one thing that ran through my mind. We were back together. Truly back together.

And, for that moment in time, it seemed that life couldn't be better.

Chapter Thirty-Four

Luke

After last night, Dalilah and I were officially back together. There were complications, of course, but we were back on track, and it felt amazing. The complications were that she was still married, and I was facing an assault charge. I was due to be arraigned, and then Dalilah and I would be heading back to Maine to spend the holidays with my family. After that, we would have to look ahead and strategize our next moves.

Was I upset that my momentum on my career was apparently back to ground zero? I was, of course. I dreamed of having my career rocket after my show, but that wasn't going to happen. I was going to have to be just like every other starving artist out there, once again, although I did hope to have some money left over from my show after taxes and legal fees for my assault. It might even be enough for me to cut back on my bartending hours and concentrate on what was important – Dalilah and hustling for more jobs.

But I was shocked on the morning of my arraignment to find out all that I was charged with. I showed up at the courthouse, Dalilah holding my hand. I hadn't yet hired an attorney, because I hadn't really had the chance. Plus, my money from my show hadn't quite come in. It was due to hit my account on the following day, so I didn't have the money to hire an attorney right at that time. But I was dressed as nicely as I could be, wearing the well-worn, by then, suit that her father gave me.

I went up to the bench when the judge called my name. I figured that I would be facing some kind of misdemeanor charge. No problem, I'd just do my community service or pay my fine, and not look back.

But, the charges that the judge read to me shocked the hell out of me.

"Luke Roberts," the judge said. "You have been charged by the State of New York with two counts of felony assault, which is a class D felony, carrying the range of 2 years to 7 years in the New York penitentiary, and one count of burglary in the second degree, which is a class C felony, carrying a range of punishment from 3 years to 15 years in the New York penitentiary. How do you plead?"

I blinked my eyes. Three felonies? Burglary? What the fuck? I didn't break into that building.

My heart started to race. Penitentiary time? Felonies? I wasn't expecting this at all. I mean, it was a little fight. Guys got into fights like this all the time. And there wasn't a guy alive who wouldn't kick Nottingham's ass after what he did to Dalilah.

The judge was looking at me expectantly, and I just said "not guilty, your honor."

The judge nodded. "This case will be remanded for trial. In the meantime, I would suggest that you hire an attorney. These are very serious charges."

I nodded my head. "Yes, your honor. I will, your honor."

He smiled and called the next case.

I went over to Dalilah, and took her hand, and the two of us walked out of the courtroom.

We got out into the street, and then both of us sat down on a bench. It was a typically freezing day, it being just before Christmas in New York, but the day was also clear.

"What the fuck," I said. "Burglary? What the fuck."

That was when I noticed that Dalilah had her phone in her hand. "I looked up burglary when the judge read the charges to you. And you can be charged with burglary here in the state of New York if you knowingly enter a building with the intent to commit a crime and you cause bodily injury in the process."

"Crap. This is fantastic. Now I'm going to have a felony record on top of everything else. Burglary. I guess I didn't see that one coming. And what the hell? Felony assault? I thought I had to cause some kind of injury for that."

"You do," Dalilah said. "So, there you go. Nottingham wasn't injured. Was he?"

I thought how he doubled over in pain after I punched him in the gut. It was entirely possible that he was injured, more than he let on. I had no idea if he sought medical attention, though.

"I don't know, to be honest. He didn't seem injured." I shook my head. "Goddamn. What's going to happen next? Thank God I'm going to be getting the money from the show in. Looks like I'm not going to have a whole lot of it left, though, after Uncle Sam gets through with me, and I hire an attorney."

I knew about attorneys, and knew that nobody good would even look at me for less than $15,000, when I was charged with three felonies.

$40,000 for taxes, $15,000 for an attorney. I still can take home around $45,000, which means that I still have a chance to cut back on my bartending hours and spend more time trying to make a go of this art thing.

I put my arm around Dalilah. "Well, let's not think about all this right now. Right now, I'm taking you home to meet pop and my crazy brothers and sisters. With any luck, you won't be subjected to Serena. But if you are, just know that she's a piece of work. An absolute piece of work. But, you've been warned so…"

"I actually can't wait," she said.

"Me neither."

But, of course, in the back of my mind, I knew that this little interlude with my family was only delaying the inevitable. Because when the holidays were over, I was going to have to face reality.

I was back to square one on my art career. I was facing three felonies and possible prison time. And Dalilah was going to have to face a divorce from that monster. Who knew what he would be capable of? I knew that I had no desire to find out.

For a few days, though, I was going to try not to think about all of that. I was going to try to relax and make sure that Dalilah was as comfortable around my family as possible.

We were going to have a good time over the holidays, goddammit, even if it killed us.

Chapter Thirty-Five

Dalilah

I was absolutely shocked that Luke would have such elevated charges, but I really shouldn't have been. After all, Nottingham was capable of anything. That would mean that he would be capable of trying to fake some kind of injury, even though Luke said that Nottingham didn't seem at all injured, just so that Luke would be faced with a felony assault. It wouldn't surprise me if he managed to pay off some doctor to tell the cops that he was really hurt. After all, without injury, Luke would have only been facing misdemeanor charges and no burglary charge. Each of those felonies were contingent upon Nottingham having sustained serious injuries.

I didn't say anything to Luke about my fears as we sat on the bus that would be taking us to his family's house in Portland, Maine. I knew that he was looking forward to my meeting his family, and I also knew that he wanted to put the whole criminal charges out of his mind for the time being.

He smiled at me as we sat there on the Greyhound bus, bound for Portland. I loved that he looked so relaxed, like nothing could touch him. He seemed to be entirely unruffled by the felonies that he faced or the fact that he couldn't get anyone to return his calls after his stellar premiere.

He lightly put his arm around me, and I put my head on his shoulder. He stroked my upper arm and looked out the window. I nuzzled him a little bit, and kissed his cheek. As I sat there on the ratty bus with him, I felt so safe and protected. Comfortable and loved. If it weren't for the fact that both of our realities were so heinous at that point, I probably would have felt on top of the world.

But I didn't. The nagging fears of what was going to happen in the near future, for both Luke and me, haunted me. I somehow couldn't believe that, at the ripe old age of 20, I had already been married, beaten, and had left behind a thriving art career. And I soon would be a divorcee. At the age of 20. I somehow believed, when I was younger, that only trashy people were divorced by age 20. I know longer felt that, of course.

"What's on your mind?" Luke asked me with a kiss on my forehead. He breathed in, as if he was trying to drink me in. Which is what I felt like doing to him, as well. To feel him, inhale his scent, listen to his words….taste him, like I did the previous evening. Just soak him in with all my senses so that I never had to be without him again.

"Just thinking about how excited I am to meet your fam," I said. "They sound really cool."

"They are. Well, except Serena, of course. But the rest of my family is pretty awesome, if I must say so myself."

"Tell me about them."

He took a deep breath. "Well, there's my pop, Michael. Twin brothers, Mark and Chris. Sisters, Amy and Serena. My pop is a bit salty, and tends not to have much of a filter. For that, I apologize in advance. Mark and Chris are awesome. Mark's in school, in his last year, at the University of Maine. Studying marine biology. Chris is still trying to find himself, like me. He's an amazing musician, and has his own band. Writes most of the songs, plays three instruments and can sing. But really hasn't gone anywhere with it just yet, so he's pretty broke much of the time. Amy is married and expecting her first. Hubby works with pop on the fishing boats."

I nodded my head and wondered if Luke would finally tell him the story of his mother.

He continued. "Serena, as I have mentioned, is the definite black sheep of the family. I mean, Chris has gotten into trouble with the law a bit. Stole a car when he was younger, roughed up a few guys. Petty stuff. But Serena…well, I have to warn you, she has an amazing exterior. Charming, beautiful, lively. But no soul whatsoever. Everybody's always taken in by her charisma, but never let your guard down and don't let her fool you. That's all I'm saying."

"Okay," I said. "Duly noted." And then I was quiet. I knew that Luke was about to tell me about his mother. I could see it in his eyes. When he was talking about the rest of his family, except for Serena, he had a look of love and adoration in his eyes. But he suddenly looked extremely sad and vulnerable.

I squeezed his hand. "Well, I can't wait to meet them," I said lightly, waiting for the story of his mom to pour forth.

"Yeah." He took a deep breath. "I wish that you could have met my mom, too." His hand flew involuntarily to his hair, and then he started looking out the window again.

"Look at that, it's starting to snow again." Then he looked back at me and smiled, and held me a little closer to his side. He kissed my forehead again, and squeezed me. "You've made me happy again. Man, when you left me…"

"I know. I felt the same way. But even moreso." I was a little disappointed that Luke still wasn't ready to talk about his mother, but I certainly didn't want to push it. "I actually thought that I wanted to die. I just didn't know how I would face life without you, and with Nottingham."

"Well, you never have to find out," he said. "And, now that everything's in the open, I hope that we can continue to live our lives without any secrets."

"Of course," I said, hoping that I truly meant that. "It was the hardest thing in the world, lying to you, and keeping all of that nonsense with Nottingham a secret. There's no way that I'll ever do that again, though. It's not in my nature to be deceptive like that. It really isn't. I wasn't raised like that."

He kissed my forehead again, and said "I'm really glad to hear that."

And then he took another deep breath, and his eyes blinked rapidly. "Well, I need to address the 800 lb gorilla. I mean, obviously, my mom is dead. I guess I should probably tell you what happened to her. I'm sure that it's going to be brought up anyhow, so you might as well hear it from me."

I nodded my head and was silent. I stroked his hair a little, as he bowed his head and put his face in his hands.

"Oh, God," he said. "When I was 10 years old, I…" And then he stopped. He obviously was having a hard time going on. "My mom and Chris went out. I can't remember why they went out just the two of them, but they went out together. I think that he was only 11 at the time." He squinted his eyes and looked out in the distance for a second, and then said "no wait, I do remember why they went out, just the two of them. I mean, she took us out individually a lot, because that was how she was. She wanted to give each of us individual attention, because it was so difficult to try to fight for her focus when there were so many of us at home."

"Anyhow," he continued, "she and Chris went to the movies. And Chris loved McDonald's. More than any of us other kids, he always wanted to go there whenever we went out."

I squeezed his hand silently, and he squeezed mine right back.

He was silent for a few more minutes, and tears started to form in his eyes. "There was a man," he said. "He was pissed off at his wife, I think. Going through a bad divorce, and the wife refused to let him see the kids. And he worked at that McDonald's until he was fired."

I felt my heart racing, as I knew where this was going. I remember reading about this when I was just 10 myself – about the McDonald's shooter who killed 15 people before the cops killed him.

But I let him go on.

"He, this man, he came into the store with an automatic weapon…the place was packed, and Chris later told me that there was a mass panic. People screaming and running under the tables. He told me that the sound was deafening, and he didn't know what was going on, there was so much chaos."

Luke was breathing harder and harder. "The gun man, he pointed the gun directly at Chris, and my mom, she stepped in front of him, and yelled for him to run. I guess he did. We found out later that my mom was actually the last person he killed before the cops got there and killed him. And the only reason why my mom was the last one he killed was that he had finally run out of bullets."

I felt tears coming to my eyes. "Oh, Luke, I don't know what to say."

He shook his head. "Not much to say. Five kids left behind, and a father who couldn't get out of bed for like a year. Serena was quite a bit older than the rest of us, so she probably should have taken the reins, because pop couldn't care for us at all. But she didn't. She was 18, and she got out of the house almost immediately after mom died. My brothers were 11, I was 10, and Amy was 13. Amy was the one who actually cared for the rest of us while my pop did his grieving."

He put his two fingers between his eyes, and shook his head. "Oh, God. Poor Chris. I mean, he didn't actually witness my mother's death, thank God, but he blamed himself so much for so long. She died saving him. It should have been me, he always said. It should have been me." Another deep breath. "And it would have been him if my mom didn't do what she did. She'd still be alive, but Christopher would be dead. Chris knew this, as young as he was, and he couldn't get over it at all."

"Luke, I…" That was all I could manage, because I felt the tears coming. "God, I just can't believe that you had to go through this. You always seem so…even-tempered. Level-headed. I have always admired that about you, because I went through years in a depressed fog just because some asshole didn't like my artwork. And here you are, having gone through something major, and you always have seemed so sunny."

He smiled. "Ah, well, I guess it's just my disposition. I mean, I've had dark periods. Not like poor Chris, of course. His wounds run deeper than mine or the rest of the family, just because the nature of what happened. The whole family has had dark periods, in fact, but what happened is no longer acute. It still aches, especially during this time of the year, but it's not something that fills us up with pain, the way that it did for years after what happened."

I put my head on his shoulder, and threw my arm around his neck at the same time. "You're very brave. I don't know what I would do if something like that had happened to me. I mean, it almost did, when I was just a little baby, but it all worked out, thank God."

"What do you mean?"

"Well, when I was less than a year old, my mother had this stalker guy, Andrew. He raped her, and then he became psychotic and thought that she was his dead wife. So, he came into the house and threatened her with a gun. And, before he threatened her, he threatened me. I had this baby-sitter, Helena, and he made her leave the house at gun-point, before picking me up and holding me. I still remember that, even though I was very young. I remember him picking me up and holding me for like an hour. He wasn't mean to me, or anything, though. In fact, he tried to get me to calm down, but there was no way I was going to calm down after what had just happened."

It was Luke's turn to be silent and look at me with sympathetic eyes. "Oh, God, Dalilah, that sounds awful."

"Yeah, well, it was. Because my mom came home, and, before I knew it, she had me in her arms and that man was still threatening us with a gun. Then she sent me away with Daniel, who was my father's personal assistant and driver at the time. And, well, my dad was shot. As I was told later on, he came in the door when that Andrew had a gun to my mother, and he deflected Andrew by pretending to be the guy who was sleeping with Andrew's wife. Remember,

Andrew thought that my mom was his dead wife, Cherry. So, Andrew decided to shoot my dad instead of my mom."

Luke's hand flew up to his mouth. "Oh, my God. What happened?"

I shrugged my shoulders. "My dad came through surgery, of course, and it was a bumpy road for awhile. My mom killed Andrew by plunging a butcher knife into his back before he shot my dad, so that was one good thing that happened. In the end, though, that whole incident just really made my mom and dad stronger together. They're fantastic people and so good together, but I guess that they had their problems in the early days. But when my dad was almost killed, they managed to really become a strong and solid unit. But that wasn't easy, because I guess my dad went through a lot of soul searching after that incident, and really beat himself up about his past."

Luke nodded his head. "I remember reading all about your father's past. Guess having something like having a near-death experience just brings it all home, huh?"

"So it seems," I said, not wanting to talk about my own near-drowning, and the reckoning that came from that. I was still a bit raw from the whole Nottingham ordeal, so talking about the rip-tide incident would bring all of that back for me. I wanted to put it all behind me as quickly as possible.

Luke smiled. "Well, this little trip has certainly turned into a bit of a downer. But I'm glad to finally have been able to open up to you about what happened. It has been difficult to talk about, as you might imagine." He got quiet for a few minutes. "In fact," he finally said, "you're the first person I have talked to about my mom, except for my other family members. And the family therapist that the state provided for us after it happened."

"Really? You haven't talked about that with Jake?"

"No," he said. "Not even with Jake. Jake still doesn't know how my mom died. I mean, he knows that she was murdered. Freddy does too," he said, referring to the homeless guy who Luke talked to quite a bit. "Freddy's dad was murdered, so I did tell him about my mom's death. But I haven't been able to really talk about how it all went down until just now with you."

I felt touched that I was the one who finally got him to bring down his walls about the subject. I touched his cheek, and kissed him lightly. He smiled and brought out the blanket that we brought, and put it around us as the bus bumped along the road.

"So, what are you thinking?" I asked him.

"Just that life seems to be really at its pinnacle now. Funny, huh? I mean, you're married, I'm probably going to be a felon, my career is in the toilet again. Yet, I couldn't be happier right now."

I laughed. "Well, if you put it like that, it certainly does seem like we're a couple of cuckoo birds for being happy right now, but I know what you mean. I'm really ecstatic myself, right now, for the same reason as you. I guess it does just go to show that, no matter what life gives you, if you have the person you love by your side, nothing can ever seem that horrible."

He kissed my lips and said "ain't that the truth."

Chapter Thirty-Six

Luke

The bus was finally pulling into the Portland stop, after a good 10 hours on the road. It was only a five hour drive from New York City to Portland, but, with all the stops, it took considerably longer on the Greyhound. Not that I minded. Dalilah and I had snuggled under the blanket for much of the way there, and it was cozy sitting there with her the whole way. She had fallen asleep in my arms, and, as I listened to her deep breathing and eventual snoring, I felt so comforted. There was a time when I honestly thought that I would never get the chance to hear her snore again, so that sound was music to my ears.

As we disembarked from the bus, Pop was sitting there, waiting for us in the snow. He grinned broadly at us, while waving his corduroy cap. He approached us, and took our luggage.

"Pop," I said, giving him a hug. "This is Dalilah."

He extended his hand to her, and she took it, but then

gave him a hug. "I'm so happy to finally meet you," she said.

"Likewise," he said, and then turned to me. "Well, you told me she was beautiful, Luke, but I had no idea."

Dalilah blushed, although I knew that she was used to hearing that sort of thing. "Oh, thank you, Mr. Roberts."

"Michael," he said. "Call me Michael. And, maybe sometime soon, you're gonna want to just call me dad."

We all made our way back to dad's ancient pickup truck. "Sorry, Dalilah, but I guess your luggage is going to get a little bit wet," he said, as he put our suitcases in the back of the pickup. "Can't be helped, though. It's been snowing for days here. I'm surprised that there hasn't been more that has accumulated, though. It just snows, and then stops, and then snows some more."

"Not a problem, Michael," Dalilah said. "A little bit of snow isn't going to hurt a thing."

At that, we all piled into the bench seat of the cab. I sat in the middle, and dad put on his wipers to clear the snow off his windshield as the ancient truck made its way back to pop's modest home.

Michael put his arm around Luke's neck as he drove along. "So good to see you," he said. "The prodigal son returns."

"Oh, come on, pop, it hasn't been that long."

"Right. Well, you just keep thinking that."

"I was home last Christmas."

"Huh. Well, you don't live that far away, you could not be such a stranger, you know."

"You too. The car goes both ways."

"I don't come to the city, you know that. Too many people, too much sketchiness." The old man shook his head. I knew my pop, and I knew the real reason why he refused to go into the city. Because of what had happened to my mom, he was afraid of the violence of large metropolises. Not that Portland was bucolic, although where my pop lived, it was pretty rural, as he didn't live in Portland proper. I always told everybody that my family was from Portland, but the actual house was situated in an unincorporated countryside that was just outside the city limits.

"I know, pop, and I'm sorry I don't visit more. But I'm here now."

"And it's good that you are. Mark, Chris and Amy are already there, and Amy's husband."

I held my breath, hoping that Serena wouldn't be there. She often wasn't, finding better things to do than hang out with the family over the holidays. But, once in awhile, she made a guest appearance, probably because she wanted to throw her wealth in all of our faces.

"What about Serena?"

"She's coming. Her sucker of a husband is finally divorcing her sorry ass, so she has no place else to go."

I looked at Dalilah. "Well, looks like you're going to meet Serena after all. Lucky you."

Dalilah just smiled, and squeezed my hand. "That's fine, Luke." And then she whispered. "As long as I'm with you, this is going to be a great holiday indeed."

Pop just smiled, as he heard her say that. "Ah, young love," he said. "I remember that well."

And then he was quiet for a few minutes. Finally, he spoke. "Uh, Luke, there's going to be somebody else there at the house."

"Oh?"

"Yeah. Her name is Carolyn. She's uh, my fiancée."

I blinked my eyes, and felt selfish as I didn't quite know what to say about that. A part of me wanted to congratulate him for moving on with his life, but another part of me wanted to slap him for betraying mom. As irrational as that was. But I just couldn't picture him with another woman, even after all these years.

"Carolyn," I said, finally, after I found my words. "You never mentioned anything about there being a Carolyn."

"Well, it's one of those things," he said. "I knew her in high school, and she looked me up on Facebook of all things."

I had to smile. My pop on Facebook. The social media giant had long since fallen out of favor with my generation, but my pop's generation still used it quite a bit.

"Oh, let me guess. She always had a crush on you."

"No," he said. "The other way around. I always had a crush on her. And, she had moved to Portland, and knew nobody, so she and I got together."

My pop had actually grown up in Wisconsin, so the fact that one of his classmates moved to his neck of the woods was somewhat remarkable.

I got silent, not really knowing what to say. I was wrestling with my emotions on this, and didn't want to admit that, because it seemed so petty and selfish. But I just couldn't imagine somebody else taking my mom's place.

But Dalilah, of course, had no such reservations. "Congratulations, Michael," she said, stepping into the void. "You must be so happy to have found somebody." She nudged me a little bit, as she obviously wanted me to say something positive about this new development between my dad and this mysterious Carolyn woman.

"Well, thank you, Dalilah," he said, a note of sarcasm in his gruff voice. "I appreciate your good wishes."

Finally, I just half-heartedly said "yeah, pop, that's great that you have somebody. Boy, I can't wait to see everyone. It's been way too long."

"Listen," Michael said. "It's been almost 11 years since your mother. 11 years. Now, I know that you don't think that I should be happy in my golden years, but you gotta suck it up. And grow up while you're at it."

I knew that. Objectively, I knew it. Emotionally, not so much. Again, I felt selfish for wishing that my pop could always just keep the image and memory of my mom pristine and not sully it with somebody else.

This was going to be a long visit.

Chapter Thirty-Seven

Dalilah

As I bumped along in the tiny pickup, I knew that I was going to have to talk to Luke when I got him alone. He obviously wasn't doing well with the fact that his father had a new woman in his life. That wasn't fair, of course, but, at the same time, I understood the impulse to feel that way. I knew that a person's head and heart didn't always match up, and that, sometimes, the heart would be the one that would win out in a battle. Luke's head had to know that his father deserved every ounce of happiness, and that nobody should have to live life devastated and alone. But his heart was apparently having problems with knowing that his mother might be replaced.

I squeezed his hand to make sure that I was there for him, and he smiled back at me, reluctantly. But the silence in that cab was deafening, and I didn't try to make small talk to fill the silence. After the whole Nottingham bullshit, I had made a silent vow to myself to live my life as authentically as possible, and filling the air with mindless chatter at that time just didn't seem to be authentic to me. So, I kept my mouth shut.

Finally, after about a half hour in the cab, we entered into a rural, tree-lined road. The truck turned left onto a gravel driveway and rested on the grass in front of a small white house. Michael got out and got our bags out of the back.

"I'll take your bags to your room, Dalilah. My son can get his own," he said, taking my bags out of the back of the truck. Luke got out of the truck, too, and got his bags and we all approached the house.

I felt nervous as I walked into the close quarters. This was a cute house, really. Walking into the house, there was a small dining room with a well-worn green carpet, and a large kitchen with a 1940s stove and 1970s refrigerator. In the kitchen was a small breakfast nook with a hand-crafted table and bench. Michael walked the short way into our bedroom, which was a tiny space with well-worn hardwood floors and just enough room for a full-size bed and one ramshackle dresser.

I put my bag down, and Luke did the same, and we then followed Michael into the living room. In the hallway leading from the kitchen to the living room there were pictures of the family. I stopped to look at one of them, and smiled as I recognized young Luke who looked to be about age 8 in the family portrait. In his mother, I saw where he got his eyes and his mouth. She had the same fascinating features as his son in this regard. Luke's mother was a strikingly beautiful woman, and it dawned on me that I didn't even know her name. Luke had only referred to her as his mother.

Luke was standing right behind me as I gazed at the

family photo. I touched it briefly and turned around. "Your mother was beautiful. What was her name?"

"Olivia. Olivia Roberts." He took my hand. "Come with me and meet the rest of the clan."

I took a deep breath and nervously followed him the short way into the small living room with the dark paneling and Berber carpet in white. There were four people sitting around a sectional couch. Two extremely handsome young guys who looked right around Luke's age were sitting on the floor with their backs to the couch. One with short hair, one with longer hair, but they were clearly identical twins. The one with short hair, who I imagined was Mark, was dressed in a sweater and khakis. He had the same dark hair and dimples as Luke. The one with the longer hair, who was probably Chris, was dressed in a t-shirt and jeans, and tattoos covered his muscular arms.

They both stood up when Luke and I walked in the room behind Michael, as did a beautiful woman who looked just a little bit older than Luke and the twins. Like everyone else, she had dark hair, but her eyes were decidedly brown, although there was a hint of green right around her pupils. She looked to be around 7 months pregnant. I would imagine she was Amy, although her husband didn't seem to be around.

The other woman on the couch remained seated, and eyed me warily. And, if Amy was beautiful, as were Mark and Chris, this woman was stunning. She surprisingly had on very little makeup, so her natural beauty shown through. She had chestnut hair that was faintly streaked with auburn highlights, and wore a tight cashmere sweater, black pants and high heeled boots. I surmised by her general attitude that this would be Serena. And she wasn't really how I pictured her. I pictured somebody much more high-maintenance looking, as opposed to this naturally gorgeous woman who was sitting on the couch.

Mark, Chris and Amy came over and gave me a hug after introducing themselves. Serena remained seated, looking at her nails.

There was a chorus of "so glad to finally meet you!" "welcome to the family!" "your pictures don't do you justice," and other pleasantries, and I felt very welcomed by the three siblings, just like I had felt welcomed by Michael. And then I was urged to sit on the couch with them, an invitation that I eagerly accepted.

As the three got to know me, peppering me with questions about how the bus ride was, how excited was I to be spending the holidays with the Roberts family, and other standard getting-to-know-you queries, Serena sat on the other side of the couch, not saying a word. I did see her eyeing me from time to time, while trying hard to look disinterested in it all.

I glanced over to her, feeling uncomfortable that she was there, while not insinuating herself into the conversation, but Amy just waved her away. "Don't mind her," she said in a conspiratorially low whisper. "She's in a pissy mood."

"I heard that," Serena said. "And yes, I'm in a pissy mood. You would be too if your fucking husband just ditched you right before the fucking holidays."

Amy rolled her eyes, as did Chris. Of the three, Mark was the one who was just a little bit less effusive. He was friendly enough, but he seemed just a bit shy. Amy and Chris, though, treated me immediately like I was their best friend.

After a little bit, Chris, Mark, Michael and Luke went into another room to play some foosball, which left Amy and I to sit and get to know one another, and we chatted like old girlfriends. But, after about twenty minutes of this, she was called away to pick up her husband, who was working on the docks that day.

"Oh, crap," she said, "I'm so sorry Dalilah, I have to leave. But I'll be back in about a half hour or so." She hugged me as she said "I'm so happy that Luke found somebody great. He so deserves it."

"That he does," I said.

I sighed as Amy left, and looked at Serena. She was glancing at me with a side-eye, one finger wrapped around her luxurious hair. She raised a single eyebrow, and I got up, uncomfortable, to try to join the boys in the foosball room.

But, to my surprise, she got in her feet as well. I looked at her quizzically, and she stepped towards me and backed me up against the wall. She put both her hands on either side of my body, and leaned down. "God, you are so sexy," she said to me, as she planted a passionate kiss on my lips.

I felt strangely drawn to her, as if she was catnip and I was a feline. So the kiss was titillating in a way that it shouldn't have been and never was with Alaina. I momentarily lost my composure, before I pushed her away from me lightly.

"What, you don't swing that way?" she said. "I think you do. Maybe you have a best friend that you've experimented with. Huh?"

I could feel my face flush warm. "No, I don't swing that way," I mumbled, knowing that she could clearly see that I was lying. And the fact that I was lying about that surprised me. I never thought of Alaina as being something that was a thing. In other words, I never thought that my flings with her meant that I was attracted to other women. But this woman...I shook my head. Luke had warned me that she was charismatic, beautiful and people were drawn to her.

He didn't warn me that she was quite this sexual, confident and bold. Not to mention apparently bisexual.

"I have to find Luke," I said, feeling my insides getting queasy. I gulped a little bit for air, and ducked underneath one of Serena's arms and stumbled towards the bathroom. "After I use your bathroom." I got through the bathroom door just as the puke came out of me. I barely got to the bowl on time.

I looked up, and Serena was standing in the doorway. "Oh, come on. I'm not that repulsive. In fact, I think that you liked that kiss. I know you did. I could feel it."

I didn't want to admit the truth, which was that her kiss was…not entirely unpleasant, and was just a little bit enticing. Much to my dismay. And I knew that my vomiting had nothing to do with her and what she did. She was magnetic. That was the only word that I could use to describe her. Magnetic.

"No, it's not you at all," I said honestly. "I think that the traveling and meeting new people just…well, I think I might be a bit stressed out. More than I realized." It was then that I noticed Luke was suddenly right behind Serena in the doorway, and he crouched down next to me, putting his hand on my back.

"Dalilah, are you okay?" he asked. "You're white as a sheet."

I nodded my head. "Yes, yes, I'm okay. I just need to lie down for a little bit before dinner, I think. All this traveling and everything that has been going on lately…I think that it's all taken its toll a little bit."

At that, I went and laid down on the bed in "our" bedroom and turned out the lights.

Chapter Thirty-Eight

Luke

While Dalilah slept in the next room, I entertained questions about her from my siblings. I worried about her a little bit, because she did look pretty pale, but I checked on her from time to time, and she seemed to be resting comfortably.

I hoped that she didn't catch a bug. That wouldn't be the best way for her to spend her holiday, to say the least.

"So, what do you think?" I asked them.

"Cool, gorgeous, talented, smart," Chris said. "What's not to like?"

At that, Amy came through the door with her husband, Jackson. She punched me lightly on the arm. "You did good with that one. She seems pretty awesome."

Even pop got into the act. "She's a keeper." And then he announced that Carolyn was on her way over to fix everybody Christmas Eve dinner.

I looked around and saw that everybody seemed just as

apprehensive as me. I felt like I was just a little bit less alone at that point, as it seemed that this was going to be a difficult adjustment for everybody. Especially Chris, who was staring down at the floor. I went over to him and put my arm around him, knowing what he was thinking. Because it was what he was always thinking this time of the year, and introducing a new woman into the mix no doubt made things worse for him.

He had such a hard time with survivor's guilt. No matter how much counseling he got, he could never understand why he survived and she didn't. As much as I always wished that there was something that I could say or do, I knew that there just wasn't.

Chapter Thirty-Nine

That night, after Carolyn made her introductions, and my siblings and I tried to make her feel welcome, save for Serena, of course, and Dalilah emerged from the bedroom after her nap, we all indulged in some Christmas dinner. This was our tradition, to have our big celebrations on Christmas Eve, which usually included all the standard ways of celebrating. Christmas dinner, followed by opening the presents and drinking some eggnog that was freshly prepared.

Carolyn, for her part, seemed nice enough. And pop sure seemed happy. So, I warmed to her for that reason alone. I was starting to realize that wanting my pop to be alone, just because I couldn't stand for anybody to replace my mom, was childish and silly. And it seemed that everybody else was good with her, too.

Over dinner, pop asked me "so, Luke, how's the art career going? Are you ready to join me on the boat yet?"

I shook my head. "No, not any time soon. I'm going to still try to make a go of it."

Dalilah piped up. "And he will," she said. "He's going to be on everybody's radar soon." She and I had discussed, at length, the effect that Nottingham was going to probably have on my career, and that was something that we were going to have to strategize when we got back – how to get things moving again, Nottingham poisoning the well or no. It was going to be difficult, but not hopeless.

I glanced at her, and she looked at me as she was about the drink her glass of wine. She took a sip, and then made a face and shook her head. She leaned over and whispered to me "this wine, it tastes funny. I think there might be something wrong with it."

I took a sip, and shrugged. "Tastes like white wine to me," I whispered back. "Why? What do you think is wrong with it?"

She shook her head. "I don't know how to explain it, but it just tastes a little bitter," she whispered, and glanced around, hoping that nobody was paying attention to what she was saying. "Do you mind drinking mine?"

"Not at all," I said, surreptitiously pouring her drink into my wine glass. I reached for the pitcher of water on the table. "Here, drink this instead. You're probably still feeling a little queasy from earlier. I hope you're not coming down with something."

"No, I feel okay," she whispered. "Aside from the wine tasting funny that is."

I put my arm around her and put my hand in her hair. Amy looked at us both and smiled.

Mark announced that he was accepted into a graduate program at UCSD for marine biology, and everybody cheered. "That's great, Mark," I said. "The Scripps program is an excellent one, I hear."

"It's one of the best in the country," he said. "And it sure will be nice to get away from these winters."

The dinner was delicious, of course, and, after the meal, Chris and I jammed on guitars in the living room, Chris having brought an extra guitar for me. We played standards that everyone knew, and everybody sang along. Even Serena, whom I caught watching Dalilah more often than I felt comfortable seeing.

In all, it was a nice time. I caught up more with Chris, as I always felt just a little bit closer to him than to Mark. Mainly because Mark was always just a little bit standoffish. He did everything right, it seemed, and sometimes I felt just a little bit judged by him. Chris felt the same way, and it was harder for him, because Mark was his identical twin, so he really should have felt more connected to him than to me. But it was the other way around.

"You doing okay?" I asked him, as we sneaked a few bong hits on the porch that night, after dinner and jamming. I looked behind me, and Dalilah and Amy were deep in conversation, while Serena was eyeing Dalilah and biting her lip. *Hmmm, wonder what that's all about.* Serena was watching Dalilah the entire evening, and it just seemed a little off.

"Yeah," he said. "You mean about meeting Carolyn?"

"Sure. And everything. I worry about you."

"Don't. I'm doing fine. My band's getting more gigs, and I swear, my song-writing has gotten fierce. At least, that's what the guys tell me. I've learned to channel, man. Channel the darkness into my music. Grunge is making a comeback, too. Everything's cyclical, and my music is going to be popular in another year or so. I've been watching the trends. So, yeah, I think I'm alright these days."

I nodded my head. "That's good to hear. You know I'm rooting for you guys always."

"I know. Too bad you're the only one. I swear, you're the one person who gets me in this family. My own twin is such a fucking cop sometimes, you know? Man, we have such beatdowns with each other because I'm not living the life that he wants me to. Dad, too. They just don't understand us artists."

"That's the way it is, isn't it? That's why I'm so lucky to have found Dalilah. She gets it. She's an artist, too, an amazing one. You should see some of the stuff that she has painted."

Chris took another hit from the bong and blew the smoke out, and waved the air a little bit. "Yeah, you're lucky. Peg and I, well, we aren't exactly seeing eye to eye these days. She's on my ass to get a real job, just like Mark. No, wait, Mark is on my ass to go to college and be like his clone."

We both started laughing. "Oh, how much we have in common," I said. "Get a real job, quit wasting your life, settle down, have a family," I said in a mocking tone. "Well, I'm on board with the settling down and having a family part, not so much on the getting a 'real job' part."

We fist bumped and Chris said "Well, I think it's time to socialize a bit more. I'm leaving a couple of days after Christmas."

"I think I'm leaving a day before you."

Then we went back in and everybody opened their presents, and then Dalilah and I announced that it was time to hit the sack.

When we got back to our room, and both of us took off her clothes and got into bed, Dalilah said "so, what do you think about Carolyn?"

"Nice, I guess."

"You're having a hard time of it, aren't you?"

I sighed. "It's that obvious, is it? I'm sorry, Dalilah, I know that I'm selfish here. But I just don't want pop to forget my mom. I mean, next thing you know, there's going to be pictures of my pop and Carolyn on the walls, and none of my mom. It will be like she never existed. That doesn't seem fair to me."

Dalilah stroked my hair. "I understand, Luke, and that's a pretty common thing. Not wanting the parent to be erased. But what is the alternative? Your father living the rest of his life alone? As much as you don't want to think of him with another woman, you also can't expect him just to be celibate and miserable for the rest of his life. He deserves love and happiness, too."

"I know that, intellectually. But I can't help how I feel. I just need some time, I guess, to adjust to all the changes there. He did kind of spring this on me and my siblings. They seem as bothered by it as I am."

"Of course, you need time. For what it's worth, Carolyn seems like a great woman, and she really seems to love your dad. So, I hope that you can find it in your heart to accept her and accept her new role in your family and in your dad's life."

"I will, Dalilah, I promise. I'm not that immature. But sometimes, I just want her back. I mean, I always do, but sometimes it just seems more acute. There is such a hole in my heart, and it just hurts to see another woman trying to fill it."

After a few minutes, Dalilah broached another subject, and, quite frankly, surprised me. "Serena. You never told me she was bisexual."

I nodded in understanding. *So that was what that whole*

thing was about. "Oh. I'm sorry for not bringing that to your attention. I guess I don't really even think of her as being bisexual, so much as she just makes her way through just about anybody attractive that she can find. If that makes any sense."

"Yeah, that makes sense."

"Why, what happened?"

"She kissed me."

I raised an eyebrow. "Do you want me to kick her ass?"

Dalilah smiled. "No, of course not. But I think that you might be wrong about her. You're a little close, so maybe you just think that she's completely conscienceless and remorseless about her behavior. I sense that she's more human than you might think."

"Why do you think that?"

"I don't know. I just get the feeling. She has human emotions, but they're buried deep behind her wall. I feel badly for her, really."

I put my arm around her and brought her closer to me. "My Dalilah. Always seeing the good in people." I felt my erection growing, and pulled away from her. I didn't want to be disrespectful and fuck my girlfriend there under my pop's roof, but, boy, was that difficult to do.

Dalilah smiled. "Perhaps sleeping naked wasn't such a great idea."

I kissed her. "Oh, what the hell. Nobody's going to know," I said, as I entered her slowly. "Just a quickie."

Of course, our "quickie" lasted the rest of the night.

Chapter Forty

Dalilah and I stayed a few more days at Pop's house, and I realized, by the end of the vacation, that I was actually happy that Pop and Carolyn were together.

"Hey, pop," I said, "I'm sorry that I wasn't thrilled at first about you seeing somebody new. It takes some getting used to the idea that, you know, mom is being replaced, but I'm really happy for you."

"Your mom isn't being replaced," he said. "And don't ever think that. This is a different thing. Olivia will never be replaced. Olivia can never be replaced. Not in my heart, and not in this house. Carolyn understands that, though. I hope you will too, one day."

We embraced, and I felt tears coming to my eyes. But it was time to make room for somebody else in my life, and that was my soon-to-be-stepmother Carolyn.

And, while I bonded with Carolyn, Dalilah was forming a strange bond with Serena of all people. Serena, after that first night, seemed to actually come out of her shell, and, just like Dalilah said, she seemed just a little bit human.

Which was weird to me, and to my other siblings. None of us quite had seen anything like it.

It started with tentative smiles whenever Dalilah was around, and it seemed that Serena was interested in watching Dalilah compose her artwork, which she did for a few hours every day. I painted right alongside her, but Serena was only interested in Dalilah's work. I soon was noticing that, whenever I would be hanging out with Chris and Mark and pop, doing guy things like playing foosball, poker and video games, Serena and Dalilah would be talking in the den. Amy was also around, but she chose to hang around her husband, as Serena was always with Dalilah, and Amy and Serena never got along. I felt a little badly for Amy, as I knew that she was interested in bonding with Dalilah more, but Dalilah seemed strangely drawn to Serena instead.

That night, I asked Dalilah what she and Serena talked about, and she told me "oh, everything. She's really having a rough time with her divorce, and she knows how much she's fucked up. She...well, I think that you need to give her a break a little bit. She's had a tough life, more than you will ever know. And that's all that I can really say. She does have a hard shell, but she seems to really want to open up to me."

I cocked my head to Dalilah a little. "Oh. I guess there are some things that I don't know about my sister."

"Yes. Things that would explain almost all of her behavior. I can't go into that, but I think that you might try to be just a little kinder to her. She might not handle things well, and she knows that. She knows how much she's hurt her family and her husband and everyone who should be close to her. I think that I've maybe even encouraged her to get some help for these issues."

"Wow. How did you become her therapist? None of us

have been able to get anything out of her but hurtful behavior."

"As I said, you're too close. I'm more of a stranger, and I think that she knows that I'm willing to have an open mind."

"I hope you're not being naïve," I said.

"Well, I'm not. I have a gift, and I've always had it. I think that I get it from my dad. But my intuition is amazing, and I can almost see inside someone's soul. That was why I was able to be in such demand when I was a portraitist, because I could get at my subject's essence and bring out what lies beneath. You can too. I see that in you. But you might have more problems doing that with somebody that you know so well, like Serena."

"You're probably right about that. I guess maybe I need to see her in a different light, and not think that she's beyond repair. It's really amazing that you're able to do that, though. Get past her apparently tough exterior to see her humanness."

She smiled, and stroked my hair a little bit. "Just give her a little bit of a chance, and you might actually be able to help her."

I brought Dalilah closer to me. "How are you feeling?" I asked her, kissing her forehead.

"Okay. I mean, my taste buds just seem just a little bit off, for some odd reason. But, other than that, I'm okay."

"That's good," I said. "God forbid you're sick. Of course, I would take good care of you, because that's what I do." I brought her chin up and kissed her gently.

She sighed, and climbed on top of me.

Our vacation was almost over, and the real world would soon be intruding. But, for just that one night, we had each other, and that was all that mattered.

The hell that awaited us back in the city would have to wait for just a little while longer.

Chapter Forty-One

Dalilah

It was finally time for Luke and I to say goodbye to his family. We had to leave the morning of the 27th, and Mark had left the day before, and so did Amy. Chris would be returning to Boston, where he was based, the following day, and Serena would be leaving as well. I had found out that Serena actually lived in the Village, which was something that Luke had never told me before, and she expressed interest in hanging out with me when we all got back to the city.

I readily agreed. Even though I knew that she was sexually attracted to me, I still felt comfortable befriending her a little more. Because I could see the hurt child that she was underneath all her crazy behavior that she had displayed over the years. And I knew where that behavior was coming from. It was coming from a deep sense of hurt that she had carried in her soul from the time that was she was just a little baby. She had confided in me that she had sought hypnotherapy over the past few years, because she didn't like who she was, and she needed to find out the root of why she was constantly acting out. It turned out that her baby-sitter had regularly sodomized her as she lay in her crib, before she turned one. Apparently that was enough for her to live her life in a constant state of fear and shame, so her behavioral issues began there and just got worse over the years.

I immediately saw that Serena was somebody who needed me, and, while I was apprehensive about helping her, because Luke was still very suspicious of his sister, I knew that it was something that I had to try to do.

As we left, there were hugs all around. Serena hugged me tightly, and tentatively went over to Luke and hugged him too. I could sense his awkwardness as he put his arms around her, and I immediately felt badly for her. Chris hugged us both, as did Carolyn, who made sure that we had an apple crumble pie to enjoy on our way home.

Michael drove us to the bus, and then, when we arrived at the station, unloaded our things, which had increased evermore, through the addition of the Christmas gifts and the pie, and hugged both of us.

"Now, you don't be a stranger anymore," he said to Luke. "I expect to see you at least once before the next holiday season."

"You can count on it, pop," he said. He brought me closer to him. "Who knows, maybe there might even be a special occasion involving this one here and me before the end of next year. Keeping my fingers crossed."

Michael put his hand on my shoulder. "You're a keeper. I've never seen my daughter Serena act like that with anybody. It's one thing for my son's girlfriend to get along with Amy, Mark and Chris. That's easy. But to bond with Serena? You're a miracle worker."

I smiled. "I guess I just have a way with people." I raised my eyebrows conspiratorially. "That's why I'm an artist, just like Luke. I can peel back the layers."

We all hugged again, and Luke and I boarded the bus for the long ride back. As we sat on the bus together, holding hands, we tried very hard to make this moment last just a little longer. The city seemed foreboding for both of us. I was going to have to file for divorce, and who knew what hell would come from that. And he would have to face his criminal charges, and do the hard work that would come with trying to find a way, any way, to salvage his art career from the ashes.

But, during the bus ride home, neither of us addressed any of this.

Chapter Forty-Two

Luke

Dalilah and I had gotten back to the city the day before, which also happened to be my 21st birthday. As 21st birthdays go, though, it was a low-key affair. I had no desire to go out and get drunk, as I was inundated with the stress of what was coming up, and alcohol would just make that worse. So, Dalilah and I just ordered in some Chinese and watched some of my favorite old movies, like *The Terminator* and *Field of Dreams.* That one always got me, because it reminded me of the overall distance I had between me and my pop, a distance that really wasn't alleviated by my recent visit.

It was just as well that Dalilah and I didn't go out for my birthday, too, at least from her perspective. Because she was really tired, and that seemed to be something that was a recurring theme anymore. Dalilah was having a difficult time, it seemed, recovering from our traveling experience, because she was tired a lot and also seemed to be nauseated much of the time. I worried about her, but she always insisted that she was okay – it was just a little bit of stomach queasiness, no big deal, and she felt that perhaps she was stressed out because of her impending divorce, so that was making her nauseated and fatigued.

While Dalilah was fighting what seemed to be an abundance of stress and a possible minor bug, I had to face what I had to face, so I found myself in an attorney's office the day after my birthday. The money from my show had come in, all $102,000 of it, and I immediately sent $30,000 of it to the IRS. No use having it tempt me. I sent another $10,000 to the State of New York for the same reason. The last thing that I wanted was to end up with a giant tax bill after all the money was gone.

So, I was anxious to see how much this attorney was going to charge and also see what I was up against. Dalilah was with me, because she, too, wanted to know everything. After our meeting with this attorney, Dalilah and I would have to proceed with the full knowledge of all that was about to go down. Neither of us could quite understand how the charges were so elevated, when clearly Nottingham didn't have any injuries. So, that would be the first thing that I would be asking this attorney, one James Francis.

This attorney was in one of the high-rise buildings in lower Manhattan, and he was somebody who was recommended by Nick, who was the best friend of Dalilah's father. Nick's father was an attorney who was familiar with many attorneys in New York, so this James Francis came highly recommended. And highly expensive, too - $500 an hour.

I wanted to go bargain hunting, and this actually caused a large fight between Dalilah and me.

"You can't bargain-basement this, Luke. You don't know

whom you're dealing with. You need somebody clever who is going to be able to get around Nottingham's bullshit, because you know that he used his power and influence to make sure that you got trumped-up charges. You know he did. He's a devious piece of shit, so you need somebody who knows what he's doing. Finding an attorney on the Internet and going with the cheapest one will find you in prison, no doubt about it."

"Oh, come on Dalilah, it's not that big of a deal. You and I both know that Nottingham wasn't injured, so any Joe Schmo should be able to get this whole thing reduced to a misdemeanor without any problem. I have to live off of this money while I try to hustle some more jobs. I'd like to cut back on my bartending hours and use that time to really throw myself into finding commissions and gallery owners who want to show me. And that's going to be harder than ever with Nottingham poisoning the well."

"Luke, you won't be able to get any commission and showings if you're in prison for years. And that's what might happen if you take your eye off the ball. There's something going on, and you need a good attorney with a good investigator to find out what that is."

I started pacing. That was what I really wanted to avoid – finding some high dollar attorney who was going to eat up most of the leftover money I got through my show. I wanted a cushion, even a small one, so that I could look at doing my art full-time. Working at the bar took time away from my art, and I really desired to be able to quit the bar and sock away the money from my show, and really make a go of it. I had no desire to pay most of my leftover money for an attorney.

"I'll gamble. I'll gamble that it's no big deal, and it's all going to go away. A misunderstanding. Or the prosecutor just filed elevated charges because that's what they do. They file trumped up charges so that they can have something to reduce them to for a plea bargain. I heard that's what happens. You get the defendant all freaked out because he's being charged with something major, so that, when the prosecutor comes with a deal that the defendant never would have taken before, he takes it, just because he's so relieved. You know, the prosecutor charges the guy with a robbery, freaks him out, and then reduces it to stealing with a huge fine. Well, if the guy was charged with stealing to begin with, he probably wouldn't take that huge fine. But, since it's a reduction from the earlier charge, he's like 'hell to the yeah, I'm taking that.'"

Dalilah nodded. "I think that does happen, but we need to know what we're dealing with here. Please, Luke, this is your future here. You don't want to be known as somebody who has a felony charge, especially one that was incurred by assaulting a powerful man like Nottingham."

"Well, maybe that's a good thing. I'm sure you and I aren't the only ones who think that Nottingham's a bastard. I'm quite sure that there are those who would like to give me a fucking medal for doing what I did. Who knows? This might actually help me."

"Listen, Luke, this isn't a poker game here. This is your life. This is your life, and you need to take this seriously. While I agree with you that you might win fans for doing what you did, because I also agree that Nottingham has made some enemies, you can't discount the fact that he carries a lot of power in this city. You don't want to mess around with him anymore than you have to. And if he has the power to put you in prison for seven years, than he will do it. He will do it, and have no compunction about it. All over two little punches. I can't let that happen. If I have to get my dad to get you an attorney, I'll do it."

That did it. Bringing her dad into it, and the threat that she was going to be the one getting the attorney. No way would I do that – let her foot the bill through her father. I wanted Ryan to stay out of this mess, and here she was, threatening to bring him into it.

"Okay, okay. I'll see that fancy attorney who was recommended to you." And, at that, I made an appointment with this guy, James Francis.

Chapter Forty-Three

Dalilah and I sat in the law firm's waiting room, each of us with a glass of water in our hands. I looked around. The waiting-room suite was as nice as Nottingham's, with dark panels on the walls, plush carpeting, and modern furniture. I could see the conference room just beyond the receptionist desk, and it had floor-to-ceiling windows that looked out over the vast city.

I grabbed her hand anxiously, wondering why I was always kept waiting by these important people. I wasn't looking forward to this, at all, because I knew that this attorney had obtained a copy of the file from the prosecutor, so he would be able to tell me exactly what was happening and why.

And I probably didn't want to know the answers to these questions.

Finally, the receptionist said that "Mr. Francis will see you now," and got up to lead us through the corridors of offices and opened the door to Mr. Francis' enormous office. Like the rest of the suite, his office had floor-to-ceiling windows, and his back wall sported a fireplace and was wood-paneled. The office was illuminated with track lighting, and various floorlamps. James Francis sat behind a huge cherry wood desk, and, to his right, were leather couches.

He stood up and greeted us as we walked through the door. "Hello," he said, "you must be Luke Roberts." He extended his hand, and I shook it, and he turned his attention to Dalilah.

"Yes," I said, "and this is Dalilah Gallagher."

He shook her hand, and said "yes, yes. I think that I met you a few times when you lived with Nick O'Hara. Good guy."

Dalilah nodded. "Probably. They had a lot of parties. You probably were at a few of them."

"Yes, yes I was. Anyhow, have a seat."

We both sat down, as did James. He took a deep breath, before launching into what he had to say. "Okay, now, Luke, I have your file. It was sent to me by the prosecutor's office. I'll be honest with you. It's not looking so good."

My heart sunk as I heard those words. "What do you mean? I punched him twice, and he seemed absolutely fine. I don't understand. There weren't any injuries."

He raised his eyebrows. "No injuries. Sorry, kid, but you must be joking. Nottingham suffered some pretty serious injuries in your altercation."

Dalilah and I looked at one another quizzically. "I don't understand. Please tell me what you know."

"Well, I've read through the medical report. Says here that Nottingham reported to the hospital and was diagnosed with a concussion and internal bleeding. Here are the photos," he said, passing me the pictures.

I looked at the pictures, and felt absolutely stunned. Nottingham looked like a prizefighter went ten rounds with him. His left eye was swollen shut and sported an enormous bruise. His lip was also swollen, and he had various cuts all over his face. I looked at the pictures of his abdomen, which showed a massive bruise on it.

I then read the medical report from Mt. Sinai, which stated that Nottingham was admitted to the hospital after complaining of a headache, dizziness, abdominal pain and nausea, and was diagnosed with a severe concussion and internal bleeding, after a CAT scan was taken, along with an ultrasound. He remained in the hospital for observation for 48 hours, after which he was discharged, as the internal bleeding apparently resolved on its own, as did the concussion.

I looked at James, feeling bewildered. No way was this medical report accurate. No.Fucking.Way. Nottingham seemed to be perfectly fine, and, in fact, I didn't punch him in his eye. I punched him in his jaw. So, this bruising and the fact that his eye was swollen shut was proof positive that there was no way that I could have done this to him.

I tried to make a joke of it. "Oh, come on. I know that I can pack a punch, but there's no way I did all of this to him."

James made a temple out of his hands and looked at me. "What do you mean?"

"I punched him twice. Not that hard, either. I wasn't trying to rough him up or anything. I was just trying to send him a message. I'm not that stupid that I would do all of this to him."

"Were you in a blind rage?"

"Hardly. I was, several days earlier, but at that time, I was angry, but not blinded by rage."

"Several days earlier," James said, interested in this. "Why were you so angry several days before this incident?"

I squeezed Dalilah's hand, and she nodded. "I have to leave the room," she said. "What Luke says to you must be confidential, and I know that, if I'm here, it wouldn't be." Dalilah knew something about attorney-client confidentiality, and knew that the presence of a third-party meant that the confidentiality would be broken.

At that, she squeezed my hand again and left the room, but she nodded at me meaningfully before going out the door.

Once she left, I told him. "Nottingham is the one who needs to be going to prison for felony assault, not me. He beat up Dalilah and really did cause her injury. How much injury, I don't know, but I wouldn't be surprised if she had internal bleeding from it, not to mention a concussion. She refused to let me take her to the hospital, though."

"I see," he said "Well, that is certainly a mitigating circumstance, at least in my eyes. Of course, whether or not that would be evidence that could be introduced in a court of law is suspect at best. It doesn't qualify as a legal justification for what you did, and you certainly cannot claim defense of others, as you went over there to see Mr. Nottingham long after he did what he did to your…girlfriend? Am I correct that she's your girlfriend?"

I nodded, and I thought I saw jealousy in his eyes as I did so. But James was too professional to say anything like "lucky guy," although I was quite sure he was thinking it.

"What qualifies as a legal justification?"

"Not much anymore. The only real justifications are self-defense, defense of others or consent – such as if the two of you were engaged in some kind of professional fight. Sometimes assault might be justified if the victim had first attempted to commit some kind of felony against the person, although even those justifications are suspect if the felony being attempted didn't involve bodily injury. But, what you did – just go into the man's office and punch him – wouldn't be justifiable under any definition, so introducing evidence that he roughed up your girlfriend probably won't be allowed. But, I can always try."

I sighed and hung my head. "Let me get Dalilah. I don't think that anything else I'm about to say to you is going to be that big of deal, so no need for confidentiality."

James nodded. "That's fine. But I'm curious why it was so important for what you just told me to be confidential?"

"Dalilah doesn't want what happened to her to get out under any circumstances. She's adamant about that, too. So, if there ever would be any occasion when you would have to testify about what I just told you, then we have to make sure that the confidentiality is secure. She doesn't want to take chances with that."

I got up and got Dalilah, and she came back in, and the two of us sat down. "Okay, then, give it to me straight. What am I facing here?"

James kinda grimaced. "Well, it's a first offense, but I'll be honest with you, that burglary charge is going to be difficult to fight. The prosecutors aren't usually willing to give you probation on a burglary charge, even if I could possibly get probation on the assault charges. You might be looking at a couple of years in prison for that, worse-case scenario."

My heart started racing. Prison? For getting into a little fight? "I see," I said, trying hard not to break down in front of him. "I mean, worst-case I go to prison, but I won't serve that much time, right? I mean, I heard that people who go to prison don't serve much of their sentences. Right?"

"Well, in this worst-case scenario, you're convicted of a violent offense. The non-violent offenders - your petty drug dealers, drug abusers, persistent shop-lifters, people like that

– they don't serve much of their sentence. Your violent offenders do."

I squeezed Dalilah's hand, but didn't look at her. I couldn't. I didn't want to see how she was reacting to this news.

"Okay," I said. "Best-case scenario."

"Well," he said. "Best case is that you somehow prove that you didn't injure Mr. Nottingham to the extent that these medical records show, and I'm able to plead you to a misdemeanor. The burglary charge goes away in this instance as well, as that charge, along with the felony assault charges, are contingent upon Mr. Nottingham actually sustaining considerable injury. But, I'm not at all sure how you're going to do that. These medical records speak for themselves."

There had to be a way…Dalilah and I were just going to have to figure that out after we left this office.

"Okay," I said. "Thank you very much. How much do I owe you for today?"

"$500," he said. "And, in cases like this, if it ends up going to trial, you're probably looking at $50,000 in fees or more."

Okay. Bye bye all the money from the show.

At that, Dalilah and I left the office, after the receptionist ran my debit card for James' fee, and we got the subway. My mind was racing a hundred miles an hour, as I wished that there was someway to turn back time so that my stupid act of punching Nottingham never happened.

As I sat there, I thought about all that I wanted to do with that money from my show. I wanted to move to the city, so that I could be in the middle of the action. I wanted to quit my job so that I could spend all my time trying to make it again. I wanted to do all of that so that I could marry Dalilah and make her happy and proud of me. So that I could be proud of me as well.

Now, it was all slipping through my fingers. Even if, by some miracle, this James person was able to plead me down to a misdemeanor, he was going to take most of my money to do it. Forget about having a trial, though. It was going to have to be a plea bargain. $50,000? I'd end up with nothing but a barrel around my ass at that point.

"Luke," Dalilah said tentatively. "We have to talk about this. We have to strategize. He can't get away with this."

"What is he getting away with?"

"Nottingham. I don't know how he did it, but he must have paid off a doctor to fake those medical records. Or something must have happened."

"Whatever," I said. "I can't think about this right now."

"You have to think about it," Dalilah said. "You can't go to prison. You just can't."

"I said that I don't want to think about it. Now, let's drop this for now until I can process it all. Right now, I just want to order in a pizza with you and get some movies on Netflix. Don't push me. I'll deal with it in my own time, but, right now, I'm pretty raw and I need to decompress. I hope that you can understand that."

So, that was what happened that night. Dalilah said nothing more about it, and we lined up some movies to watch. My vacation from my job was almost through, and I would have to go back to work the next day. It would have to be an early night.

We sat on the couch and watched a couple of movies and ate pizza from the pizzeria down the street. On tap was a new movie, *Dead of Night*, which was a slasher pic, which I was in the mood for, because I wanted to indulge my dark fantasies about doing to Nottingham what was being done on screen. I also wanted to watch one of my favorite old movies, *Fight Club*. I happened to love the director David Fincher, and this movie, in particular, was one of my top movies of all time, even though it came out well before I was born.

Dalilah and I sat there and watched the movie, and there was something about this movie in particular that I wanted to see. I wasn't sure…it had been years since I had seen the film. But when it came upon the scene when the narrator beat himself up in his boss' office, so that the narrator could get the company to keep him on the payroll for doing nothing at all, therefore he wanted to blackmail the boss, I paused it excitedly and looked at Dalilah.

We looked at each other. "Are you thinking what I'm thinking?" I asked.

Dalilah nodded. "Nottingham is just psycho enough to do that to himself." Dalilah got up and started to pace the floor nervously. She started talking. "He would do that to himself. Of course he would. Anything to make sure that he gets revenge upon you. But, what if he didn't do that to himself? What if he got somebody else to do it to him?"

"Go on…" I said.

"He goes to a fetish club, right? Right? So, he goes down there, and asks somebody to rough him up, and then checks himself into the emergency room and says that you did all of that. He would do that. I know that he would do something like that. It sounds just like him and his fucked-up mental state. Anything to make sure that you pay for being with me. It's not enough that he destroys your career. He apparently wants you completely destroyed as well."

"Okay," I said. "That gives us something to go on, at least. Does he go to just one club, or many? Who can we talk to about that, and how can we prove that I didn't do that to him?"

"We could get James to subpoena the cops. They can say that Nottingham looked fine when they arrested you. But, then again, Nottingham might come back with saying that the injuries showed up later. The bruises and the internal bleeding and all of that. It's going to be more complicated than we might realize."

"So, Nottingham goes to his fetish club…"

"Yes. And those people are pros. So is Nottingham. He probably knows just how much beating he could take that would put him in the hospital, without causing too much long-term damage. You know that Nottingham would never risk having the person going overboard and really hurting him so that he has some kind of permanent injury."

"Okay. So what do we need to do?"

"We need to figure out which fetish club Nottingham goes to, and ask around. Talk to the people around that club who might have seen Nottingham come in on the same day that you punched him, and ask them what kind of treatment he got that night." At that, Dalilah got out a copy of the medical record that James gave to us. "Yes, see, it says that Nottingham presented to the ER at 2 AM. He said that he sustained those injuries around 12 hours earlier in the fight with you, but that he didn't come to the hospital until his symptoms got worse," she said, paraphrasing the medical records. "That's it! We find the person at that club who might have done this to him, and see if we can get that person to agree to testify or something."

I started to feel hopeful and excited about this, but then immediately started feeling discouraged again. "But Dalilah," I said, "those places are confidential. They aren't going to just talk to us schmos, especially since we aren't cops or anything. They'll tell us to hit the road."

At that, Dalilah got quiet. "You're right about that. We aren't exactly regulars, and neither of us know anything about that world. It would be very difficult to just go on in there and try to get information. But there is somebody who might be able to help us."

"Who?"

"Your sister Serena."

Chapter Forty-Four

"Serena? Serena? You're out of your fucking mind, Dalilah. That girl wouldn't lift one finger to help me. If I was lying on the street, bleeding, she'd be dialing her nail salon as she stepped over me. That is, if she didn't decide to put her foot on me, just to add further insult to injury. Nice try, though."

"Oh?" Dalilah said. "Really? Well, for whatever reason, that girl is captivated by me. I don't know what it is, but she and I really bonded while I was there. She told me things that she said that she hasn't told anyone. She said something about feeling that she and I were old souls and she understood me, and felt that I understood her. Again, I can't explain it much, either, but Serena was quite taken with me. And why didn't you ever tell me that she lives in town? She lives in the Village."

"Oh, she does? News to me. I guess because she never told me that she lived in town, and I never asked. No offense, but I have always tried to say as little to that girl as possible."

"Well, she lives in the Village. She's lived there for like 10 years. Really, Luke, it's shameful…"

"Oh, no. You're not going to guilt-trip me. You spent a few days with her. I spent a lifetime. A lifetime of putting up with her crap. I will never forgive her, either, for blowing off my mom's funeral. Never, never, never."

"Luke, she told me about that. She was grieving, too, but she covered it up. She covered it up by acting like she didn't care, but she did. She did care. It devastated her greatly. Listen, Luke, she reminds me a great deal of Nick, my father's best friend."

"Oh? You mean, Nick is also a no-good two-timing cheat who…"

"Yes. He was. He was all of those things until he met the woman who finally tamed him. Man-whore, arrogant, you name it. Had a hard shell. At least that's what my dad told me about him. But Nick was hurting, so he put up this enormous wall around him. If you didn't know him, you probably would have thought he was the biggest asshole in the world. But underneath it all, he was really a big pussy-cat. He endured tragedies, and that was just how he dealt with it. By having a hard shell."

"Well, guess what. Maybe Nick came off like that to strangers and showed his loved-ones a different side. In this case, *I'm* supposed to be Serena's loved-one. I'm family. So, I should be the one that she's nice to, and you should be the one who she treats like shit. But it's apparently the other way around."

"Well, the analogy isn't perfect, but I'm telling you, Serena is a good person underneath all her bluster. She carries around a great deal of guilt about how she has treated everybody, and an enormous burden about how she treated your mother before your mother died. I mean, I know that she stole from your mom, but she was just a kid. A fucked-up kid. And she's dealing with an awful lot of heartache."

I looked at Dalilah, trying to decide if I should believe her about my sister. How could she get to this soft inner core of my crazy sister, when I never could, nor could anyone else in my family? I mean, Dalilah just knew Serena for a matter of days, and suddenly she's her best friend? Or only friend, for that matter - I never knew Serena to have a friend, period.

I shook my head. "I don't get it…"

"You don't have to. All you need to know is that she can help us. I hate to betray her confidence, but I feel that it's necessary here - Serena is into that lifestyle like Nottingham. Who knows? She probably has been with Nottingham a time or two. But she knows about the East Village clubs, and I hear those are the ones that Nottingham frequents as well. She knows people there. She can be like our Virgil, guiding us through hell."

Dalilah was referring to Dante's guide in *Inferno*. It seemed an apt enough allegory, really. Dalilah and I were complete virgins when it came to the underground world that we were going to be seeing. We were going to need somebody to guide us around and try to find out what it was that we were going to need to know. To help us find the right person who might be able to give us information about Nottingham.

"So, what, we find somebody who can tell us that he beat up Nottingham on the night that he went into the ER. And then what? I don't know how that information would even help out at all, except for if we had a trial, and James could use the information to show some alternative reason for Nottingham's injury. That still would mean that I would have this case hanging over my head, and I would be out a minimum of $50,000."

"It's better than going to prison, I would think."

"Sure it is. But it's not a magic bullet. That's all I'm saying."

"It's a start. Besides, maybe we could use the information we get to go straight to the prosecutor's office and get them to drop the charges. Or maybe the information can be used to get James to be able to negotiate a plea to a misdemeanor."

Dalilah took a deep breath and started looking pale.

"You okay, Dalilah?"

"Yeah," she said. "I just felt a little woozy, that's all. I'm so sorry, I have to lie down for a little bit. But when I get up, I'm calling Serena, and I'm not taking no for an answer here."

I sighed. When Dalilah got something in her head, God love her, she went with it. Far be it for me to stand in her way.

Serena. Who would have thought I would be doing anything with that woman? I shook my head as I realized, anew, that fate was a crazy thing.

Chapter Forty-Five

Dalilah

Luke is a man. He doesn't necessarily know the signs of early pregnancy. Which was a good thing, because I had a feeling that I was preggers. It was exceedingly early, of course – I had surreptitiously taken several pregnancy tests, and they all were negative. Still, after I started feeling woozy, tired and especially after the wine started to taste bitter, I knew. I looked on the Internet to see if pregnancy signs occurred so early, and, sure enough, there were reports of women having symptoms within days of conception, as crazy as that sounded.

I did some calculations in my head – Luke and I had sex a matter of days before we went to see his family, and that was when the symptoms started. I could only assume, and hope, that Luke would be the father. Not that I could possibly keep the baby, which was why Luke probably couldn't know about it. I knew enough about New York divorce law to know that if I conceived while I was married to Nottingham, that there not only couldn't be a divorce until the child was born, but that Nottingham would be the presumptive father. This would mean, automatically, that he would have custody of the child, and, knowing him, he would do everything in his power to wrest sole custody from me. I didn't trust him, at all, and I couldn't let that happen. Even if he got split custody, I couldn't let it happen. No way. I would never have any child of mine subjected to his depravity and cruelty.

So, I wasn't at all sure that I was pregnant, and I hoped and prayed that I wasn't. Not that I didn't want Luke's child. Of course I did, even though both of us were still very young and neither of us was established. I still had faith that everything would work out for Luke and his career, and that this criminal charge would be resolved as soon as Luke and I could prove that Nottingham is a freak who essentially got somebody to beat the crap out of him just so that he could frame Luke. I also had faith that I would be able to get my own career on track. I had started up with my painting when I was on vacation with Luke, and I was finding, once again, that I was getting my voice back. I could envision my future with Luke, and it would be filled with commercial success for both of us. So, supporting a child wouldn't be a problem, soon.

But the specter of Nottingham, and how much crap he was going to put me through if I were pregnant, made me pause. It would break my heart, absolutely break it in two, if I had to surreptitiously terminate my pregnancy, especially since the baby probably would be Luke's, not Nottingham's. If it were Nottingham's, I would be far enough along that it would show up on a pregnancy test. So, that gave me comfort. But terminating Luke's baby...I didn't know if I could go through with it. I didn't know if I could live with myself if I did that. But, then again, could I live with myself if I brought a child into this world who would be claimed by Nottingham? The baby would legally be Nottingham's, after all, as the conception was during the marriage. A DNA test would certainly prove that Nottingham wasn't the father, but I knew that Nottingham would still have rights to the baby, and would fight it every day in court if he had to.

I shivered, thinking about my choices, and said a silent prayer that I was only coming down with something. I wanted a baby with Luke, but not until I was officially divorced from Nottingham, so that there could be zero question that Nottingham could never be a part of the child's life.

You can't think about this right now, Dalilah. You have to think about the more immediate situation of making sure Luke stays out of prison. As crappy as I felt, I knew that I was going to have to get ahold of Serena and see what she could do to help us in finding out information about Nottingham. So, this was next – after I got up from my rest, I would give her a call.

After just a few minutes, though, I started to feel better. Less queasy, less fatigued. I realized that I really just needed to lie down, and that a nap wasn't even in order. So, I got out my phone, where I had entered Serena's contact information, and looked it up and dialed.

"Dalilah," Serena said on the second ring. "I was hoping you'd call."

"Yes," I said, feeling guilty that I was calling her for a favor. She obviously sounded like she was eager to talk to me. "Listen, I don't want you to think that I'm only calling you because I need something. It just so happens that I do, though."

"Sure," she said. "What do you need, Dalilah?"

"Um, can we meet for a drink somewhere? I don't think

that I'm going to bring Luke just yet, though. I know that you guys have to mend fences."

"Yeah," she said. "Where?"

"In your neck of the woods," I said, thinking, accurately, that it would be more than rude to have her come to Brooklyn, when she was the one who was going to do us the favor. "How about Gotham's tomorrow at 6?"

"Gotham's it is," she said. "I'm happy to hear from you, Dalilah."

"Well, I'm glad to be calling. Although you might not be so thrilled when I ask you what I need."

"I'm on pins and needles to find out," she said. "See you tomorrow."

I went out into the kitchen, where Luke was sketching in his book while sitting on the floor. I knew that he did that to relax, and his painting came better when he was already under less stress. He stood up when he saw me. "You feeling okay, honey?" At that, he got up and poured some hot water into a cup. "Here's some tea with honey and ginger. My mom always made this for me when I was feeling crappy."

I smiled and took the proffered cup. "I'm fine, really. Just have a little bug, I guess. Hope I don't give it to you."

"Well, if you do, you do. Anyhow…."

"I got ahold of Serena. We're meeting at Gotham's tomorrow evening."

Luke nodded. "As much as I don't like the idea of my sister getting involved in this, I suppose you're right. Serena might be valuable to us in this investigation. Sorry for giving you a hard time about her earlier."

"Not a problem. All that I ask is that you have an open mind about her."

"I'll try. It's going to be difficult to overcome a lifetime of her disappointing and hurting me and the entire family, but, at the same time, I really would like to think the best about her. If you found her good side, then I'm all for trying to get to know her in a new light."

I was a bit taken aback by Luke's change of attitude, but I realized that he seemed a great deal calmer than he earlier did. I supposed that he had the chance to really think things through, and realized that, with his freedom on the line, he probably shouldn't look any gift horse in the mouth.

"Okay, then, I'm glad to hear that. I do want to talk to her alone, though. I hope that's not a problem."

"No, I understand. I mean, we aren't the best of friends just yet. As stupid as it sounds, as this is my case, I probably would be the in the way right now."

I sipped my tea, and found that I did feel better. I looked at Luke, wanting so bad to tell him my suspicions about the fact that I felt like I could be pregnant. But I really needed to see a family law attorney first. Lay everything on the table, and see what I could expect. See if there was any way for me to cleanly divorce Nottingham if I was expecting a child, although I knew in my gut, and intellectually as well, that that would be asking way too much.

"Ah, well," Luke said. "I think that it's time for bed. Let's pull out the futon and hit the hay. I have to work early tomorrow a double shift."

The two of us then got naked, and got under the covers. Luke stroked my body gently, and my minor queasiness was forgotten. His touch was still so magical to me, and I kissed him eagerly. He took a deep breath and got on top of me and entered me. I threw back my head in ecstasy, not wanting it to end. I put my hands behind his head and brought his face down to mine. His soft lips were gently brushing mine as I felt him stroking in and out. Then he groaned softly and rolled over. "Sorry that was a quickie," he said. "I'll make it up to you tomorrow, I promise."

I didn't care. I orgasmed as usual. That was one thing about Luke – he could make me orgasm with just the slightest gentle touch. I didn't think that I could ever be as captivated by another person. And I knew how much stress he was under. Everything was hitting him at once – the felony charges, the fact that nobody from his show would return his calls, and going back to work. I really looked forward to the day when everything was resolved and we could get our lives back on track.

But would it be resolved? If I were pregnant, that would definitely put a huge wrench into the entire thing. So, as I lay there in Luke's strong arms, I looked up to the sky and silently said a prayer to the one that I believed in sometimes, other times not, that I wasn't pregnant. I figured it couldn't hurt to pray, even if I didn't necessarily believe, because there was always the off-chance that there was something there who would hear me and make sure that my wishes were answered.

Chapter Forty-Six

While Luke worked his shifts at the bar, I caught the subway into the city and met Serena at Gotham's Bar and Grill in the Village. This was not a typical bar and grill, at least what I used to always think of when I thought of bars and grills. Rather, it was more like a nice restaurant, with white tablecloths, and a gorgeous tiled floor. The enormous windows looked out into the city life, and the ceilings, like so many other finer restaurants and drinking establishments, were a good 20 feet high.

Serena was already there, and stood up when I came through the door. She was dressed casually in black pants and a green sweater, with an Hermés bag that matched her red fingernails. I went over to her, and she gave me a hug. I wondered, as I sat down across from her, how it was that everybody was so wrong about this woman. I saw her as a beautiful woman with a hard shell, and, behind this hard shell, was this innocent and hurt child. Everybody else in her life only saw the shell, I guessed.

I took a deep breath as the waiter came around for my

drink order. "I'd like a glass of sparkling water," I said, handing him back his menu.

Serena narrowed her eyes. "I knew it. How far along are you?"

I sighed. "I have no idea. I mean, not far along enough that it shows up on a pregnancy stick. And how did you know?"

She put her hand to mouth. "You mean, aside from the fact that you looked like a sheet at my old man's house, and puked your guts out when I first met you?"

I smiled. "Touché."

"No, seriously. I'm sensitive. I can sense things. See things that others can't. You used to have that ability, too, when you were a kid. But you don't use that so much anymore, do you?"

I thought about her words. When I was very small, I did know things that others didn't. But that was a normal thing with kids, and it was something that I thought that I outgrew. Maybe I didn't, though, which was why I was always able to see behind a person's eyes and façade and understand what was going on underneath. And I wondered if that was the real reason why Serena took to me so quickly. She recognized somebody who was "sensitive" like herself, even if I didn't necessarily still acknowledge it in my own self.

I smiled. "I guess you're right. As you know, I used to make quite a lot of money as a portraitist. I did that when I was a kid, but my other passion was in the genre of urban expressionism. But I was very good at the portraits because I was able to paint their inner soul. At least, that's what they always said. No matter how they seemed on the outside, I saw what was roiling beneath, and that was what I painted. I was unique in that way."

She nodded her head and sipped her wine. "You really should tap into that more, Dalilah. I can help you do that. It would be a shame if you went through the rest of your life ignoring your God-given abilities."

I felt uncomfortable hearing her talk like that, but I had no idea why that was. I guess because I didn't want to feel like a freak, and acknowledging that maybe I did have another sense that was underdeveloped would do just that. "Yes, Serena, maybe you can help me with that."

She looked skeptical. "Alright, I won't push. But you wanted to talk to me about Luke, I guess. He's in trouble, isn't he?"

I blinked my eyes, knowing that I didn't specify why I wanted to see her. How did she know that I wanted to see her about Luke's troubles? "How did your entire family never know about your abilities?"

She shrugged. "My dad always shunned me because of what I could see and sense. So, I kept quiet about it. My family hated me, anyhow, for good reason. I always was a brat. Acting out, though, but nobody could ever hear me. They didn't want to, so I had no use for any of them."

I took her hands. "Serena, this might all be fate. My meeting you, and you helping us. It might be the way that you and your brother can mend fences, and maybe he can talk to the rest of the family about doing the same."

I saw tears forming in her eyes, and she swallowed hard and took a sip of her wine. Then she took a deep breath and said "so, beautiful lady, what is it that you need from me?"

"Augh. Well, I hope that this isn't inappropriate. But, desperate times call for desperate measures." I then told her the entire story about Nottingham, from the beginning until the very latest developments. She followed along silently, nodding from time to time.

"Wow," she said, after I finished. By that time, she was on her second glass of wine, and we had decided to go ahead and order dinner. "You guys certainly have gone through a lot. I can't believe that you would put yourself out there with that creeper, just to help Luke. I hope he appreciates you."

"He does. I appreciate him, too."

She nodded. "Well, let's see. You said that you have a good feeling that he belongs to the Rose Club?"

"Not positive, but I think so. At least, that was what I understood from people in the know."

She flattened her mouth and took another drink of her wine. "I'm afraid that I would be of little use, there. That's a very exclusive club, and you have to be invited to be a member. Which I'm not. I go to Eve's myself. Little bit less hardcore."

I felt deflated, thinking that this entire idea wasn't going to pan out. I didn't quite know what to do, except maybe talk to James and see if he had any ideas about issuing subpoenas or something of the sort. But I didn't know if that were even possible, because this entire thing was based upon a hunch to begin with.

She patted my hands. "All isn't lost. Don't look like that." She smiled. "Listen, if you don't mind doing something slightly illegal....no, sorry, very illegal. But, anyhow, I happen to have some fake police badges that we could all use. We go in there like we own the place – that's the key to getting the information you want, you gotta be confident and not back down – and we start shaking everybody down. We'll find the dom who roughed up that creeper in no time. Listen, that place is underground – they don't want any trouble. Once we find who we're looking for, it's just a matter of threatening subpoenas and legal action, and they'll give us what we need. An authorized statement would probably do, wouldn't it?"

I brightened. "Yes. That would certainly be a start. I don't know what James, Luke's attorney, would need to present to the prosecutor's office, but I would imagine that a notarized statement would probably be some pretty good evidence." I cocked my head at her while I sipped my water. "You sound like you've done this kind of thing before."

"You'd be surprised at the things I've done. Let's just say that if you need something done, and you don't mind doing things extra-legally, I'm probably your girl. And, in your case, I would think that extra-legal would be the way to go."

I knew that. I had consumed enough legal books in my life to know that a subpoena of this place, without some kind of probable cause, would be quashed. And a hunch, which is what I was working with, wasn't probable cause for such a search, so I doubted that James would be able to get the information that we needed in this case. And, as secretive as a place like this was, it was going to be exceedingly difficult to do things above-board.

I felt reasonably confident that Serena was going to be able to get what we needed.

"Okay," I said. "So, let's do it. I don't want to ask where you got those badges, though."

"No, you probably shouldn't. Just know that they look really authentic, and they work every time."

"Is it going to look okay that there's three of us going in there?"

She shook her head. "Actually, no. I was going to tell you that. Probably just Luke and I should do it. Sorry about that, but these places are used to seeing one or two cops at a time. But three would be overkill, and I don't think that we need to draw attention needlessly."

"Agreed," I said, feeling a little bit disappointed that I wouldn't be able to come along, but I understood, at the same time. "I hope that you guys can do this together without wanting to kill each other."

Serena smiled. "I know what you mean. But his ass is on the line, and, besides, I feel that I probably owe him this much. It's time to make amends, and this will probably help that along."

"Of course, Luke is going to have to wear some kind of disguise. I mean, he can't be recognized. You never know, the case might come to trial, so we certainly can't have the people from that club looking at him and saying 'say, you look like that cop who came in here investigating us.' I imagine that wouldn't be such a good idea."

Serena nodded her head. "He'll wear a cap, thick glasses and a beard and moustache. That should be good enough. Good thinking, there, Dalilah. You probably are going to end up saving his ass, too."

We clinked our glasses and ate our food, which had just arrived. I knew that Luke probably wasn't going to be entirely comfortable doing this with his sister, but he was just going to have to get over it.

Chapter Forty-Seven

Luke

I was sitting in the front seat of Serena's Porsche, in my disguise, feeling like a total idiot for going to this Rose Club in the West Village. That morning, Dalilah broke the news to me that Serena and I would be going to this place, and I was apprehensive, to say the least. Not just because I was going to do something that was clearly illegal – impersonating a police officer – but also because I had to spend the evening with Serena.

"She doesn't bite," Dalilah said, as she put the beard and moustache on me, not to mention makeup. She gave me some enormous glasses and baseball cap with a large brim, and smiled, satisfied. "Now put on your big boy pants and do it."

Which was how I found myself in the car with Serena, heading to this fetish club. "Now," I said. "We're agreed that if this Nottingham happens to be there, we leave immediately, right?"

"Well, I'm thinking about that one," she said. "He doesn't know me, so maybe I just keep on going and you high-tail it out." She looked at me. "Don't be so nervous, kid. It's going to be fine."

"Easy for you to say. You're not the one who's out on bail. I'm sure that impersonating a police officer would probably be one of those things that would get my bond revoked. Call me crazy."

She sighed. "You know, you always called Mark the cop, but I think that you have more than a little cop in you, too. Lighten up. As I said to Dalilah, you have to walk in there like you own the place. You can't be intimidated and embarrassed. You have to act like a real undercover detective would. No shaking, and you have to look everybody in the eye."

I shook my head. "Why are you doing this? I mean that sincerely. You've never wanted to help me or anybody in the family before."

She looked straight ahead. "I've found some things out about myself recently. I can't go into that just now, but I've had a breakthrough in therapy. And meeting Dalilah...I don't think that you fully appreciate what you have there with her. She's special, even more than you know. Yeah, she's a genius and artistic prodigy and all of that, but there's some untapped potential in her, too. I can see that. So, I'm doing this for her, too. But I admit that I don't want my baby brother serving time for something he didn't do. Although you probably should think twice before trying to beat down psychotic billionaires in the future. Word to the wise."

I chuckled in spite of myself. "Not my most shining moment, that. But my intentions were good."

"Of that I have no doubt. You were sticking up for your

girlfriend, and that's noble. Not the smartest thing you've ever done, but noble nonetheless."

I relaxed, and tried to bring down my walls, which, I admit, were always up with her. *Stop being so suspicious. Dalilah loves her, and take her at her word. She wants to change, she wants to be a part of the family again. Let her help you, and don't question it.*

We finally arrived, and I took a deep breath. "I really hope that I can pull this off."

"You can," she said, putting my face in her hands. "Look me in the eyes."

I obeyed. She did have a strong will.

"Okay. Now. Here's how it's all going to go down. We go in there, and we ask to speak to Mistress Claire. We tell the person who's admitting the clients that we're investigating an assault case. And that's all that we say. They'll let us in once we flash our badges."

"Yes," I said. "And then we talk to Mistress Claire and we give her the story. Which is the true story, right?"

"Right. Now, I've done my homework, and this Mistress Claire is the head-mistress, and probably would be the one who works over the really important clients like this Blake Nottingham. So, she's the best place to start our inquiry."

"Are you sure that telling the truth is the best thing here?"

"Yes. We need Mistress Claire to know exactly what we're looking for. If we tell her a lie, then it will come out, sooner or later. And forget about getting a good statement then."

"And what if she lies? She's going to want to protect Nottingham, I would think. These clubs are very confidential and they want to protect their clients as much as possible."

"That's when we begin the shake-down. We threaten

subpoenas and guarantee that the cops will be watching their place very closely from now on. They don't want any trouble, believe me."

"Yeah, but I'm quite sure that Nottingham is a VIP there. They're not going to want to lose his business for sure."

Serena shrugged. "They're going to have to choose between losing his business and inviting the cops in to monitor them closely. As an underground club, you can bet that they'll be willing to sing like a canary rather than invite increased scrutiny. At least, that's the gamble."

"And what if they call in our badge numbers, or something like that?"

"It'll check out. I'm not that stupid."

I shook my head. "What do you mean, it'll check out?"

"I got connections. Somebody legit gave me these badges."

"What do you mean-"

"You ask too many questions, kid. Too many questions. Now, let's move."

I took a deep breath, but felt much more confident now that I knew that, somehow, these badges were "official." I shook my head. Somehow, having a sister who didn't mind doing things "extralegally" and had some powerful connections, was paying off for me. I realized how little I knew about my sister, and I was actually starting to warm up to her, little by little.

There was a lot that I was going to learn about her. Not all of it was going to be pretty, but that's life.

At that, we got out of the car and went to the nondescript door of the Rose Club.

Chapter Forty-Eight

Before we went through the door, Serena looked at me and pointed. "Remember, like we own the fucking place. Got that? Follow my lead."

I nodded, feeling nervous. Serena sure had the confidence to pull this off. I, on the other hand, had just turned 21 years old, and I felt like I looked like a kid still. My disguise didn't quash those feelings one bit. I always pictured undercover officers as being quite a bit older, so I felt self-conscious. But Serena opened the door and strutted right up to the lady who was behind a podium that looked almost like a movie box-office. She was heavily made-up, and was dressed in a leather bikini and high-heeled stiletto boots. In her hand she had a whip. She cocked her head at the two of us.

"May I help you?" she asked, fingering her whip.

Serena flashed her badge. "I need to speak to Mistress Claire."

The woman nodded, and looked at me. "And you are?"

Like I own the place. I went right up to her and flashed my badge as well. She looked at mine at little bit longer than she did Serena's, and I felt my heart pounding wildly. I could imagine myself behind bars, again, and facing yet another felony – that of impersonating an officer.

Finally, after what seemed like years, but probably was only seconds, the woman buzzed the heavy red door in front of us, and Serena and I walked on in. I let out my breath, and tried to shake it off as I watched my sister strut through the door.

Something told me that this wasn't her first rodeo in doing this.

"Come with me," an enormous black lady said. She was dressed in flimsy lingerie that barely covered her huge breasts and legs. She had long red talons, and, like the woman who guarded the door, she had on high stilettos, but hers were strappy, as opposed to being gladiator boots. There was a large event space with a stripper pole and a trapeze, and a stage with a nude woman sitting in a chair, her legs spread open, with a guy between her legs and another behind her, fondling her breasts. From that room, there were several windy hallways which passed by several different rooms, all of which had glass walls, so that Serena and I could see everything that was going on in there.

Each of the rooms appeared to cater to a specific kind of kink. There was a room that was a cold-looking medical examination room, complete with a sterile metal table with stirrups. On the table was a woman who was tied up, and another woman was giving her what looked like a typical pelvic exam. Another room was a room that looked like it was reserved for people who had tickling fetishes, because there was a large bed in this room and various items that would be used to tickle people. On the bed was somebody who was doing just that – tickling another woman with a large feather.

I tried hard not to seem like a looky-loo, reminding myself that I was supposed to be a professional, therefore I couldn't stop and marvel at what I was seeing. But I felt like doing just that. I realized how much of a virgin that I was when it came to this type of thing.

Finally, our guide led us to a room that was clearly outfitted for BDSM practices. This was a large room, and, in the middle, was a St. Andrew's Cross, which was like a regular cross, but it was shaped like an X instead of a T. There was a man who was chained up on this cross, bound by both his wrists and his ankles, and he was completely nude, except for a cock ring. He had a gag on his mouth, and nipple chains that were being pulled by a beautiful woman in a tight-fitting red leather gown. She had a whip in one of her hands and a dildo in another.

I guessed that this woman was Mistress Claire, although she hardly looked large enough to be able to inflict the kind of damage that was wrought upon Nottingham in those pictures that I saw. I wondered if she had some kind of assistant, or if there were men who did this kind of thing as well.

I felt uncomfortable watching the torture of this man, who was writhing and trying to cry out in pain, but his leather gag stopped him from doing so. But the woman looked at us, and smiled, and went to the other side of the man and lashed his thighs. She obviously didn't mind putting on a show, and, I figured, that the guy on the cross didn't mind, either, although he couldn't very well voice his consent to us watching his torture right at that moment.

Serena watched with me, her face impassive. Again, I felt that this was probably just old hat with her, because she seemed not fazed by it all. I nudged her. "Perhaps we should come back at a better time?"

"No," she whispered back. "The performance is almost done."

"How can you tell?"

"I just can," she said.

And, sure enough, within five minutes, the man was released from his cross, and he got down on the floor and literally crawled while Mistress Claire kicked him along with her boots. He crawled along to a room that was just off to the side of the torture chamber, and Mistress Claire came over to us.

"Can I help you?" Her voice was surprisingly melodic and soft, in contrast to what I imagined the voice of a dominatrix to be.

"Yes," Serena said, flashing her badge. "I'm Detective Robinowitz, and this is Detective Stetson." She nudged me, and I flashed my badge as well. Flashing the badge was getting easier and easier, I found, but I didn't exactly want to get overconfident.

Mistress Claire looked wary, but she nodded and said "follow me." We did, to a small room that was adjacent to the dungeon. It was a typical office, really, with a cherry desk, two chairs and a computer. Soft music was playing, some kind of dreamy electronica. The walls were red, which seemed to be a theme throughout this place, and there was a Picasso knock-off on one of the walls, and an enormous fake tree was in the corner.

The dominatrix sat down behind the desk, and motioned for Serena and me to have a seat on the other side of the desk, which we did. "Okay," she said. "What can I do for the two of you?"

Without hesitation, Serena said "You have a client here, by the name of Blake Nottingham."

Mistress Claire shook her head. "Doesn't ring a bell."

At that, Serena brought out the picture of Nottingham with the bruised-up eye.

The dominatrix looked at the picture. "Oh, that guy. Okay. Well, most of our clients don't use their own names, and he's no exception. What do you need to know about him?"

"He came in here on the night of December 18. Correct?"

"Let me see," she said, popping on her computer. "We have the schedule here of who came to visit, and it looks like…yes. Yes, he was here that night. What's your order of business?"

"He presented that night to the ER with signs of being battered. Concussion, internal bleeding. He used his injuries to try to frame another man for felony assault. Obviously, it sounds as if there was an alternative explanation for these injuries. I need for you to make a notarized statement that I can present to the prosecutor."

"Are you going to subpoena these records?" Mistress Claire asked.

I held my breath. I doubted that what we were doing could be the basis for a subpoena, as the entire conversation would probably be considered to be hearsay.

Serena raised her eyebrow. "Well, we can do this for you the easy way or the hard way. The easy way is you give us the statement that we're asking for, and, in return, you won't be harassed by the NYPD. The hard way is that you make us get a subpoena, and you get a special task force that will be dedicated to coming down here and inspecting all of your practices. I'm quite sure that you're familiar with the laws and the codes of this city, and how many of these codes you violate on a routine basis. This place will be shut down in no time."

Mistress Claire tapped her fingers on the desk, obviously trying to decide whether to turn in an important client, or to risk having the wrath of the police force rain down upon their establishment. I felt myself holding my breath, knowing that, if she called Serena's bluff, I would be SOL.

"Everything we do here is safe, sane and consensual," she said, repeating the BDSM mantra. "But we don't want any trouble. What kind of statement do you want?"

"A statement that he was here on the night in question, and what kind of treatment he got here."

"Well, it looks like he was being attended to by Mikael that night. I'll go see if Mikael is around, and he can give you the details of what kind of service Mr. Roberts got that night."

"I'm sorry, did you say Mr. Roberts?" Serena said.

"Oh, I apologize. That's the assumed name that this Blake Nottingham uses. That slipped out and it shouldn't have."

Serena flashed her badge again. "What's the full name that Mr. Nottingham uses when he comes here?"

"Luke Roberts," Mistress Claire said. "I'll be right back." And, at that, she left.

As soon as Mistress Claire got out of earshot, Serena started laughing. "What's so funny?" I asked her.

"Boy, this guy has a hard-on for you, kid. Not literally, but he really wants to get you in trouble all the way around. Using your name as his assumed name at a sex club? That's pretty priceless right there."

In spite of myself, I started laughing as well. It *was* kinda funny in a slanderous kind of way, really. "He really will go to any lengths to get revenge on me, that's for sure."

But the levity of that moment gave way to serious apprehension as the moments clicked by, and Mistress Claire didn't reappear, and neither did Mikael. I took a deep breath, imagining the worst. Usually in the movies, whenever somebody leaves the room, they would come back with the actual authorities, and the fake cops are busted right then and there. I could imagine the Mistress returning with some uniformed police officers who would announce that Serena and I were both under arrest.

Serena looked at me. "That's not going to happen, now stop thinking that."

I cocked my head at her. "What's not going to happen?"

"That woman isn't going to come back in here with uniformed policemen. You have to relax. It's all going to work out, just trust me."

I furrowed my brows. "How did you-"

"Don't ask so many questions. Things are going to be fine, you'll see."

"But I don't understand."

She sighed. "It's written on your face. You're terrified of getting busted. I've done this fifty times, kid, and I've never even come close to being busted. Now, just relax, please. If you keep looking like a deer in the headlights, this Mistress Claire person might really feel that you're trying to put one over, and then you just might end up in the clink."

I shook my head, wondering if this was what Dalilah meant when she told me that my sister was unique. She seemed to have some kind of sixth sense, as she was completely tuned into my wavelength and thoughts.

Serena shrugged. "You're getting easier for me to read, now that you don't hate me so much. When you bring your walls down, I can tune into your energy much better. I like this much more than before, really."

"I didn't say anything."

"You don't have to. You're one of the easier people to read, really, just because there's no artifice to you. What you see is what you get with you. Your girlfriend is a different story, though. She's pretty complex, but I'm really starting to get to pick up on her story as well. I love that girl, but she's capable of great deceit, much more than you. Step lightly there."

I felt that I needed to defend Dalilah. "She was only deceitful to save me. You shouldn't say that about her."

"You act like being deceitful is always a bad thing. Trust me, it has its positive uses. Case in point," she said, flashing her fake badge at me. "I think if Dalilah were here with me, she'd be as unruffled as a military bunk bed. She has that ability to cover up what's really going on with her. You, not so much."

"How do you know…" I said, but I never got to finish my sentence, for Mikael came through the door at just that instance. Serena and I both rose to our feet to greet the hulking man, who was dressed in a leather g-string, with gladiator shoes and two leather belts that criss-crossed his hairy chest. He was around 6'5" and at least 220 lbs of solid muscle. He definitely looked like somebody who would be capable of roughing up Nottingham.

I tried hard to stifle a smile, as I imagined this guy working over the stiff, prim and proper Nottingham, while Nottingham begged him for more. I looked over at Serena, but her face, as it had been that entire time we were there, was impassive.

"Hello," the Hulk said. "You're here to talk to me?"

"Yes," Serena said, all business. "My name is Detective

Robinowitz and this is my partner, Detective Stetson. We're here to talk to you about a man whom you might know as Luke Roberts. I understand he's a regular here."

Mikael looked at both of us suspiciously. "We try to keep our clients' identities confidential. That's the only way that a place like this can stay in business. Once our clients know that we're willing to sell them out, then this place will not be in business much longer."

"Okay, let me give this to you straight. Your business is already under investigation for allowing minors in this door. You've already invited close scrutiny for that. If you don't give us what we want, this scrutiny will be stepped up. How long do you think that you'll be in business after our sex crimes division gets through with you? Now, I can call off the dogs, but only if you dance. I need an authorized statement from you that this man, whose name is Blake Nottingham by the way, not Luke Roberts, was here on the night of the 18th, and you beat him badly at his request. I'm going to show you some pictures, and I need for you to make an authorized statement that you were the one who caused the injuries in these pictures." Serena got out the pictures, and showed Mikael them, and I could tell by his expression that he was the one who roughed up Nottingham, for he looked non-plussed. "Make an authorized statement, or risk being shut down. Your choice."

"We don't want no trouble," he said.

"Then give us what we need."

Dayum, Serena was good.

The poor guy knew that he was defeated. He looked at the pictures again, and then reluctantly said "okay, I'll sign whatever statement you need me to sign."

I bit my lip. I almost felt sorry for this guy, and for this club, because Nottingham was going to raise an absolute stink if he ever found out what transpired here. I hoped and prayed, really, that he never did find out. He shouldn't, anyhow. He should only be able to find out that the prosecutors dropped my charges to a misdemeanor, and that would be that.

Serena gave him a statement that she and I had prepared that essentially said that Nottingham's injuries were sustained by Mikael that evening. Mikael signed it, and Serena notarized it. She told me beforehand that she actually was a legitimate notary in the State of New York. That was one legitimate thing that went down.

"Thank you," Serena said. "My partner and I will see our way out."

Mikael nodded, and, as Serena and I were leaving, I looked back and saw him and Mistress Claire arguing. I would imagine that Mikael probably wasn't supposed to fold like an accordion, because I saw him make gestures to her that essentially said *what was I supposed to do?*

We passed by the same rooms that we passed on our way in, and I saw a woman on the medical exam table being surrounded by three different people who were busy giving her breast and gynecological exams while her feet and hands were tied up. That was an odd fetish for me, just because every girl I knew who went through that sort of thing absolutely hated it. But, then again, I didn't think that having a person tug on a nipple chain would be the most pleasant experience in the world, but lots of people would beg to differ.

Serena and I got into her Porsche, statement in hand. After we were a safe distance away, I put my hand on her shoulder. "Hey, uh, thanks. I really owe you."

"Yeah, you do," she said. "After all, I don't think that I can go to that place now." But then she smiled. "Kidding.

My kink runs just a little bit less towards pain, although I really do enjoy being bound and humiliated."

"TMI," I said. "But, really, you didn't have to do that for me."

"Don't thank me yet. This notarized statement might or might not get those charges dropped. You might have to get that lawyer of yours to send an actual investigator over, and have their records subpoenaed. I don't know, legally, what's necessary to accomplish what you need, but, with any luck, this might be enough. At any rate, this statement gives James probable cause to issue a subpoena, I would think."

"How did you know about them admitting minors?"

"I didn't. I just figured that they probably did, though. You might say that I got lucky, but, really, that wasn't such a wild hunch. That's probably why that club is underground in the first place."

"And how do you know so much about legalities and all of that?"

"Jack of all trades, master of none. I know a little about a lot, unlike your girlfriend, who knows a lot about a lot."

"Yeah, she does, but how do you know about all of that?"

"She's an old soul. Has lived many lives. Carries the knowledge of these lives with her, which is really unusual. How do you supposed Mozart composed all those wonderful symphonies, starting from the age of 5? He probably had many past lives in which he was a musician, and he was somehow able to retain the knowledge of his previous selves."

I really didn't know what to say to her rambling.

"You don't believe," she said. "What, are you agnostic? Atheist? Believe in heaven and hell?"

"I don't know what I believe. I guess I'm agnostic." This conversation was certainly taking a turn for the surreal.

"Well, for what it's worth, with your talent, I think that you're probably an old soul, too. Lived the life of an artist over many generations and incarnations."

"How do you know about my talent?"

"Come on. I've been following your career for years. I've talked you up to some pretty important people. They usually have given you a shot, even if they didn't entirely pan out like you might have hoped. But hang in there. That show you had opened some doors, even if it doesn't seem like it."

"How do you know-" I began, and then stopped. I was starting to realize that Serena just knew. There was really no point in wondering how or why. It just was. "I'm sorry, Serena, I have to process all of this. You've talked about me to important people? I mean, I have gotten some pretty good bites over the past year or so, places where I thought that I would have a commission or two, and sometimes I got something. Nothing like what happened with that show, though."

"Well, win some, lose some. The point is, you're on your way now, even if you don't really feel like it. Talk to me in a year. You'll be in a much better position."

"Well, hopefully in a year I won't be in prison, thanks to you. I never would've thought…"

"What, that I'm actually human and I really do love you and Mark, Chris, Amy and dad? I've acted like a shit all of these years to you guys, and I really didn't do much to help myself over the holidays, as much as I promised myself before I got there that I was going to make an effort to show everyone that I'm in the process of changing. Changing is always a process, too, never a destination. The second you think of change as being a destination is the second that you're gonna backslide." She shook her head. "I really wanted to open up, but, somehow, I only ended up opening up to Dalilah. And that's because I recognized that she was going to understand me. But maybe there's a chance for you and me yet."

"There is," I said, putting my hand on her shoulder. "There is, Serena."

She smiled. "Well, kid, we're back at your place."

"Would you like to come up and have a beer? See Dalilah?"

She shook her head. "Early morning tomorrow, but thanks. Besides, I don't think that Dalilah has been feeling so good."

"She hasn't. She seems to be under the weather somehow."

She nodded. "Under the weather. Well, kid, hopefully you won't be a stranger, huh? If you need me for anything, you know where to find me now."

"I won't be a stranger," I said. "I promise."

And I somehow knew that I would be as good as my word.

Chapter Forty-Nine

Dalilah

I was actually happy to have the evening off. It had been almost two weeks since the night that I think that I might have conceived, and, sure enough, there were apparently enough hormones in my body to finally turn the pee stick pink. Now, there was no doubt in my mind about my situation, and, quite frankly, I was really confused about what to do.

Great. This is just great. 1% of pill users get pregnant if they never miss a single pill, and you're one of the lucky ones. I sighed, knowing that this had to be fate. There was no way around it. But that didn't mean that I wasn't tempted to go into a doctor and get a procedure before anybody would be the wiser.

You can't do that, Dalilah. This is Luke's baby. Of that, I was sure. There was just something in my gut that told me that the baby was going to be Luke's, even if Nottingham would legally have the right to him or her.

I made a mental note to see an attorney in the morning, first thing, to see exactly what my options were. I had already researched enough on the Internet, though, to know. Nottingham would be the presumed father, and, if he wanted to halt a DNA test to prove that he wasn't, then he had the power to do so. Granted, a court could order a DNA test if I requested one, but something told me that Nottingham would fight that with a high-powered attorney, and just might win. Best interest of the child and all of that. The judge would have discretion on whether or not a DNA test would be warranted.

I really had gotten myself into quite a pickle, and I cursed fate. *Why couldn't you have waited until I divorced that bastard?* I asked, shaking my fist at nothingness. *Seriously? Why now? I could have gotten a quickie divorce in a matter of months, and then I would be home free. But no. You choose now.*

I felt like screaming in frustration.

What next? What was going to happen next? When was that stupid Nottingham going to be cleanly out of my life? Out of Luke's life?

Never, that was when. Never, never, never, never. If he wasn't trying to destroy Luke by framing him for causing injuries that didn't happen, he was trying to destroy Luke by turning all of his powerful friends against him in the art world. And, once he got through with ripping Luke to shreds, he was going to turn on me and the unborn baby whom he was going to claim. I knew that as sure as I sat there on that couch.

I looked into the future and saw Nottingham destroying mine and Luke's child with his depravity and his cruelty. Hating that child because he was going to know that the child didn't belong to him. Taking all of his anger, which he no doubt harbored because I rejected him, out on this child.

He was going to be delighted to know that there was an impending baby, for no other reason than the fact that he was going to know that he would finally be able to exact his revenge upon me.

I couldn't let that happen. I just couldn't.

But I couldn't terminate Luke's child. I couldn't live with myself.

I was certainly in another dilemma. It seemed that ever since I met that horrible man, I was going from the frying pan into the fire constantly. Just when I thought that everything was going to work out, something else happened to ensure that I was going to continually pay for my original sin of leading Nottingham on in order to help Luke.

Chapter Fifty

Luke finally got home, and he presented the first piece of good news that I had in awhile. "Well, we got it," he said, coming over to me on the couch. "We got the statement. I need to get that to James ASAP and see what has to happen next. Hopefully the prosecutor will just take it and reduce the charges, but Serena said that there's the possibility that the records that showed that Nottingham was there that night will have to be subpoenaed. But you'll never guess what alias he uses while he's there."

I raised an eyebrow. "Luke Roberts?"

Luke looked at me with his mouth open. "How did you know?"

"Sounds like something he would do. He really wants to make trouble for you everywhere he goes, doesn't he?"

"That's just what Serena said."

"Well, Serena is a wise, wise woman. You need to listen to her."

"I am. She's not so bad. I think that she might actually be a part of my life from now on. Imagine that. Serena, a part of my life." He looked excited. "Dalilah, I can feel it. I can feel that we're coming out of this nightmare, and things are going to come together. I'm going to get those charges reduced, and I'm not going to have to pay James $50,000, more like $5,000, so I'm going to have some money to maybe move you and me to the city in a few months. We're both going to make a killing in the art world. I have a feeling that Serena might be able to help, of all people. She seems to know people. Important people. Things are turning a corner, Dalilah. I know it. I can feel it. Can't you feel it?"

I didn't have the heart to tell him about what was really going on. So, I just smiled and said "you're right, Luke. We're almost out of it."

"Yeah. Now, tomorrow, I need to see James, and you need to see a family law attorney about getting a quickie divorce from that bastard. Hopefully, in a few days, well, not a few days, it's almost New Year's Eve, but after the New Year, things are really going to be new for us. New, Dalilah. You and me against the world, huh? You and me against the world."

You and me against the world. Oh, Luke, if you only knew how wrong you are.

Still, I just smiled. "You and me against the world."

Chapter Fifty-One

Luke

I was very worried about Dalilah, for she seemed to not be able to shake her lethargy, nausea and malaise. If anything, she seemed to be getting worse by the day. But, when I offered to take her to a doctor, she begged off every time.

"It's nothing, Luke. I feel fine," she would say as she picked through her food and pushed it away.

"Maybe you have mono. That's pretty common in people our age." I went over to feel her head, and she didn't seem to have a fever. "Well, maybe not. I would think that you'd have some kind of temperature."

"Luke, don't worry about me. Now, go and see James with that statement. He's in the office today, but won't be tomorrow, as tomorrow is New Year's Eve. So, skedaddle. I would love to come with you, but I'm so sorry, I'm having problems just getting out of bed today. But I love you, and I'll see you when you get back."

I nodded my head. "I'll be back as soon as I see James."

I made a mental note to stop by a Jewish deli and bring back Dalilah some hot chicken soup. That always did the trick for me when I was sick.

So, as I made my way to James' office on the interminable subway ride, I was feeling hopeful and strangely pessimistic at the same time. Something wasn't quite right this morning. I could feel it in the air with Dalilah. It wasn't just that she was sick, it was that she was hiding something from me. Of course, when I saw her last night, I was so on top of the world after having gotten that statement that I didn't even think about the fact that Dalilah seemed off.

I shook my head. The last time I had a bad feeling about Dalilah, and tried to ignore it, she ended up dumping me. Oh, god, was that about to go down again? After we fought to get back together – in my case, literally fought – would it all go to shit again?

I took a deep breath, and tried to calm myself. She wasn't going to dump me again. She wasn't going to dump me again. I had to repeat that to myself a hundred times, as I closed my eyes and tried to block out everything around me. But I couldn't fight the bad feeling that had suddenly come over me. The feeling that something was indelibly wrong.

I finally got to James' office, and waited for him to be ready for me. I had explained to him earlier in the morning that I would be by his office, because I had a piece of information that would be helpful for him. He agreed to meet with me for fifteen minutes, because he had to wedge me into his schedule. I gave him mental props for being able to see me last minute.

The receptionist finally told me that James was ready, so I walked on back there and had a seat. I fingered my manila folder in my hand, the folder that hopefully held the key to my freedom.

"Okay," James said. "What do you have for me?"

I took a deep breath. "I have an alternative explanation for Nottingham's injuries," I said. "He goes to a BDSM club, well fetish club, really, and he went in there on the night that I punched him and asked to be worked over by this guy who goes by the name of Mikael. And, well, I got a notarized statement from Mikael that this is what went down."

"Let me see that," James said, and I handed it to him, and he examined it. "Well, this certainly wouldn't be admissible in court, this statement, not unless this Mikael took the stand. But, it might do for the prosecutor on this case. Between you and me, the prosecutor, Jamal, has no love for this case anyhow. I talked to him and told him what you told me, and he says that sounds about right. You're clean, other than this assault case, so that helps you, too." He sighed. "Worst-case scenario, I have to subpoena the records, but I don't want to have to do that, especially since these people rarely use their own names in these kinds of clubs."

"So, you think that things might be okay?"

"This certainly helps. How did you get this statement, anyhow?"

"Well, I can tell you, because it will be confidential. But my sister has these fake police badges and…"

"Oh, no, say no more, please. I don't want to know. Sorry I asked." He put his fingers to his temples, like he suddenly had a severe headache. "Oh, what the hell, go on with the story. It's not like you're confessing to your crime or something like that."

I looked at him quizzically.

"You know, because if you confess guilt, then I can't put

you on the stand, knowing you're about to perjure yourself if you try to say otherwise. Ever wonder why defendants often don't take the stand? That would be a big reason why. That's also why attorneys never want to know for sure whether or not their client is guilty. But go on."

Fascinating. I momentarily lost my train of thought. "Oh, so if you have a murder client and you want to put him on the stand to say that he didn't do it, you can't put him on the stand if he tells you that he really did do it?"

"Yeah. It's called suborning perjury. But, please, go on with your story."

"Yes, my story. Well, my sister has these fake police badges, and we went in there and shook Mikael down, basically. That was how we got a statement out of him."

James' mouth went into a grimace. "Well, that's illegal as hell, as you probably know, and now this statement really won't be allowed in court. And I now don't have probable cause to subpoena those records. So, I wish that I'd stopped you before you could tell me all of this. Ah, but then again, it's better it comes out now than be embarrassed by it later."

"This statement isn't probable cause for a subpoena?"

"No. Fruit from a poisonous tree, we call it. When things are obtained illegally, then they can't support probable cause for anything. Law 101, really."

"You mean, my sister and I did all of that for nothing?"

"Not for nothing. I mean, Jamal just might take your statement without question. Between you and me, though, I'll be putting my license and ass on the line by giving him that statement. But Jamal and I work pretty well together most of the time, and he owes me a few favors. It's a gamble, though, for sure."

My heart started to sink. This wasn't a slam dunk, after all.

James shook his head. "You really didn't think this through, did you?"

"I don't understand?"

"You went in there with your sister. You're the defendant in this case! Didn't you think for even one second that it would all blow up in your face if this thing ever came to trial? Could you imagine – I'd have to call Mikael to the stand to testify about Nottingham being in that club, and he'd take one look at you, and the jig would be up, my friend. The jig would be up."

"Well, I had on a disguise," I said. "I wore these enormous glasses, had a fake beard and moustache and wore a hat."

"Oh, well, there's that. At least you did that much." He shook his head and chuckled. "And here I was imagining that you went on in there as easy as you please, with no disguise at all."

I felt embarrassed that James thought of me as so callow. But, then again, I *was* callow. I felt that way sometimes, even though Serena insisted that I was an old soul who had lived many lives.

"So," I said, "you're going to get in touch with the prosecutor and see if the charges can be reduced?"

"Yeah, I'm going to do that right now, if you don't mind. Let me scan in this statement, and I can email it to Jamal. I know that he's not in the office the entire day because of tomorrow being New Year's Eve and all, and I also know that you probably have zero desire to have this hanging over your head during your holiday. What are you doing for New Year's, incidentally?" he asked, as he scanned in Mikael's statement.

I thought about Dalilah, and how bad she was feeling. "I don't know. Dalilah doesn't seem to be doing so good these days. We might just stay in and order take-out, like we did for my birthday."

He nodded his head. "Sometimes that's more fun than fighting the crowds, anyhow. I did Times Square one year, and I swore, never again," he said with a smile. "Now, let me call Jamal."

I held my breath, praying that Jamal was actually in the office.

"Hey, Jamal," James said. "I need to talk to you about a case you have. A Luke Roberts....yes, well, apparently your victim went to a BDSM club on the night that he went to the ER and got himself beat up there, and tried to frame my client for the serious injuries...emailing you the statement right now," he said, as he clicked his mouse.

James mouthed to me "he's looking for your file now." He swiveled around in his chair while holding the phone, and hummed lightly. "On hold," he said. "Man, they need to update their hold music."

I smiled. I could relate to that. Everybody could, really.

"So," James said, his phone to his ear as he addressed me. "You're staying out of trouble this New Year's. I'm probably going to end up looking for trouble myself." Then he smiled. "Not really, just kidding." He shook his head. "Boy, when you told me about how you obtained that statement I..."

Then he turned his attention to the phone. "Yes, Jamal. You got the statement and you have the file....oh, come on, give the kid a break. It's his first offense, and he was standing up for his girlfriend. He just turned 21....come on, you don't have to go through all that trouble, subpoenaing those records. The statement was authenticated...okay, that's probably going to be great. But I'll call you back and let you know…you have a good New Year's, too, and I'll talk to you soon."

At that, he got off the phone and smiled at me broadly. "Am I a miracle worker, or what? Jamal will drop the burglary charge and reduce both of your assault charges to misdemeanors. He was going to do some independent investigation, but he's pretty swamped, and, quite frankly, he's happy to have one less major case to worry about."

My heart did somersaults. "Really? Misdemeanors and no burglary? Really?"

"Really. If you want to take that deal, we can set it up on the docket for tomorrow morning. The court is taking pleas for half the day tomorrow before knocking off for the holiday."

"Oh, hell to the yeah," I blurted out, wishing that I had Dalilah next to me to share in my joy. "Call him back, let's set up a plea."

At that, James called Jamal back, and gave me the thumb's up. He got off the phone. "Tomorrow morning, 9 AM. You know where the courthouse is, right? Meet me there at Division 28, and don't be late."

I nodded my head rapidly, wanting to hug James. "Tomorrow at 9. Tomorrow at 9. I'll see you then."

As I left his office, I thought *things are finally looking up for sure. It's going to be a great New Year's after all.*

I excitedly went home to Dalilah, and burst through the door.

But, to my surprise, she wasn't alone. A handsome man, about 50 years old, was sitting on my couch with her. I didn't recognize him at all, and I was momentarily jealous. Dalilah, however, didn't seem to jump when I came home, so I assumed that I had nothing to worry about.

"Luke," Dalilah said, as the man got up off the couch. "I'd like you to meet my father's oldest friend, Nick."

Chapter Fifty-Two

Dalilah

Once Luke left, I knew that I had to do something. I couldn't just sit around, worrying. Yet I didn't have the energy to get off of the couch and go into the city and see a lawyer. So, I did the next best thing – I called Nick.

"Dalilah," he said, his voice friendly. "Long time, no hear."

I started to talk into the phone, but nothing but a sob came out at first. "Uncle Nick, I need to talk to you. I need your advice so bad right now."

"I'll be right there. Where are you?"

I gave him the address. "You're not working right now?"

"Nothing important. It's almost New Year's. Everybody's in down mode right now. Give me forty-five minutes and I'll be there. I'll get Charlie to drive me."

So, Nick appeared at my place within the hour. "So," he said. "What's the emergency?"

"I'm sorry, I didn't know who else to call," I said, feeling guilty that I didn't want to call Alaina for this. I loved Alaina, and she and I were trying to mend fences, but, for this dilemma, I needed somebody with experience and a sure hand.

"Okay," he said. "By the way, I love you, but you look like hell. Have you been sick?"

"No. Not sick. Just pregnant."

Nick looked at me quizzically. "Well, I can certainly see where that would be unwelcome news at your age and your…" And then it seemed to dawn on him. "Oh, shit. It's not-"

"I don't think so. I honestly think that it's Luke's. The timing makes me think that, plus I just have an intuition about it. But that doesn't matter. Nottingham is going to have claims to the baby, just because I'm still married to him. He's the presumed father under the law."

"A rebuttable presumption. Don't forget that. A DNA test can clear all that up."

I shook my head. "No. Not if the judge decides that's not in the best interest of the child. I mean, I could get a private DNA test, sure, but the judge has discretion on whether to allow that. And you know that Nottingham will get the best attorney in the city to fight it. You know that. He hates me. He hates Luke. He wants to destroy both of us, and this baby will be the perfect opportunity to do so."

"I have no doubt on what you're saying. But what are your options here? Your plans?"

I took a deep breath. "Do you think that I should terminate?" And, at that, I just started bawling. Nick wrapped his arms around me, and held me as I cried. "Oh, god, I haven't said that word aloud to anyone yet. I can't do it. I just can't do it. This is Luke's child, I know it. I know it. I can feel it. What am I going to do?"

"Shhhh, Dalilah. You can't look at this emotionally. I suppose that's why you called me. I can objectively assess the situation."

"Of course. Of course. But I can't not look at this emotionally. This could be the perfect situation if Nottingham weren't involved. I mean, yeah, Luke and I are young, but we're also very much in love. And he gets me. He wants to give me the world, and he'll be a great dad. He's so even-tempered and level-headed." *Well, except for the fact that he punched Nottingham, but no need to go into that.*

"I hate to even ask this, but, I hope that you weren't careless enough to not use protection while you're still married to Nottingham."

"Of course I wasn't careless. I've been on the pill for quite awhile. Been taking it faithfully, every single night before bed. So, I don't know what happened, except that I apparently am one of the unlucky ones who got pregnant anyhow. There's like a 1% failure rate, and I'm apparently in that 1%."

Nick nodded. "Not that it would have made a difference if you were being careless, but glad to know that you weren't."

"Okay, so what do I do? Have the baby and gamble that the judge won't let Nottingham have rights? Or do I do the unthinkable without telling Luke? That would certainly be cleaner. I would be able to divorce Nottingham and have no ties to him, and move on with my life with Luke. That's all I want, Uncle Nick, is to move on with my life. Start fresh with Luke. Leave this whole sorry chapter behind me, and just look ahead to a bright future."

I put my head in my hands. "Oh, but that sounds so selfish and cold. What am I saying? I'm going to abort Luke's child so that I can get away from Nottingham cleanly? Really? Is that the person that I've become?"

"I hate to say it, Dalilah, but I think that you've made your decision. It sounds that way, anyhow."

"What would you do? April comes to you with a problem like this. What would you advise?"

"I'm the wrong person to ask about this. I've lost a child. Not the same thing, of course, not the same thing at all. But, take it from me, it's one of the most devastating things in the world."

I nodded my head, trying to tamp down my nauseated feeling in my gut. I had no idea if that nauseated feeling came from being pregnant or from being in this awful dilemma. I rubbed my stomach, but it did no good. "Excuse me," I said. "I'll be right back." And, at that, I ran to the bathroom and puked. I shook my head. *It's starting this soon, the morning sickness? It's going to be a long nine months.*

I came back and sat on the couch. "Why can't things just go smoothly? What's wrong with me?"

"Well, you got involved with the wrong guy. You got involved with a devious, manipulative and callous man. It's not really your fault, Dalilah. You're young. You're probably the most intelligent person I know, book-smart wise, but you still have lots to learn about the world and about human nature. It just goes to show that a psychopath can suck just about anybody into his web."

I nodded my head. Once again, I was uncertain. Nick was right. Nottingham *was* a psychopath. Did I want to take the chance that a man like that would have rights to this kid? How would that be fair to the child, bringing him or her into the world, only to lose the child to Nottingham's manipulations and games?

I was in an impossible situation, no doubt about it. And, surprisingly, Nick was of no help. I thought that he could help me bring clarity to the situation, but he really wasn't able to. Still, it was good to talk to somebody about it. Get the words out in the open, even if Nick had no good advice about what to do.

"Well, Luke will be home any minute. Whatever happens, I can't talk to him until I make a decision. I hate to say it, but, if I decide to, you know, I probably will never tell him that I was ever pregnant. That's shitty of me, though, isn't it? I just think that some things are better off not being known, though."

"It's up to you, Dalilah. But, just remember, it was keeping secrets from Luke that got you into this whole mess in the first place. You have a good guy, there. I'm quite sure that he'll be more than willing to be by your side, whatever you do."

I shook my head. "Not with this. I can't see how he would ever forgive me if he knew the truth. That is, if I decide to terminate. How could we possibly move forward? The whole point of doing something like that would be so that Luke and I could move forward together, cleanly, without any Damocles swords hanging over our heads. No, I'll make that decision on my own. Of course, if I decide to keep the baby, then Luke will be a part of the team. We'll fight this thing together. I hope that you and dad will also be, of course."

"Goes without saying."

I shivered. "Dad will want to kill me, though. He was so against the whole Nottingham marriage to begin with. I'm quite certain that he'll be thinking that I brought all of this on myself. And he wouldn't be far wrong."

"Don't forget your mother."

"Oh, I know. I know. She's at her wits end with me, though. Mom and I have never seen eye to eye, I'm sorry to say. God love her, but she doesn't understand me, and I think, sometimes, I drive her up a tree."

Nick smiled. "That's what you're supposed to do. Drive your mom and dad up a tree. Make them worry every minute of every day about how you're fucking up your life. Just remember that they went through their fair share of mis-steps, to say the least, so I'm quite sure that they relate more than you know."

"Yeah. Well, mom never considered aborting me. I mean, she was afraid and alone and didn't really know who my father was while she was pregnant with me. But she stuck it out. She was strong." I shook my head. "Maybe I need to be strong, too. Maybe that's just what I need to do."

I got up and paced. "God, this is an impossible situation. It is."

Nick patted the couch. "Sit down, Dalilah. Sit down, and let's think this whole thing through."

But, just then, Luke came through the door.

I made the introductions, and Luke was friendly with Nick, and Nick was the same with Luke. Then Luke said to me "Dalilah, uh, can I talk to you? In the kitchen?"

"Sure," I said. I turned to Nick, and he waved at me as if to say *don't mind me. Pretend I'm not here.*

Luke and I got to the kitchen. "What is it?" I asked him.

"I'm pleading tomorrow to a misdemeanor assault. Two misdemeanor assaults. I'm not sure what the judge will do with that, but I'll probably pay a fine and be done. Isn't that fantastic?"

My heart leaped with joy for Luke, and, for a brief moment, my awful dilemma was forgotten. "Oh, that's great, Luke. I knew it. I knew that you could get out of it." I kissed him on his cheek. "That's like the best news I've heard in a long time."

"I know. I can't believe our little plan worked. I have to call Serena to tell her the good news. I honestly don't think that I could have done it without her."

"You do that," I said. And, at that, Luke dialed the phone and talked to his sister. I went back to the couch and sat next to Nick, who was busy trying to look like he was not listening to a word that Luke and I were saying.

Luke got off the phone, and Nick said "well, Dalilah, I probably should be going. I'll be in contact with you, okay?"

"Yes, thanks, Nick." I gave him a hug, and he left.

Luke looked at me questioningly. "Nice guy, at least he seems like it," was all he said. I knew that he wanted to question me on why Nick was here, but he didn't. And I didn't volunteer the information, either, as I honestly had no idea what to tell him.

"He is. So, tomorrow. I hope that I'm feeling up to going to court with you. I'd really like to support you."

Luke tousled my hair, and brought my head onto his chest. As always, I smelled his cologne and felt his hard pecs, and I was instantly comforted. Luke just had a way of calming me down, no matter what kind of circumstances were facing us. "I brought you some chicken soup," he said, bringing out a sack and a little cardboard cup with a lid. He got up and got a regular bowl, and poured the soup into it. "It should still be hot," he said, bringing it over to me on the couch.

I was touched by his gesture, really, even though I

thought that the soup probably wouldn't help. "Thanks, Luke, that's very sweet of you."

"Well, I have to take care of my girl."

God, I hate having secrets from him again. I swore, the last time, that I would no longer keep secrets from him.

But I had to keep this secret, at least until I figured out which route to take.

Chapter Fifty-Three

Luke

The next day, I went with Dalilah down to the courthouse, an enormous art deco structure in Midtown. We went to the division where I was supposed to plea, and realized that there were hundreds of others who were in his same position. Luckily, James was there, waiting for me. "Don't be intimidated by this big crowd," he said. "We're fifth on the docket, so we won't be here long."

I nodded and squeezed Dalilah's hand. "What do you think is going to happen? What will this judge give me, as far as a sentence goes?"

"Jamal is recommending one year probation, no fines. Basically, as long as you keep your nose clean for a year, you'll be okay. If something happens during that year, though, and you get into trouble, then you will not only be facing some kind of jail time for this offense, but you also will be facing the penalties for your new one. So, please, Luke, don't get into trouble for that one year."

"I won't," I said. "I'm generally not a trouble-maker. This was the exception."

"Of course," he said. "I know you're clean, which is why I was able to work this deal for you. I'm a little surprised that Jamal agreed to the deal so easily, but, then again, not really. He's dealing with people who have a rap sheet a mile long, so, as I said, he had no love for this case and was happy to see it gone."

Holding Dalilah's hand, we went inside the courtroom and had a seat. As we waited for the judge to appear, we sat, silently. Finally, the judge did appear and began the docket. He called several cases, and each person went up and pled guilty, and the judge pronounced their sentences. My name was called, and I went up to the bench with James.

"Luke Roberts, you have been charged by the State of New York with two counts of misdemeanor assault. How do you plead?"

"Guilty, your honor."

The judge nodded his head. "Upon recommendation of the prosecutor's office, you will serve one year in the county jail. Your sentence will be suspended, contingent upon completing one year of probation. The conditions of your probation are that you will complete an anger management course and you will obey all laws of the State of New York. And good luck to you." At that, I walked away from the bench and followed James outside of the courtroom.

"My heart almost stopped when that judge said that I was going to jail for a year. You probably should have warned me about that."

"Yes, I apologize. Basically, though, if you violate probation, you will serve your sentence in the county jail. So, please, stay clean. I'll also give you the information that you need to enroll in your anger management course."

I shook James' hand. "Thanks," I said. "For everything. And, you don't have to worry. I'll make sure that I stay clean for the year. In fact, I'll make sure that I stay clean from now on."

James smiled. "I believe you. Have a good holiday."

"You, too."

Dalilah and I then left the courthouse. "Well, Dalilah, the nightmare is almost over for us. Now, let's concentrate on you getting your divorce, and we can truly move on."

Dalilah nodded her head, and said nothing.

I furrowed my brow. Something was going on with her, still.

I was scared to death to find out what.

Chapter Fifty-Four

Dalilah

Five Days Later

There was one good thing that came out of Nick's visiting me – he was able to give me the name of a highly-recommended attorney who was familiar with Nottingham. That was important to me – to find an attorney who literally knew what I would be facing if I kept this child. And I had to make a decision, soon, because Luke was starting to get suspicious and had been harassing me about seeing a doctor. I guessed that he was relieved from the stress from his criminal case, he was able to concentrate more on my problems.

"Come on, Dalilah, you've been feeling like crap for weeks now," he said. "I think it's about time that we go in for some tests. I've been reading on the Internet, and it sounds like you might have some kind of virus. Epstein-Barr is something that I've been reading about. It causes mono, which is another thing that I worry about, but it also causes problems all on its own. Or chronic fatigue syndrome. I don't know, Dalilah, there's something wrong, and I think that we need to find out what it is."

"Luke, please, I don't want to see a doctor right now. Just give me a few days, and I think that I'll be feeling better."

"Okay, but if you are still feeling crappy by the end of the week, you're going."

"Agreed."

So, I knew that I had to see an attorney as soon as I could. Nick arranged for this attorney to fit me in, because Marissa Herschel was the most sought-after family law attorney in the city. I was grateful that she had an opening, and I was able to squeeze in.

I got to her office, and went right back to see her. She was a petite woman, only about 5'2" and a little over 100 lbs. With her black hair in a tight bun, glasses and conservative clothing, she looked like a kindly aunt. But I knew her reputation, which was that of a ball-buster, so I knew that appearance belied her underlying true grit.

"Dalilah," she said, "have a seat. I know that you were referred here by Nick O'Hara, so I'm really glad that I was able to fit you in."

I sat down. "I'm really glad that you could fit me in as well."

She looked at me with a smile. "So, tell me why you're here."

"I need a divorce and I also need legal advice."

"Well, you've certainly come to the right place."

"I specifically need advice about the man that I'm married to, Blake Nottingham."

At that, Marissa's demeanor changed. "Blake Notting-

290

ham. Well, what can I tell you? He has Steve Singleton as his attorney on permanent retainer. I don't know if you know the reputation of attorneys in this town, but Singleton is known to be the most aggressive."

"Okay. Well, let me tell you my situation. I'm pregnant. I don't think that the baby will belong to Nottingham, because I'm with somebody else. Somebody else whom I love very much. This other guy, I think he's the father."

Marissa nodded. "Well, as you probably are aware, Nottingham will be presumed to be the father of the baby in this situation, but that's a rebuttable presumption."

"Yes, I understand that," I said. "You know Nottingham and you know this Steve Singleton. I understand all about judicial discretion and best interest of the child standards and all of that. How likely do you think that Nottingham will have claims on this child, even if DNA definitively proves that the baby isn't his?"

"There's different factors to take into consideration," she said. "What judge we would get is a large factor. Unfortunately, Mr. Nottingham is very friendly with most of the judges on the bench, but there are a few that he isn't friendly with. And there are judges who would be much more likely to allow DNA evidence to rebut the presumption than other judges. Because some of the judges are old-school and believe that a child born of the marriage is a child born of the marriage, while others have a more liberal attitude. It really will be the luck of the draw in this situation. I wish I could be more definitive, but that's the way it is with judicial discretion."

"Okay. Best-case scenario."

"I would give you a fifty-percent chance of prevailing and being able to rebut the presumption of paternity."

"Worst-case."

Marissa screwed up her mouth. "Worst case, we get a judge who not only is friendly with Mr. Nottingham but is also old-school. If that happens, I would say you have very little chance of prevailing. Maybe a 2% chance in that case."

"And that's assuming that Nottingham's attorney doesn't play any kind of dirty tricks." I knew *that* would be a part of the bargain.

"Well, his attorney, Mr. Singleton, is certainly known for his aggressiveness. You definitely have to take that into account as well."

I nodded my head. "Well, I think that you gave me the information I need. How much do I owe you?"

"Nothing. I'm doing this as a favor to Nick. But if you decide to hire me, then I do charge $400 an hour."

I knew that was really a discounted rate, probably because of her close ties with Nick. "Thank you. You've been very helpful."

I trudged out of her office, and took a deep breath. It was freezing, so I pulled my coat tightly around me and, shivering, I went into a coffee shop and ordered some treats.

I was putting off the inevitable, but I was more clear, after talking to Marissa, on what it was that I had to do.

I sat at the coffee shop, though, because I wanted to be the person that I was just a little bit longer. There would be no turning back after I made my decision. I would be a woman who terminated a pregnancy. I didn't know how indelibly changed I would be if I did this. I didn't know if I could look in the mirror after this, let alone sleep at night.

But there was one thing that I did know. It all became clear to me as I sat there in that coffee shop, contemplating my options over a cake pop and cup of hot cocoa. There was no way that I could do this and hide it from Luke. That would be an absolute recipe for disaster. There would be, forevermore, something between us, and he would never quite know exactly what that something was.

But it would be something that might end up destroying us.

I took a deep breath. My hands were shaking, and I could feel the tears threatening. Too many tears wasted on a psychopath. I made a mental note not to shed another tear about anything that man did to me. Not to mention to Luke. *No more tears, Dalilah. He's not worth it.*

Luke had to be a part of it. He either was going to hate me, or he was going to understand. Most likely he would hate me. But I would surely hate myself if I didn't tell him, and I could tell that I would also end up irrationally blaming him. I didn't want to lash out in anger and frustration, when the only person that I should be angry and frustrated with would be myself. The air needed to be cleared, and he had to be there with me. It was his baby, too, so we would have to do our grieving together. It was the only path forward, and I was glad that I at least came to that conclusion. God forbid I didn't. God forbid.

My heart was in my throat. I had to make the phone call that I hoped never to.

"Luke," I said, picking up the phone. "We need to talk."

Next in the Fearless series

vinci-books.com/trapped

She's trapped in a dangerous game with her devious husband. Will her unborn child pay the price?

Dalilah Gallagher's unexpected pregnancy while still married to the conniving Nottingham has left her feeling cornered. With Nottingham believing he's the father, Dalilah knows she must find a way to shield her baby from his malicious influence.

Turn the page for a free preview…

Trapped: Chapter One

Luke

Dalilah had just called me, and, once again, I started to feel apprehensive. I hated that she just said those words again – that we need to talk. The last time she said something like that to me, she dumped me. At any rate, those words sounded just ominous to me.

"Okay, Dalilah, are you coming home, or would you like to meet me somewhere?"

"I'm in the city," she said. "Could you meet me on the corner of 5th and Park? I'm in a *Starbucks* here. I'm so sorry, I would like to come home, but I need to stay in the city, too. There's something that I need to do, and I need you by my side to do it."

That sounded more encouraging to me. That she needed me by her side, as opposed to something else. I relaxed a little bit. "Okay, I'll be there. Just give me about an hour or so. I'll see you in a bit."

"Luke?"

"Yes?"

"I love you. I really, really do." At that, she started to cry softly, and I got concerned. What was going on? Did she see a doctor without telling me? Was she really sick?

"I love you too. I'll see you in a few."

I shook my head as I got into the shower and got dressed. It was my dream that we had made it through our traumas, and came out the other side. But did we? Was there something else, something worse than ever, which greeted us? I couldn't imagine what that would be, but Dalilah wasn't the kind of person who would just start crying for no reason at all.

My apprehension grew as I boarded the subway to make it to Fifth and Park. My heart was in my throat, absolutely. I didn't know why it seemed that happiness was always in reach, yet always so very far away. Too far away, it seemed. It was like the Greek myth about Tantalus – the fruit was always just beyond his reach, and the water was just beyond his mouth to drink. That was his fate. That was his punishment. It seemed appropriate, because I had felt like Tantalus since the day that I met Dalilah.

Happiness was just around the corner, until it wasn't.

When I got to the *Starbucks*, and saw Dalilah's tear-stained face, I knew. I knew that happiness was just out of reach, once more.

"What is it, Dalilah?" I asked, sitting down next to her. I took her hand and kissed it, and then kissed her forehead. "Please don't tell me that you're really sick." God forbid. Maybe she had a terminal disease. I tried to put that thought out of my mind, but it still crept into my brain until it became something that I simply couldn't shake.

She shook her head, but just cried more. Finally, after a

few minutes, she just said "I don't know what to say. How to say this. I just don't know."

"That's okay," I said. "You can tell me when you're ready."

She cried for a few minutes, and then took a deep breath. "Okay," she said. "Before I tell you what I need to tell you, I first have to give you a kind of dry lecture on New York family law. I know that this is going to seem out of place, but you need to know this so that you can know that what I have to do is something that is absolutely necessary. I've tried to think my way around this, but nothing is coming to me just yet."

I relaxed a little bit. It sounded like she wasn't, in fact, going to tell me that she had a terminal disease or a severe sickness. I nodded my head. "Okay, go on with the dry lecture," I said with a smile.

Another deep breath from her. "So," she began. "There's this concept in New York law, and most any state law, really, called putative father. That means if there is a child conceived during a marriage, that child is presumed to be the child of the husband in that marriage."

My heart started to quicken. I suddenly knew exactly where she was going with this, and all of her sickness in the past week or so was starting to make sense. Still, I didn't interrupt. She obviously had to tell me everything, and I was going to let her.

She nodded her head. "There's also a standard used by judges known as the best interest of the child. That means that a judge has discretion on anything legal that involves the child. There are no hard and fast rules when it comes to issues such as child custody and whether to allow DNA evidence or a paternity action during a divorce proceeding."

I took a deep breath. "Dalilah, I know where you're

going with this," I said. I suddenly felt like jumping for joy that she was pregnant, hopefully with my baby. But that feeling was tempered by the sobering thought that the baby might not be mine at all, and that Dalilah apparently was none too happy about it. I knew why- from what she was telling me, it sounded like Nottingham would have rights to the child, no matter who was the actual father. Just because he blackmailed her into marrying him.

She started crying harder. "Yes, Luke, I'm pregnant. I'm not sure how far along I am. Not very, because the home pregnancy test I took just recently indicated pregnancy. But I am pregnant. I know that it's yours, Luke. I can feel it in my gut."

"I don't understand," I said. "How can that be? You started to feel nauseated right after you and I made love. Don't those symptoms come on later?" My heart started sinking. Perhaps the baby wasn't mine at all.

"Yes, usually," she said. "But sometimes women start feeling it right away. Nobody can explain why, but sometimes it just starts really early. Within a couple of days."

I wasn't convinced. I understood that Dalilah had sex with Nottingham. She had explained that to me when she and I got back together – that she felt that she needed to submit to keep him happy. Another sacrifice that she made for me, and that was the worst one of all, she said.

How could she really know who was the father in this situation?

"Okay," I said. "Now, calm down. We'll get through this. No matter what, I'm not running. We'll get through this together."

Even as I said those words, though, I wasn't convinced. I knew as well as she that the child would be Nottingham's, no matter what, and that Nottingham would screw up that child royally.

She shook her head. "Oh, Luke, you don't know the things that I know. The children of men like him – they're awful. No morals, entitled. Not to mention the fact that he's abusive. What kind of a chance would my child have with that kind of an influence in his or her life? I would be bringing in a child that would have little chance of living a normal and happy life. I mean, I will provide as much guidance and love as I can, as will you, I know, but I will only be half of the equation. I just don't see how it can work."

I got up abruptly and started to pace. Dalilah helped me out of my jams, so now it was time for me to do the same. "Okay," I said, "let's brainstorm this." That was my first instinct. I didn't want to look at the situation emotionally, because if I did, I knew that I would demand that she keep the child. Because I knew in my own gut that the baby would really be mine. "Is there any way that a judge will allow a DNA test to prove who is really the father?"

Dalilah nodded her head. "I saw an attorney today. She said that it would entirely depend on what judge we get. Some judges will allow it, others won't. Unfortunately for us, Nottingham is friendly with most of those judges, which complicates matters further."

"But you and I can still do a DNA test to show that I'm the dad, right? I mean, there's nothing stopping us from doing that, right?"

"Of course," she said. "We can do a private DNA test, but whether or not it's allowed in court is another matter. And, even if it is allowed in court, whether or not a judge will actually sever Nottingham's rights is still another matter." She shook her head. "It's all so complicated."

"So," he said. "A judge doesn't allow it, and we appeal that decision. What about that?"

"Appeals courts won't overturn a decision unless it was some kind of gross error. Gross error means that no reasonable judge would make the decision that the trial court judge made, given the facts and circumstances. In this case, there's no way that an appeals court will strike down the trial court if they deny the request to admit the DNA evidence. Nottingham and I were still together under the same roof right before this baby came into being. It would be entirely reasonable for a judge to decide not to disturb Nottingham's rights to the child."

I shook my head. Dalilah had done her homework, of course. "Sounds like you've been reading up."

"I did look at case law," she said. "Of course."

I put my hands behind my neck and lowered my head. "Dalilah," I said. "I can understand the predicament that you're in. I really can. And, if it weren't for this whole Nottingham situation, I'd be over the moon with joy. I know that we're young, but I'd love to have a child with you." I didn't express the fear that I couldn't really provide for the child. I knew that I had to use the fact that a baby was on the way to work harder than ever to get a foothold in the art scene. I would be a great provider for both Dalilah and the baby, I just knew it.

"Well," Dalilah said. "I would be overjoyed, too, Luke. It's my dream to have a beautiful baby with you. But that's not the situation that we're looking at. The odds are long that Nottingham won't have at least split custody with this baby, and I can't bring a child into the world knowing that Nottingham is going to have a chance to make the child's life hell. Not to mention the fact that his hatred for me would probably cause him to take all of that out on the baby. How can I bring a baby into the world knowing all of this?"

I paced the floor. "Dalilah, please. Don't make a hasty decision. You just have to have faith that it will all work out fine. We'll find a judge who will allow DNA evidence and will be willing to sever Nottingham's parental rights. Or we'll prove that Nottingham will be an unfit father, which will give you all the rights. Something can be done, Dalilah. You just have to believe that it will all work out in the end."

"Luke, don't be naïve," she said. "Nottingham's attorney, according to the attorney I saw this morning, is an aggressive shark. Don't even think that we can prevail in a custody action if the judge refuses to allow DNA evidence. It won't happen. I'll be lucky if Nottingham doesn't end up with sole custody, as soon as everything is said and done."

I bit my lip. "There's a way out of this, Dalilah. There has to be. I mean, if this is my kid, I don't think that…" I shook my head, as the enormity of what was about to happen came down on me. Dalilah maybe was carrying my child, and she wanted to kill him or her. I fought back tears. "Do you believe in something, Daliah? Something larger than us?"

Dalilah took a deep breath. "I don't know," she said. "Intellectually, I don't. Emotionally, I'd like to believe that this world is not all there is."

"But nobody really knows," I said. "Is that safe to say?"

"Of course. Everybody thinks that they know, but nobody really does."

"So, what happens to this baby? Does this baby just lose his or her only chance to live? Or do you think that maybe the spirit will just go on and have a chance with somebody else?"

"Luke, I know what you're saying," she said. "I've actually had the same questions myself. Which is why this decision is far from easy."

"But what if it is this life is this child's only chance? Maybe he or she will be the next Beethoven or Madame Curie."

"Or the next Ted Bundy or Hitler," Dalilah said. "I'm not persuaded by that argument."

"Okay," he said. "But think about all the children who came into this world unwanted. Some of them have gone on to do great things. And there are plenty of children who aren't necessarily great, but the parents can't imagine life without them. Children aren't always convenient, Dalilah. They're often a surprise. But the parents usually love them anyhow, and are so grateful that they didn't terminate them when they had the chance."

"I understand all of that," she said. "But this is a unique situation, don't you think? In this case, there won't be two loving parents bringing the child up. There will be one loving one and one abusive monster involved. The chance that this child is going to grow up being completely messed up is exponentially more than with children who come into the world with two sane people as parents."

"But what if it's mine?" I said. "I think that it is. I know that I also have a gut feeling that I'm the dad. When you told me that you were pregnant, I just had the feeling that you were carrying my child. I don't want....I really don't want my child to die."

Dalilah, all at once, started to look angry. "I know that, Luke. Don't you think I know that? I want this child so much. I really do. If I weren't married to Nottingham, it would be a welcome thing. Even though we're young, and neither of us have much money, I still would want this baby with you. But that's not the situation here."

I sat down, and took her hands. I looked into her eyes. "Dalilah, I'm not a religious person at all. I don't know what I believe. I think that I do believe in something. Not sure what. But I do believe in fate and faith. You have to have faith that this will all work out for us in the end. Something will happen that will ensure that Nottingham won't get his depraved hands on this baby. It's going to be stressful, and it's going to be hell, but it will work out in the end. But if you terminate now, there's no chance for it working out in the end. And you might deprive both of us of something really wonderful."

Dalilah started to shake her head. "Luke, please. I don't want this to come between us."

"How can it not? Even if the baby is legally his, it might actually be mine. How can this situation not come between us?"

"What if I'm pressured into having the baby, and everything that I predict comes true? Nottingham gets custody, and proceeds to make the child's life hell. I'll be dealing with that for the rest of my life. Won't that come between us, too? You're going to resent me for terminating, but I might resent you for talking me out of it."

I sat down, and put my head in my hands. Another impossible situation we were in. Damned if we did, and damned if we didn't.

I wished so much that I had a crystal ball that would tell me how all of this was going to shake out. She was absolutely right – there was a chance that this baby was going to cause an interminable amount of grief. I foresaw a heated custody battle, and Nottingham doing his best to screw up the child. Dalilah was going to go through hell, and so would I. There probably would be no way around it.

So, I blurted out the first thing that came to my mind.

"We run. We go and live in another country, and Nottingham won't find us. We change our names and our identities, and we run. That's what we do. That's what we do, Dalilah. We run."

To my surprise, Dalilah actually looked hopeful. "That could work," she said. "I have some Irish relatives. Distant ones, for sure, as they're the descendants of my grandma Maggie's cousins. At least one of those descendants is living in London as we speak. His name is Liam. I don't know much about him, but maybe my dad could get in touch with him and see if he could put us up for a spell. Just until we can get used to that city and find our way around it."

I nodded my head. London actually sounded like an awesome idea to me. The art scene there was thriving, especially for my kind of cutting edge works, and Dalilah's, too. And Paris was just a train ride away. "London," I said. "I love that idea. But what if Nottingham tracks us down there? I was actually thinking of something more like Siberia or Bora Bora." I was only half-joking, really. London sounded like a heavenly idea, but it wasn't exactly the most inauspicious place. Nottingham Industries was international, which meant that Nottingham would be doing business in London. The chances of us running into him would be slight, but still a problem. And if he runs into us and sees that there's a child…I shuddered to think such a thing.

"No, Luke," she said. "We'll just have to do a good job of covering our tracks. Living like two people in the witness protection plan. I don't quite know how we're going to be able to change our identities, but perhaps that won't even be a problem. London is a big place, Luke. We could get lost in there. Nottingham won't know to look there for us, either. And, best of all, we'd both have a fresh start with our art.

I'll be sad to leave my family, of course, but Nick owns a house in Italy, and my dad has a winery there, too. They go to Europe all the time. We'll still be able to see them."

Was this going to work? It didn't matter, it had to be done. Even if it didn't work, we had to at least try. It was a plan, which was better than the other plans that we managed to cook up. It was infinitely better than terminating the child, and also infinitely better than letting the child be ruined by Nottingham. Of that, I was sure.

Of everything else, I was less sure.

Trapped: Chapter Two

Dalilah

So, we were going to run. Was it the ideal situation? Hell, no. The ideal situation would be that there wasn't a baby at all. But it did seem to be the best solution, considering the circumstances.

I really didn't see any way around it. That I would be charged with possible kidnapping if Nottingham ever found out about the baby and the fact that I ran to keep it from him, was not even on my radar. Luke and I were going to have to take a chance that we would never be found.

But, deep down, I knew that it was fruitless. Nottingham was going to track me down. If he had to send private investigators to every part of the globe, he was going to do it. Even if he didn't know about the baby.

I had to try, though. At the very least, I had to give Luke and me some distance from the whole Nottingham situation, so that I could think about my next move. There was a way out of this, I knew it, that didn't necessarily involve

Luke and I running from place to place for the rest of our lives, like fugitives. I just didn't see it, but it would come to me.

In the meantime, though, I had to tell my mom and dad about all of this mess. Like it or not, I was going to have to tell them. If nothing else, dad might be able to contact Liam and see if I could stay with him. I didn't know much about Liam, except that he was some kind of mogul over in London, and was very wealthy. He was young, only 27, and had made a fortune in the music business, representing some of the hottest acts in the world, before establishing his own record label. Last I knew, he was literally a self-made billionaire.

I personally had never met the guy, which made it strange that I was going to try to see if I could stay with him for the time being. But he was the only relative that I knew who lived in London. All the other Gallaghers were scattered around Cork, Drogheda and Dublin. As much as I had always wanted to live in Ireland, secretly, I knew that London had a much hotter art scene. This would give both of us a fresh start, which Luke was desperately needing after the apparent rejection from all of the people he met at his premiere. I looked forward to getting a fresh start, myself.

So, a few days after Luke and I had made our tentative plans to run away from the whole Nottingham situation, I found myself waiting for my mom, dad, Nick and Scotty to meet me for dinner at Wolfgang Puck's. I dreaded talking to them, but I asked Nick to at least give mom and dad a heads-up on the topic of discussion that day. Mom had already called me, hysterical at the thought that I was thinking of terminating my child. I had to talk her down off the ledge, but I managed to get it under control when I reassured her that I wouldn't be depriving her of a grandchild after all.

They met me, and we all sat down.

"Okay," I said, addressing the four people at the table. The four people who, aside from Luke, meant the absolute most to me in the world. "I guess Nick has filled all of you in on the fact that I'm pregnant, and what that means, considering my situation with Nottingham."

"Yes," my dad said. "I've already gotten in touch with some of the best family law attorneys in the city. I've gotten a few lined up that will help you fight this one all the way."

I shook my head. "You'll be fighting fire with fire. Whoever you find to represent me, Nottingham will have better. You aren't the only billionaire involved in this situation, dad. You can't throw money at this and hope that it resolves itself."

"I don't understand," mom said. "You assured me that you would keep this child. And you don't seem to want to fight Nottingham in court. So, what is your plan?"

I took a deep breath. "My plan is to move to London and start fresh. Luke and I have already talked it through, and we know the possible consequences."

My dad was shaking his head. "No, you can't do that. That is essentially kidnapping, I hope you know that. You're going to be acting like a criminal by doing that, and you will also be treated like a criminal when Nottingham finds out what happened. You have to face this. I didn't fight enough when I found out that you were going to marry that man, but I'm putting my foot down now. You can't do this."

I sighed. I was prepared for this. "Dad, once again, it's not a matter of my asking permission. I'm an adult. You can't stop me. And believe me, I've thought about this situation eight ways to Sunday. I see no other solution. Yes, there could be devastating consequences if Nottingham sees what I've done, but I'll just have to face them if it comes to that. The other solutions to this situation are untenable. Either I terminate or I let Nottingham ruin this baby. Neither of those are options for me. I mean, I admit, the first idea I had was to have an abortion. But Luke made me see that there was possibly another way. And I'm going to take it. The odds are against us living our lives in peace, but I like the odds of Luke and I getting away with this a helluva lot more than the odds that Nottingham won't get custody of this child."

Dad was still shaking his head. "I won't see my daughter become a criminal."

I took a deep breath, and looked at Nick, who, surprisingly enough, wasn't saying a word.

I raised an eyebrow. "Sometimes, dad, you have to break the law if a situation is bad enough. I would think that you, of all people, would know this." I looked at Nick again, pointedly, and he shook his head.

Dad looked over at Nick, and then back at me. "How did you know?"

"I just do," I said. "I was a bratty kid, and wanting to learn how to do subversive things. I taught myself to hack, and I found out about Paul Lucas, and what really happened to him. And all that I can say is that Uncle Nick is in no position to…"

Scotty's face got white, and I immediately felt bad. Nick looked like he was going to come over to my side of the table and strangle me with his bare hands. He turned to Scotty. "Scotty, honey, I need to speak with Dalilah alone."

Scotty just put her hand on his, and said "no need. I

know. I've always known what happened to that bastard. I've just never told you that I knew."

I immediately felt terrible for bringing up this can of worms, especially since that was apparently some kind of secret between Nick and Scotty all of these years.

"Crap," Nick said. "Then I guess I need to talk to you alone. Later, though." He shook his head and addressed me. "When are you going to stop bringing this up, Dalilah? It happened, it was years ago, and he got what was coming to him. Let it go."

It was my dad's turn to look mystified. "Wait," he said to Nick. "You knew that Dalilah found out about that, and you never told me?"

He shrugged. "I didn't find it to have any relevance. Dalilah promised, on her word, that she wouldn't let that whole sorry incident out of the bag, but, apparently, she's not good with her word."

"Listen," I said. "I only brought that up to let you guys know that sometimes you have to make solutions that are not exactly legal, when you're up against the wall. That's what I'm going to do, here."

Dad looked like he wanted to slap me, which is a look that I had never seen on his face. "Two wrongs don't make a right," he said. "Listen, I've made mistakes in my life. Nick has, too. Your mother has made mistake, Scotty too. We've all made mistakes. Some of them were pretty huge ones. But that doesn't give you *carte blanche* to repeat the pattern."

"That wasn't a mistake, Ryan," Nick said. "Paul Lucas wasn't a mistake. He got what was coming to him, and you know it."

"That's not the topic of conversation, here," dad said to Nick. "The topic is whether or not my daughter will commit a felony by doing what she's planning on doing. Dalilah is the topic, here, not what you and I did 17 years ago to a pervert who didn't really deserve to live."

"Huh, dad," I said. "Nick made himself judge, jury and executioner of that man. And you're going to lecture me on what I'm about to do?"

At that, my dad slapped my face, hard. I put my hand up to my cheek, and looked at him. He had an expression that I had never seen in my entire life. His face was red, his eyes menacing, his mouth turned down. "You will never talk to me like that again," he said. "How did you turn out like this? So devious, so underhanded. I didn't raise you to be a criminal. And you will never bring up Nick's past to try to justify your shitty actions. You will face up to what you wrought by doing what you did with Nottingham – using him, getting trapped by him, and marrying him for the wrong reasons – and you will do it within the bounds of the law. Do I make myself clear?"

"Crystal," I said, thinking to myself that I was just going to have to run away with Luke without his blessing. I looked over at my mother, who wasn't saying much. She at least seemed to have a little bit of humility, considering all the devious things that she did in her own youth. Namely, running away from my dad when she was pregnant with me. She, essentially, did what I was proposing to do in this situation, only my motivation for doing so was much, much different than her motivations for running away all those years ago.

Ironic. For once, my mom really seemed to understand me. At least, if I read her expression correctly, she understood me. It seemed that she was furtively trying to give her non-verbal approval for what it was that I was going to do.

My mom put her hand on my dad's. "Calm down,

Ryan," she said. "Listen, you and I have to talk about this later."

"There's nothing to talk about," dad said. "I know what you're thinking, beautiful, and it's not the same thing at all. You running from me when you were pregnant with Dalilah wasn't the same thing as what Dalilah is proposing to do."

"It's not?" mom asked. "What's the difference?"

"For one, you knew that I wouldn't press charges for kidnapping. At least, I hope that you knew that."

"Regardless, it's the same thing," mom counteracted. "If you're going to call Dalilah a felon, then you're essentially saying that I'm a felon, too. Really, if you get to the heart of the matter, that's true."

Oh, god. Now, I was turning everybody against each other. I never wanted to drive a wedge between my parents, let alone Nick and Scotty, yet it seemed that everybody was angry with one another all of a sudden.

I dug up their pasts in a way that I probably shouldn't have. I essentially opened the long-festering sores that lay deep underneath two seemingly rock-solid marriages. I immediately tried to put a lid on it, while telling them that I was still going to run, and they couldn't stop me anymore than they could have stopped me from marrying that bastard in the first place.

I put my hands in the "time-out" position. "Listen, let's focus, here. I'm really sorry that I'm bringing up sore subjects. I never meant for this meeting to result in there being hard feelings between all of you. But I also want to let you guys know that you should empathize with my situation. You guys have been in impossible situations before, and you took care of it how you saw fit."

I looked at my mother, and took her hand. "Mom, you ran from dad when you were pregnant with me. I understand why, too, considering that whole Natalie mess. Dad forgave you, and you two moved on."

Then I looked at Nick. "You plotted the death of the man who was doing horrible things to Aunt Scotty. I'm quite sure that you didn't want to do that, but you did. You did, because you understood that doing that was the only real solution to an impossible knot of a problem."

My father shook his head. "What kind of an example have I set for my own daughter?" He no longer looked angry, but, instead, looked extremely sad. "Dalilah, please understand. Everybody at this table has done terrible things. With the possible exception of Scotty. But, please don't repeat the pattern. I know it sounds hypocritical and like I'm telling you to do as I say, not as I do."

I felt sorry for him, because he looked so defeated. I saw in his face that he was beginning to understand that nothing that he could say or do would stop me from doing what it was that I felt was necessary. I also saw in his expression the shame and guilt over his own actions in the past, and the apparent effect that these actions had on me. He knew that he had little moral ground to stand on in lecturing me, and this devastated him beyond measure. I knew that, just by reading his facial expression and body language.

Of course, I had no idea exactly what role my dad played in the Paul Lucas affair. I did know that he at least knew about it, and probably approved of it. This made him as guilty as Nick in my book. This would be why he was coming across as so guilty.

Grab your copy...
vinci-books.com/trapped

About the Author

Annie currently lives in San Diego with her two fur-babies, Bella and Toby, and her significant other, Joey. When she's not writing, she's busy reading, cycling all over town, watching cooking shows or classic old movies on TCM (Cary Grant is her favorite) and occasionally watching trashy television shows.

About the Author

www.ingramcontent.com/pod-product-compliance
Lightning Source LLC
Chambersburg PA
CBHW011743010726
47498CB00012B/2910

* 9 7 8 1 0 3 6 7 0 3 0 6 6 *